PRAISE FOR *DECANTING A MURDER*

"This debut mystery has a sympathetic main character with secrets in her past, well-drawn secondary characters, a possible love interest, and fascinating detail on wine, wineries, and wine making skillfully woven through the story."

—*Booklist*

"Nettmann's lead character Katie Stillwell, aka 'The Palate', as an amateur sleuth is a perfect pairing in this intricately crafted sommelier mystery. At turns fascinating and suspenseful, I was thoroughly captivated by the story and enjoyed every turn of the page. Uncork me another!"

—Jenn McKinlay,
New York Times bestselling author

"The quiet hillsides and vineyards of California's famed Napa Valley have produced many famous vintages over the years, and first-time mystery author Nettmann knows this territory well … The first in a very promising series."

—Brendan DuBois, a multiple award-winning
author and a three-time Edgar nominee

DECANTING
a
MURDER
—— A SOMMELIER MYSTERY ——

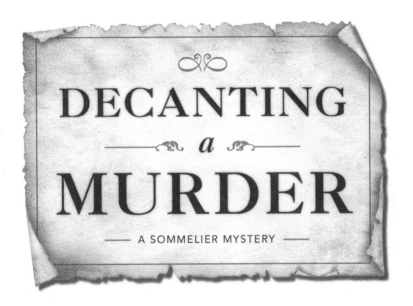

DECANTING
a
MURDER

— A SOMMELIER MYSTERY —

NADINE NETTMANN

MIDNIGHT INK
WOODBURY, MINNESOTA

FIRST EDITION
First Printing, 2016

Book format by Teresa Pojar
Cover design by Kevin R. Brown
Cover Illustration by Pierre Droal/Deborah Wolfe Ltd.
Editing by Nicole Nugent

Midnight Ink, an imprint of Llewellyn Worldwide Ltd.

Library of Congress Cataloging-in-Publication Data

Names: Nettmann, Nadine, 1980– author.
Title: Decanting a murder : a sommelier mystery / by Nadine Nettmann.
Description: First edition. | Woodbury, MN : Midnight Ink, [2016] | Series: A sommelier mystery ; 1
Identifiers: LCCN 2015044614 (print) | LCCN 2016002246 (ebook) | ISBN 9780738748504 | ISBN 9780738748863 ()
Subjects: LCSH: Wine—Fiction. | Murder—Fiction. | Mystery fiction.
Classification: LCC PS3614.E526 D43 2016 (print) | LCC PS3614.E526 (ebook) | DDC 813/.6—dc23
LC record available at http://lccn.loc.gov/2015044614

Midnight Ink
Llewellyn Worldwide Ltd.
2143 Wooddale Drive
Woodbury, MN 55125-2989
www.midnightinkbooks.com
Printed in the United States of America

DEDICATION

*For everyone involved in creating wine and
everyone who enjoys drinking it.*

ACKNOWLEDGMENTS

Because my publishing dream took ten years to come true, there are many people whose support was invaluable along the way. Although I'm unable to list everyone, please know that I appreciate each and every one of you.

I would like to thank my wonderful agent, Danielle Burby, for her guidance, hard work, and editorial insight. Thank you to Josh Getzler for seeing promise in this book from the beginning. My deepest gratitude to Terri Bischoff and the team at Midnight Ink for believing in this series and taking a chance on a debut. A tremendous thank you to Melanie Hooyenga for her professional encouragement, friendship, and willingness to read different versions of this book as it evolved.

I am indebted to Fred Dame for picking me out of the crowd and putting me on a wine panel in 2010. You changed my life. Thank you to everyone who welcomed me into the wine world, especially Geoff Kruth, Debra Peterson, Kent Torrey, Shaun Prevatt, Elena Prevatt, Bill Burkhart, Kyle Kaplan, Danny Novicic, Mario Miranda, Eduardo Bolanos, and Matt Woody.

My heartfelt gratitude to Jennifer Bosworth, Laura Konopka, and Edith Cohn who read early drafts and provided valuable feedback. Thank you to Amy Scher for her encouragement and positivity on our parallel publishing journeys. Many thanks to Michelle Steffes, Wendy Harvey, and Wendy Brousseau for letting me bounce ideas around and discussing this book at length. My sincere appreciation to Kelsey Hertig for her winery insight, advice, and camaraderie. Thank you to Irene Phakeovilay for making sure my details were correct.

I am grateful to my publishing pals for their advice and unwavering support: Gretchen McNeil, Julia Shahin Collard, Jennifer Gray Olson, Jess Brody, Leigh Bardugo, James Matlack Raney, and Brad Gottfred.

Thank you to my parents for their constant encouragement and especially my mom for ten years of steadfast proofreading. And finally, a special thank you to my husband, Matthew. Your love and support makes everything possible.

ONE

PAIRING SUGGESTION: CHAMPAGNE—ÉPERNAY, FRANCE

Ideal as an aperitif to get you started.

❧

ONE THOUSAND SEVEN HUNDRED and forty-two. That's how many flash cards I had studied over the last two years. Yet, as I waited for the results of the Certified Sommelier Exam, I knew they weren't going to call my name. Maybe it was because the exam was notorious for being difficult and held a 60 percent failure rate. Or maybe it was because my anxiety had appeared during the blind tasting section, raising my pulse and muddling my thoughts. My tasting group liked to call me The Palate for my calm and collected ability to decipher any wine, but with the clock ticking, the Master Sommeliers watching, and the other participants frantically scribbling on their papers, The Palate was replaced by a scared and confused taster blankly staring at the glasses of wine.

I forced myself to push through, identifying a vintage, varietal, and wine region for each glass, but I knew I hadn't come close. It was like firing a gun in the Police Academy trials. You could be a sharpshooter all year long, but if you missed the target during your final exam, you missed the target and the test was over. There were no second chances that day, only an option to try again at a future date.

I took a deep breath and stared at the door, my hands clenched as I waited for the revered Master Sommeliers to enter with the results.

The other forty-nine people around me all wore their game faces—the practiced pose necessary for sommeliers. It was important to remain outwardly serene while dealing with all types of restaurant guests on a nightly basis. I was used to gracefully listening as a guest yelled at me over a bottle of wine or smiling without comment as a group enjoyed a special bottle that they had brought in, even though I could tell that the wine was clearly spoiled.

The six Master Sommeliers entered and I straightened my shoulders. The first Master stepped forward as I eyed the stack of papers in his hand. "We have your results," he said, his gray hair slicked back and his game face perfect, cemented in place by decades in the wine profession. "Unfortunately it was a low pass rate today. A lot of you found the trivia portion to be your downfall."

One thousand seven hundred and forty-two, I reminded myself. Every free moment over the last two years had been filled with memorizing flash cards. The trivia section had gone well, and I was extremely confident about the service portion of the exam. Everything had been great except the blind tasting.

I stood in a sea of professionals, all masking their nerves behind their sommelier game faces. I hoped I seemed as calm as my neighbors. I clapped as the first three names were called and the recipients walked to the front to receive a certificate and the purple pin. They were one step closer in the four-step process to the coveted position of Master Sommelier, a title held by just over two hundred people around the world and only a small percentage of them female. With the title comes respect, honor, and a guaranteed paycheck.

I stared at the large red pin on the Master Sommelier's lapel as he read out names, my hand absentmindedly fidgeting with the dime-sized introductory pin on the lapel of my coat. I wanted to wear the Master Sommelier pin with such passion that an ache stirred deep in my chest.

I folded my hands together and waited, a small tremble running past my elbow. The pile of papers in the Master Sommelier's hand was shrinking.

"We have only one name left. The last person to join our group today is …"

But it wasn't my name.

I stood back, fighting to keep my game face on as I watched the group of newly minted Certified Sommeliers stand together for a photo, their purple pins shining in the overhead light. Their next step would be the Advanced Exam and the desirable green pin.

"Don't worry, kiddo," said a voice behind me. I turned to see Bill Andrews, my boss and manager of Trentino Restaurant. "You'll get it next time." Bill was in his fifties and always had a broad smile on his face. He was meticulously stylish with his salt-and-pepper hair neatly trimmed and a navy blue sports coat as his permanent accessory—even when he wore jeans.

"Thanks," I said. "I don't know what happened. It was during the tasting—" I broke off, unable to continue.

"You're a great taster, okay? Don't let this shake you." He stepped closer and put his hands on my shoulders. "We can go over it on Monday with the tasting group, but I know you. You're good at this, okay? Don't let this get to you."

I nodded as I swallowed my disappointment. "Thanks." I glanced at my watch. It was four thirty and I still needed to change. "I have to go, I'm going to be late."

"Is this for Frontier? Man, I'd love to switch places with you. I want details on everything, okay?" Bill lowered his voice as he motioned to the sommeliers surrounding us. "I bet some of them would trade their new certification to get into Frontier Winery. Everyone wants to go there."

I allowed a smile to break through. Bill was right. And a party was just what I needed. "Thanks. I'd better go. I'll see you at work tomorrow." I grabbed my purse and headed toward the door.

"Wait, Katie." Bill pointed to a table covered with envelopes. "Your results."

I took a deep breath and scanned the table for the envelope that contained detailed notes written by one of the Master Sommeliers, letting me know how I failed and why. When I found my name, I scooped it up and stuffed it in my jacket pocket unopened. I tried to focus on the upcoming party at Frontier, but the tightness in my chest threatened to consume me.

———

It wasn't until the vineyards of Napa Valley appeared outside my car window that the tightness released. The perfectly organized vines brimming with bright green leaves in geometric rows never failed to bring calm and order to my life.

The familiar sign approached, WELCOME TO THIS WORLD FAMOUS GROWING REGION, its warm message welcoming strangers and friends to the renowned Valley. Nestled between the foothills of Northern California, Napa Valley possessed a reputation acknowledged all over the world for its picturesque setting, culinary expertise, and award-winning wineries.

The first commercial winery opened in Napa in 1861, and now there were more than 450 wineries in the Valley, including Frontier, a historic winery known throughout the wine world for its secrecy and its exquisite red wine.

I lowered all four windows, encouraging the scent of the vineyards to float inside. The damp earth, the clipped vines, the plump grapes, and the crisp Napa air—all the elements that create a bottle of wine, a bottle of wine with a story to tell to anyone who listened carefully enough.

I always listened.

Just like every bottle had a story, every person had a story and I handled people better when I thought of them as wine. Some wines I loved and eagerly anticipated, while other wines were difficult to swallow, their delicate structure spoiled. Expose a wine to air long enough and it will turn to vinegar.

I thought of the people in my life as specific grape varietals. My dad, stoic and stern, was like a Barolo—an Italian wine that needs years of aging before it is drinkable and, even then, needs to be paired with a heavy steak. My best friend Tessa was clearly Merlot—sometimes smooth, sometimes with a bite, and struggling with a soiled reputation that it didn't deserve.

Merlot's reputation was damaged in 2004 when a pop culture reference made it "uncool" to drink. It became the wine you didn't order and the wine you didn't dare take to dinner at a friend's house. Merlot, the most widely planted grape in Bordeaux, no longer received the same affection in California. Vintners all over the state ripped out Merlot vines and replaced them with more popular varietals such as Cabernet, Syrah, and the newly famed Pinot Noir.

Tessa had lost her reputation around the same time. She became the girl parents didn't want their kids to be around, the outcast at school. Her grades slipped and she never went to college. Instead, she jumped from job to job, never managing to last long at any of them.

The black matte invitation fluttered on the front seat, the parchment overlay flapping in the breeze. I moved my purse on top to keep it still, the short note from Tessa barely peeking out from under it.

Hope you can make it.

I glanced at the time. I had promised Tessa I would be early, but the Friday night traffic out of San Francisco had delayed me more than I had hoped and it was already twenty past six, only ten minutes before the party started. I pressed harder on the gas pedal as the vineyards flew by my window.

The entrance of Frontier Winery came into view, the gates surrounded by a stone wall that lined the property. Frontier wasn't open to tasting appointments or tours. In fact, Frontier was never open. The gates remained closed, a constant reminder that some places in life are off-limits. Today, however, the gates were wide and welcoming, the driveway stretching through the trees. A white sign decorated with cursive letters announced, *100th Anniversary. Private Event. Invitation Only. Do NOT Enter.*

The Prohibition years had wiped out many of the wineries in the Valley, but not Frontier. Long gone were the days when this winery survived on crafting sacramental wine, which could escape the laws of Prohibition. Now, Frontier produced a limited-release wine that boasted three-figure price tags and was available only to the Frontier Wine Club and an exclusive list of big-city restaurants.

I paused in front of the sign before proceeding through the gates. A man in a black suit stood on the left side of the driveway, flanked by three valet attendants in red vests.

"Name?" he asked, his dark sunglasses hiding any evidence of emotion.

"Katie Stillwell."

He flipped over the pages in his hand.

"I'm a guest of Tessa Blakely. She works here."

He circled something on the paper and a valet stepped forward, but the man put his hand up, shooing the valet back to the line of red vests.

"She's requested that you park in front of the offices instead of valet. Continue straight and you'll see her silver car. You can park in the space next to it."

"Thank you." I pulled forward. Mature oak trees lined the gravel driveway and rows of green vineyards began past the trees. They opened to a view of a two-story stone building covered with small leaves of creeping ivy, which hugged the windows like a winter sweater.

A covered wooden walkway draped with vines extended to a second structure that mimicked the century-old stonework but was clearly built years, maybe even decades, after the winery.

I parked next to Tessa's car and stared at the exam envelope on my front seat, the words calling to me from inside. Now would be as good a time as any. I slid my finger underneath the flap and removed the letter. My eyes scanned the page, the black ink soothing even as the words shook me. I had passed theory and service, but the blind tasting had been my downfall. *Needs a lot of work,* the Master Sommelier wrote.

The hours, weeks, and months I spent blind tasting ran through my head as I stared at the hillside behind the winery. A fallen tree lay at the bottom of the slope, its broken limbs splayed in a forgotten pile beneath the vines that staked a firm hold in the soil, the perpendicular rows segmented only by the occasional oak tree.

"Needs a lot of work," I whispered to myself as I got out of the car, the scent of fermenting grapes thick and heavy in the air.

The side door of the offices opened and a tall blonde jumped down the two steps. "Yay, you made it!" Tessa cheered, running toward me, her curls bouncing on her shoulders, her low-cut navy blue dress doing little to hold back her bulging chest. "I tried to call you. I was worried you weren't coming!" She threw her arms around me, floral scented shampoo wafting from her hair even though most wineries, and most likely Frontier, forbid employees from wearing scents of any kind.

"Of course I was coming!" My reply was muffled as Tessa hugged me. "I'm even two minutes early."

Tessa finished the hug. "You didn't answer my texts."

I felt my purse and looked at Tessa. "My phone's in the car. Why, what did they say?"

Tessa shook her head with an amused smile. "You're so organized, but you never have your phone."

"I don't like to be available to everyone twenty-four/seven."

"Clearly." A grin spread on Tessa's face, her smile revealing the tooth she had chipped by falling out of my tree house when we were young.

"Why are your teeth purple? Have you been drinking already?"

"I work at a winery, Katie. It's basically part of the job description."

"You never change."

"Why would I? It'd be a shame to ruin perfection." Tessa tapped my shoulder. "So, spill it. How did the test go?"

I breathed out, focusing on the vineyards, their organized lines dotted with plump bunches of dark red grapes. Harvest would be any day now.

"Earth to Katie. Where are you? Stop ignoring me."

"Sorry, I'm not." I turned to Tessa. "It's just ..." I took a deep breath. "I didn't pass the exam."

Tessa stopped. "Are you serious?"

My chest tightened. "I guess I wasn't ready."

The smile drained from Tessa's face. "But you never fail at anything. Please tell me you're kidding."

"Let's talk about it later." I glanced up at the buildings. "I'm here now. I want to enjoy this."

"Yes, but are you okay?" Tessa raised her manicured eyebrows, her eyes sympathetic.

"I'm fine. Really. In fact, I'm better than fine because I'm actually here at Frontier."

"Okay." Tessa brightened and squeezed my arm. "So what do you think of my place?"

"Your place?" I laughed. "You've worked here for four months."

Tessa shrugged. "Details, details." She motioned to my dress. "I remember this dress. Looking to get lucky?"

I looked down at my black cocktail dress with its high neck and low hemline that fell an inch above my knees. "I actually thought it was pretty conservative."

"I'm being sarcastic. Come on, Katie, would it kill you to show a little cleavage once in a while?"

"You mean like you?"

"If you've got 'em, flaunt 'em." Tessa shook her chest as she kicked out her leg, the edge of her three-inch heel barely missing my shin.

"How do you walk in those?"

"Practice. Plus, they're my new favorite shoes. Come on." Tessa looped arms with me. "Let's get you something to drink." She pulled me toward a lawn peppered with round tables and white tablecloths.

"Wait, can I see the place? I've been dying to come in here for years."

Tessa pointed to the buildings behind us. "It's right here."

"No, I mean a tour."

"This building holds the offices and the owners live on the top floor. That one is the winery where all the fun stuff happens, and behind it is a creepy old wine cellar. Good?"

"Really? That's all I get?" I took a step forward. "Is there at least a bathroom I can use? It was a long drive from the city."

"Let's go inside the offices. We've ordered fancy port-a-potties for tonight, but I'd never do that to you."

We entered the first building into a long hallway with a dark wood floor and beige walls that appeared darker than they should due to the poor lighting. The same musty smell that seemed to inhabit all older buildings was heavy in the air.

Tessa pointed to the second door down. "The bathroom is through here, past the break room."

"I'll only be a second."

"Good, 'cause we have a date with a bottle of wine." Tessa winked as she crossed her arms and leaned against the wall.

I stepped inside the break room. It was the same as any other break room with a microwave, coffeemaker, and a round table with chairs. It was almost strange to see something so normal at a place I had always thought of as practically mythical.

I shook off the disappointment and headed to the bathroom where I took a moment to reapply my eyeliner and lipstick. I never used much makeup, but Tessa had taught me years ago to keep eyeliner and lipstick in my purse as a quick fix for any occasion.

I returned to the break room and paused at the table, where a newspaper was open to the games and cartoon section. The sudoku was partially filled in and I stared at it, the numbers moving in my head. After a moment, I met Tessa back in the hallway.

"About time, slowpoke."

"You know if you put a nine and a four in the top row of that sudoku and then an eight and a six in the left middle box, you'll be able to solve the rest."

"You and your puzzles," said Tessa. She held up a pair of black three-inch heels. "I have something for you to wear."

I looked down at my shoes. "What's wrong with these?"

"Katie, it's a special night. You're finally here at Frontier and you can drink amazing wine while chatting with gorgeous men. Don't you think heels will make it all the more glamorous?"

"Maybe." I stared at the heels in her hand. "I guess. For one night."

"That's all I ask." Tessa crouched down to replace my shoes.

I lifted one foot at a time as Tessa placed the heels on my feet. My ankles wobbled as I stood with the new height. "I can't wear these. I'll trip and look drunk."

"Then you'll fit in with the party guests!" Tessa opened a door and tossed in my shoes. "Don't forget they're in this closet." She grabbed my hand and pushed open the door to outside. "Come on, let's get to the party and start drinking."

"Okay, but not too much. I have to drive back to the city tonight." I took the steps one at a time, my heels sliding when I reached the gravel driveway.

"So law-abiding!"

"Always." I shuddered as a distinct memory came to my mind.

"You okay? We need to get you some wine. The '08 Cabernet will help. It helps everything. Besides, there are some fun surprises planned for tonight. Be prepared to have your socks knocked off. Not that you're wearing socks." Tessa smiled with her lips closed as we approached the lawn.

"Wait, I know that smile. You're up to something."

"I don't know what you're talking about," said Tessa as she stepped onto the grass, her blond hair swaying as she walked. "What did you always say? That I'm like a wine?"

"Yes." But unlike Merlot, which was making a comeback with wine drinkers everywhere, Tessa's reputation was getting worse. When a wine is left out and turns to vinegar, it's never the wine's fault. Tessa's reputation over the last twelve years wasn't her fault either. It was mine.

TWO

PAIRING SUGGESTION: SPARKLING WINE—SONOMA, CA

A crisp wine which pairs well with parties and celebrations.

LONG STRANDS OF LIGHTS with white paper lanterns stretched high above the lawn, poised to illuminate the area as soon as the golden hues of daylight were replaced by the blackness of night.

My borrowed heels dug into the soft earth and the green aroma of freshly cut grass floated in the air as I counted ten round tables, each carefully positioned to eliminate any chance of a table slant from the slight uphill of the lawn. Vases overflowing with full white flowers and purple irises adorned the center of each table.

"How many people are coming tonight?"

"Only our wine club members—about one hundred people, I guess," said Tessa. "It's not exactly an event open to just anyone."

"I would expect nothing less. After all, it is Frontier." My fingers grazed the smooth petal of a stargazer lily as we walked past a table. "These kind of remind me of our prom flowers."

"I know, right? But these are much better. You know why?" Tessa grinned.

"Because we don't have to deal with Marcie and Tina acting like they own the place?"

"I was gonna say because I ordered them, but I like your reason better." Tessa nudged me with her shoulder. "I'm so glad you could come tonight. You're my date for the night."

"I'm your date? Really? I'm surprised you don't have a new flavor of the month."

Tessa stopped and looked at me. "Who says I don't? I bet we can find you one tonight, too."

"Unlikely."

"You work too much."

"I love my job."

"You love excuses." Tessa faced me. "Katie, you have to keep your eyes open. There are available guys everywhere." She looked around at the empty tables. "Okay, maybe not yet, but there will be once more guests arrive." She pointed to the far side of the lawn, where two long tables were covered with wineglasses next to the catering booths. "The wine stands are my favorite part of tonight. Come on, let's go get a drink."

"So tell me," I said as we walked, "how exactly did you get a job here? You never told me."

Tessa shifted uncomfortably. "It's a long story."

I thought I saw something stir in Tessa's eyes, but I left it alone. "Well, thanks again for inviting me, I really appreciate it."

A man and woman stood near the far booth, a clipboard in the woman's hand. She pointed at the clipboard while the man leaned against the booth and nodded.

"Tessa, who are they?"

"The owners."

"Mark Plueger, right? And I bet that's his wife, Vanessa. I've heard the winery's been in his family for generations."

Tessa shrugged. "Something like that."

I paused, my heels wobbling. "Can we meet them?"

"Let's get a drink first." Tessa continued toward the table.

"Come on, it will only take a second."

Tessa turned and faced me. "Why do you want to meet them?"

"Because—"

"I know, I know," interrupted Tessa. "You always want to know the story behind a place. Come on." She walked in their direction as I followed.

The woman looked up first, her platinum blond hair pulled back into a French twist. She was in her early forties and had a large scar, approximately three inches, which ran down the left side of her cheek, a thick layer of foundation barely concealing it. She nudged the man next to her with her elbow. He looked up, his soft brown eyes acknowledging both of us as we approached.

"Mark and Vanessa Plueger, this is my friend Katie Stillwell. She's a sommelier at Trentino in San Francisco."

Vanessa extended her professionally manicured hand toward me, a jasmine fragrance along with it. "It's nice to meet you," she said in a gentle voice as she shook my hand. "I've dined at your restaurant. Great salmon."

"Thank you."

"Yes," said Mark, who was older than Vanessa, with gray hair sprouting alongside his temples and deep grooves in his face. "I've heard a lot about you from Tessa." His handshake was strong, his skin rough from winery work. "Congratulations, I heard you just became Certified with the Court."

I glanced at Tessa. "Oh, well," I stalled. "The test was today."

Mark leaned back against the booth and put his hands in his pockets. "Tessa also mentioned that you can tell the vineyard location and year of a wine by tasting it."

"Sometimes." The results of the exam went through my mind as heaviness weighed on my heart.

Tessa's arm flew around my shoulder. "Oh please, her wine tasting group calls her The Palate." She shook me as if trying to reassure me, but the effort was lost. "She needs to learn how to brag about herself," Tessa continued. "She knows wine and yes, she can tell the year of the wine and all that stuff."

"How do you do that?" asked Vanessa. "I can tell a glass of Frontier wine apart from any other glass, but I don't think I could do any old wine."

I put my game face on as I focused on the conversation. "Blind tasting is a process. You learn the different aspects of the varietals and regions, and then when you have the wine in front of you, you break it down into sight, smell, taste, and draw key clues in a deductive way so when you get to the end, you have a narrow idea of what the wine should be. It's like a puzzle. You have all the pieces in front of you, you just have to solve it." I paused and glanced at Tessa, then Mark and back to Vanessa. "I'm sorry, I'm rambling. I do that when I talk about wine."

Vanessa smiled in a way my mom used to when I talked about my day at school.

"Well, I look forward to hearing your opinion on my wine," said Mark. Vanessa gently placed her hand on his arm. "Sorry, *our* wine," he added.

"I've been selling your Cabernet at the restaurant for years. It's a great wine."

"That's what I pay people to tell me but you're not on my payroll. So I want to hear an honest opinion after you've tasted tonight's wine." Mark's kind eyes looked directly into mine and he smiled.

I returned the smile. "Absolutely."

Tessa cocked her head. "Can we open something fun tonight?"

"What do you mean?" asked Mark.

"Something neat, something historic. Katie likes the story of a wine, so how about a wine that tells something about Frontier? Ooh, like a bottle of Merlot. Katie is a huge fan of Merlot." Tessa's hands flared out to the side to reference a space that would fit a baby elephant. "Like huge."

"Tessa." I shot her a look.

"What?" Tessa shrugged innocently. "You are."

I returned my focus to Mark. "I like a variety of wines."

"But Merlot especially?"

"Yes," I said as I nudged Tessa. "I do really love Merlot."

Mark pulled his fingers through his peppered hair. "Well, we're serving Cabernet tonight, but why don't you grab a bottle of the '94 Merlot from the cellar." He unclipped his phone from his belt and looked at the time. "The reserve bottles won't come out for a few minutes, but let's start celebrating."

"Sweetheart, aren't we serving Merlot tonight?" said Vanessa.

"We have one bottle on the menu, but it would be nice for them to have a special bottle. After all, it is a celebration." He squeezed Vanessa's hand and then looked at Tessa. "Enjoy the '94 Merlot."

"Wow, thanks." Tessa linked her arm around me. "We'll go right now."

"Thank you so much, it was very nice meeting both of you," I said as Tessa's arm pulled me away.

"Quick," Tessa whispered as she led me back up the lawn, "before he changes his mind."

The stone walkway curved around the winery to a spacious concrete area shaped like half an octagon, the middle section set back as if it held up the hillside.

I paused and rubbed the ball of my foot on the concrete pad, outlining the small stones methodically placed into it. "The cellar isn't original?"

"Why do you say that?"

"All the concrete. It's new."

"Nah," said Tessa as she pulled the right handle of two wooden doors that arched in the center of the wall. "It's been here since the winery opened, but they redid the outside earlier this year. Or maybe it was last year. I don't know." She held the door open for me.

"It's not locked?"

"Would that matter?" Tessa waved her fingers in the air. "I learned a few things in the joint."

"Tessa, stop."

"Get over yourself, Katie. It's always open during business hours."

I stepped inside, the light from the door casting a small rectangle of white onto the stone floor in front of me. The beam faded to obscurity as Tessa closed the door behind us.

Darkness with a mixture of oak and damp surrounded me. "Tessa? You have a flashlight?"

No reply.

"Tessa?" My heart rate began to escalate.

"Calm down, scaredy-cat. I'm getting to it. Hey, we should open a bottle of wine right now. Would give new meaning to blind tasting, right?"

I waited for my eyes to adjust, but the black abyss remained. "Tee, are you going to turn a light on anytime soon?"

"Still don't like the dark?" There was a giggle to Tessa's voice.

"Tessa!" My voice echoed through the cellar.

Lights flared to life behind barrels stacked two high on either side as the tunnel curved deep into the hillside.

"One day you'll stop being afraid of the dark." Tessa tapped her finger on her lips. "Hmm, maybe we should try that again." She reached for the light switch to the left of the door.

"Not funny, Tessa."

Tessa turned around. "I'm just kidding." She pointed to the cellar. "Now you've seen it. Is it as fun as you expected?"

"I can only see barrels. Are there bottles in here, too?"

"Yep," said Tessa as she walked forward, her heels echoing around us. "Remember that party freshman year in Kelly's basement? This would have been much cooler. And it's fully stocked."

The ceiling changed from stone squares to etched bedrock as we went farther into the cellar.

"I bet they carved this all by hand."

"I guess," said Tessa. "Sounds like a headache."

We passed the first side tunnel, which snaked into the hill at least twenty or so feet, crates of wine stacked on the floor to the right and racks of wine to the left.

"What wine is this?" I motioned to the crates.

"I don't know. New wine?"

"Really, Tessa?" I laughed. "You work here."

"I work for the wine club, not the wine cellar. All I know is that I don't open that stuff," she said as she pointed to the crates.

The next tunnel was only four feet deep, followed by another tunnel that went at least ten feet into the hill. The non-uniformity of it gave me a chill, and I put my hands over my arms.

Tessa looked over her shoulder at me. "Are you cold?"

"No, not really. I'm fine."

"Don't worry, we won't be in here long."

I glanced at the tunnels as we passed, the round bottoms of bottles protruding from the shelves in perfect symmetry, their dark glass reflecting in the glow of the overhead bulbs. Certain bottles appeared more illuminated than others. "The lighting makes it look like there's white wine in here, too."

"There is."

"I didn't know Frontier made white wine."

"They don't. It's from next door," said Tessa. "Jim Garrett is a friend of theirs and they sometimes swap bottles."

"Why aren't they all together in one place? They're randomly on different shelves and in different tunnels."

"Welcome to Vanessa's method of organization."

"Effective."

We continued through the cellar as it went deeper into the hill.

"This place is pretty big considering Frontier is a boutique winery. I'm surprised."

Tessa shrugged. "Maybe they were preparing for greatness when they built the place." She flicked her eyes at me. "They knew I was coming."

"Tessa," I groaned.

We reached a wrought iron gate that blocked off the rest of the cellar, which curved an additional fifteen feet before stopping.

"This is where the stuff gets good." Tessa lifted up the large padlock on the gate. "And they keep this one locked." She turned the base of the lock to the left, then the right. It popped open and the gate swung to the side. "It's an insider secret." She pointed at the labels of the next few tunnels. "'99, '98, '97, '96, almost there."

"Pretty generous of Mark to let us have a '94. I'm sure it sells for a lot, since the current releases run so high."

"Yeah, he's sweet." Tessa turned down a side tunnel labeled 1994. "Here's the Merlot." She motioned to the three alcoves in front of her. "Those over there are the Cabernet, and he didn't make Pinot back then."

Bottles of red wine lay carefully stacked on top of each other in alcoves in the stone, a layer of dark black mold covering several of the top bottles, except for three bottles of white wine. The labels on those were unblemished, the words *Garrett Winery, 2012 Chardonnay* in wide cursive writing above the image of a meadow with orange, yellow, and green brush strokes.

"A 2012 in the '94 section?"

"Vanessa." Tessa shrugged and picked up a small wire basket designed to keep older bottles level during transportation so the sediment remained undisturbed.

"Look at you, so knowledgeable about wine. You even have a basket to decant the wine."

"I don't want to drink a mouthful of sediment. Besides, not bad for four months on the job. I know a lot now."

"What are the main grapes found in Bordeaux?"

"I meant about this wine, show off." She leaned closer to the first alcove. "Which bottle shall I choose?"

I let out a small laugh. "Aren't they all the same? And when have you ever been picky?"

Tessa stuck out her tongue. "I'm picky."

"Give me two examples."

"My shoes."

I nodded. "Okay, good. Another one?"

Tessa tapped her lips. "My men."

"Seriously? You mean you pick up a lot of men."

"Funny. No, you'd be proud. I'm picky these days. Like my current boyfriend—he's financially successful."

"Wait, you have a boyfriend? But you don't like to be tied down."

Tessa put her hand over her mouth, her voice dropping to a whisper. "Well, sorta a boyfriend." She bit the knuckle of her index finger and looked at me. "We haven't made it one hundred percent official yet. But he adores me, he's super cute, and he's great in bed. There's even been mention of the M word. I chose a good one this time."

"Okay, I need to hear more right now. Why don't I know this?" I stepped back and my hand hit the rack behind me. A bottle on the top wobbled and went crashing to the floor, wine and glass scattering across the space between us. "I'm so sorry!" I leaned down and tried to stop the wine with my hands as it flowed across the cellar floor.

Tessa stepped past me and returned a few seconds later with towels, a brush pan, and a bucket.

"Tessa, I can't believe I did this. So sorry!"

"Don't worry, you're not the first and you're definitely not the last."

I pressed the towels onto the wine. "This is probably five hundred dollars' worth of wine."

"I know," Tessa laughed. "Vanessa would be pissed. She's all about the bottom line."

"I don't do stuff like this, I never break bottles. I think the exam unsettled me ... I don't know." I stuffed the wine-soaked towels into the bucket while Tessa brushed the glass into the pan. "Will you get in trouble?"

Tessa shrugged. "Nah. I think we're doing a good cleanup job."

I sat back on my heels. "Look at me, I'm messing up your life again. You invite me to your work and look what I've done."

"Messing up my life again?" Tessa stopped brushing. "Are you talking about ..."

I nodded.

"You still think about that?"

"Yes." I locked eyes with Tessa, the soft lighting casting a yellow shadow on her face.

"But why? That was what, twelve years ago?"

"I know, but I feel … I don't know."

Tessa stood up and grabbed the bucket. "Don't worry about it. I'm fine. Okay? You would have done the same for me. Right?"

The thought went through my mind.

"Right?"

"Yes," I breathed out.

"Okay, good. Then let's leave it. Come on, let's get the wine and get out of here."

"What about the bucket?"

Tessa handed it to me. "Put it by the door before we go out."

"And it'll be okay?"

"Of course." Tessa smiled with her mouth closed. "There's no way I can get fired from here."

THREE

PAIRING SUGGESTION: ROSÉ—CÔTES DE PROVENCE, FRANCE

A refreshing wine with a dry finish.

THE DAYLIGHT HAD TURNED soft, the bulbs above the lawn doing their best to replace the lost light as the sun lowered behind the hills. Caterers raced around with trays while guests pulled up at the valet.

"Find us a seat, I'll be right back," Tessa said as she handed me the basket and skipped to a booth. I sat down at a table on the far side of the lawn next to a hedge that separated the property. Tessa returned with two glasses and a decanter. "I'm glad I got these before the line started. People are going to get super drunk tonight."

"Here, I have a wine opener." I reached into my purse.

"I love that you leave your cell phone in your car, but still carry a wine opener. Don't worry, I have one." Tessa pulled a wine opener from the pocket of her dress.

"A dress with pockets, nice."

"Effective fashion, Katie. I'm telling you, it's the way to go." Tessa cut off the foil and pushed the opener into the cork. The dark wood handle glinted in the overhead lights as the stainless-steel body turned. An engraving caught my attention. *Tessa B.*

"Nice opener."

"I know, right? Mark bought it to thank me for all the great work I've done."

"Expensive gift."

Tessa shrugged. "I guess." She removed the cork from the bottle. "Want to decant?"

"Sure. But we need a light."

"Here." Tessa took a lighter out of her pocket.

"I thought you quit smoking."

"I did."

I tilted my head to the side. "Why do you have that?"

"Listen, Katie, you never know when you might need a lighter. And right now is one of those times." She smiled. "I'm ready, are you?"

"Oh, sorry." I lifted up the bottle of wine and poured it into the glass decanter as Tessa held the lighter under the neck of the bottle to illuminate the line of sediment. When the line reached the neck, I stopped pouring, the sediment returning to the bottom of the bottle along with the last few ounces of wine as I placed it in the middle of the table next to the flower arrangement.

Tessa filled two glasses from the decanter, drops spilling onto the white tablecloth. "Oh well, I'm sure it's the first of many spills tonight." She handed a glass to me. "Not by me, of course, but by everyone here." Tessa held up her glass. "Cheers to old friends and the best future Master Sommelier I know."

I clenched my jaw. "I don't know. Maybe."

"What do you mean *maybe*? You'll get the Certified next time." Tessa nodded, her curls falling in front of her face.

I swirled the wine in my hand, the droplets forming tears as they ran down the glass. "No, I think I'm done."

"Bullcrap." Tessa shook back her hair. "You don't give up. I mean, that Police Academy thing—that was just for your dad, to follow in his footsteps. Your heart was never in it, even before the final test. But you'd never give up on wine."

"Listen," I interrupted as I held up my glass, "let's toast to something positive."

"Yes! Like how awesome we are?"

I laughed. "Sounds great."

"Or," said Tessa as she leaned forward and we clinked the glasses, "how about my upcoming promotion?"

"You're getting a promotion? Already? Cheers to that!"

"Actually," said Tessa as she swallowed a mouthful of wine, "it's a gray area. And only sort of a promotion. And it's hush-hush around here, so *shh*." She took another long drink.

"Meaning?"

Tessa waved her free hand dismissively and shrugged.

I held my glass away from my face. "Tessa, what you are up to? Be honest with me."

"I'm always honest with you," said Tessa. "When have I ever lied to you?"

"Sixth grade. When you kissed Tommy Beeman."

"Oh please, so one time in twenty years?" Tessa lifted up her glass. "Can't I get an appeal, Judge Stillwell? I've served my time."

A string quartet started playing from the corner of the lawn. As classical music flowed throughout the area, I focused my attention on the wine. More than twenty years of aging, more than twenty years since the grapes had been pressed and fermented, more than twenty years since the story had been formed, waiting to be uncorked.

I swirled it around the glass, watching it splash up the sides before I took a deep breath. Although muted from age, currants, blackberries, black cherries, and a hint of cocoa emerged from the wine.

I took a sip and let it fall over my palate, washing away the events of the day as I focused on the subtle flavors in the wine. It made me smile and I felt myself moving in time with the music.

"Um, what are you drinking?" A young man with dark brown hair and brown eyes stood next to the table, his gaze focused on the label of the wine.

"It's not one of yours, Seb, so don't worry about it," replied Tessa.

Seb reached for the bottle, a tremor in his hand as he picked it up. His face was narrow, with small defined features, and his body was thin, nearly rail-like, as if that of a boy, although his face indicated he was in his twenties. He held the bottle in both hands as he examined the label. "A '94 Merlot, huh? Are you kidding?"

"What?" said Tessa. "It was a good year."

"Um, Vanessa is gonna be pissed. You're done for sure." His hand shook as he put the bottle back on the table and it fell over.

"Please." Tessa picked up the bottle and righted it. "You need to relax once in a while."

"I'm serious. Does Mark know that you're drinking that?"

"Does Mark know what?" said Mark as he approached the table. He glanced at the bottle and then at Tessa. "Yes, Mark does know she's drinking that." His focus shifted to Seb. "You want some?"

"Um, no. Not ready to start drinking." Seb hesitated, his left leg shaking as he drummed his fingers on his faded pant leg and glanced around the area. "Um, I'm gonna check with Alan to see if he needs help." He took off toward the winery.

"He's such a liar," whispered Tessa. "He's been drinking since three."

"What does he do?"

"Assistant winemaker."

Mark sat down at the table. "I love this time, right before the flood of guests arrive."

"There are some already here." I pointed toward the first booth, where four couples held empty glasses about to be filled.

"Yeah, but they're busy drinking right now. I won't have to start talking to people for another ten minutes or so." Mark glanced over his shoulder. "Vanessa's handling the last-minute details, so as long as she doesn't see me sitting..." He motioned to the glass in my hand. "What do you think?"

"It's beautiful. Balanced and smooth. And I love the age on it."

"I'm glad you like it. The '94 is my favorite year. Although I should pretend that every year is my favorite as it's a business, but I can't. The '94 is the best." Mark leaned back in his chair and looked across the lawn.

Two of the couples previously at the booth now sat at one of the round tables, their glasses of red wine contrasting against the white tablecloth.

"Can you believe it, one hundred years?" Mark's voice contained a softness reserved only for moments of pure truth. "For one hundred years, my family has been on this ground, making wine. My dad, his dad, and his dad before that. My great-grandfather started with a dream and it's still going." He waved his hand in the air. "He only had a few workers when Frontier began and he did most of the work here himself. We still have his old wine press in the back. He did nearly everything by himself." Mark's eyes shifted back to the bottle of wine. "I'm fortunate to have a great team so we can all share the work." He looked at me. "Your family in the wine business?"

The table rocked as Tessa stood up and walked over to the booths.

I returned my attention to Mark. "My uncle owns a winery."

"It's not an easy business. So much can go wrong." Mark picked up the bottle and ran his thumb over the label. "But so much can go right. When everything comes together in harmony, you have a perfect bottle of wine. It's the only thing I've ever wanted to do. Create great wine and have it be appreciated by those who savor it."

"My uncle feels the same way. He said making wine made his life worthwhile."

Mark put the bottle down. "Is his winery here in the valley?"

"No, South West France actually. Just outside of Cahors."

"Nice. Have you spent a lot of time there?"

"Used to," I replied. "When I was little."

Tessa returned to the table with a new glass, which she filled from the decanter and placed in front of Mark.

"Thank you, Tessa." Mark picked up the glass. He held it up to us. "*Salute.*"

"*Salute,*" Tessa and I said in unison.

I took a sip of the wine, which now carried a depth it didn't have before. The work Mark had put into the wine, the efforts of his great-grandfather to create a winery for his family in California, the years that the winery had been in Napa. It all came together in the glass with a story to tell.

"There are some people," started Mark, "who think I should open the winery to the public." He stared at the glass, a noticeable sadness in his eyes. "Produce more wine, have an open tasting room, give tours. Elements that will drive more of a profit. But it was never like that. It's always been about the care put into the product, about making great wine, even if it's a limited quantity. I can't destroy my great-grandfather's dream." His eyes met mine as a soft glistening came into them.

"People aren't always right, Mark," inserted Tessa. "You need to do what you want."

"You're right." He closed his eyes and lifted the glass to his chin, the wine trickling into his mouth, followed by a smile that clearly conveyed that he savored every aspect of the wine. "Perfection in a bottle," he said after swallowing. He opened his eyes and held the glass up, the sparkling overhead lights creating bursts of cranberry colored orbs in the wine. "Everything was perfect that year. The weather, the yields, the process. I'd give anything to go back to '94."

"I was seven," Tessa snickered.

"Thanks," retorted Mark. He glanced across the lawn. "I guess I should go check in with Vanessa and greet the guests. She's probably wondering where I am." Mark stood up from the table. "Enjoy your evening, ladies."

"Thank you." I raised my glass to him. "And thank you for sharing your wine with us."

"My pleasure." Mark turned from the table, his gait slow and reluctant across the lawn.

When he was halfway across the grass, I turned to Tessa. "You finally have a good job and a really nice boss. I'm happy for you."

"Thanks. Not bad for a delinquent, if I do say so myself. And I do." Tessa beamed, the purple stain across her teeth much darker than before. "Ooh look, here's Alan. I'm going to try and get him to talk. This is fun, watch."

An older gentleman with a white beard and a cowboy hat ambled near the table.

"Hey, Alan, having a good night?"

Alan's head slightly nodded, the only acknowledgment that he had heard Tessa's question.

"Want to join us for a drink?"

Alan shook his head and tipped his hand to his hat as he sauntered away.

"Okay," said Tessa. "Maybe later." She turned to me. "Man of few words but he makes a great wine. Been here for thirty years or something. One day, I'm going to find out what goes on in that head of his. I bet he has some good stories to tell." Tessa poured herself another large glass of wine.

"It's still early, Tee. Don't you want to pace yourself?"

Tessa rolled her eyes. "It's a winery celebration, Katie. We're supposed to drink. A lot. In fact, you have some catching up to do." She topped off my glass and then took a gulp of her own wine as she studied something in the distance.

I turned and followed her gaze. A raven-haired girl with perfect posture and a fitted black dress paraded around the tables as she gave directions to a young man in a white apron.

"A friend of yours?"

"Hardly. That's Mark and Vanessa's assistant, Lisa. She doesn't play nice."

Lisa paused when she saw Tessa, her white pearls still swinging with movement. After a moment, she continued looking around as if searching to give instructions to someone, anyone.

"Is she in charge tonight?"

"Nope, she just acts like it. That's Lisa for you. She takes credit for everything. She's my *favorite*." Tessa stressed the last word. "She tells Vanessa if I clock in even one minute late from a break and she went on a rant when I poured slightly more than one ounce for a guest. Even Mark had to tell her to relax."

"She sounds charming."

Tessa's eyes remained on Lisa. "Whatever." She took another drink. "I keep my distance." She topped off both glasses with the rest of the wine and placed the empty decanter back on the table. "Come on, let's mingle. Maybe we can find you a guy. Should be a lot of rich ones tonight."

31

"Is money all you ever think about?"

"Makes the world go 'round, Katie."

We stood up and walked through the tables, the caterers filling the serving dishes as we passed.

A waiter approached with a tray of canapés decorated with delicate folds of salmon slices. "Would you care for an hors d'oeuvre?"

"Ah, no, thank you. I'll wait till later."

"I'll take one." Tessa grabbed two and popped them in her mouth.

"Tessa, shouldn't you save those for the guests?"

"Nah, I am a guest," Tessa said as she chewed. "Tonight at least. You're a guest too, so I ate yours."

I shook my head. Tessa might have held down a steady job for the last four months but she was still Tessa.

"Sorry, they're not serving pasta tonight," she said.

"Tessa. I eat things other than pasta, you know."

"But if you had a choice?"

I hesitated. "Pasta."

"Exactly."

"My favorite wine lady, there you are," said an older voice with an affected tone. "What a fabulous dress you're wearing."

The gentleman, in his midsixties with silver hair in tight curls and a gray handlebar mustache, stepped closer to us. "I've been looking for you all night." He smoothed down a red ascot with his free hand and adjusted his gray tweed jacket.

"Garrett, I figured you would be here," said Tessa. "Nice to see you."

"Yes, my dear, lovely to see you as always." Garrett's eyes moved to me and he raised his eyebrows.

"Oh, this is my friend, Katie. Jim Garrett, but he goes by Garrett."

"I think last names are so much more regal, don't you?" Garrett swirled his wineglass as a clinking noise came from it.

"Is that ..." I paused. "Are there ice cubes in your glass?"

"Of course!" Garret lifted the glass. "I love a glass of cold white wine."

"Doesn't it water down the wine?"

"Only if you let it sit there." He downed the wine, leaving the ice cubes golden-colored at the bottom of the glass. "But I don't." He flashed a smile. "Katie, are you a connoisseur of wine? And by a connoisseur, I mean do you drink it?" He looked at my glass. "I guess you do. Smashing. You'll have to try mine, too."

"Garrett owns the place next door. Garrett, why don't you tell Katie how long you've owned your winery?"

"Oh me?" He emitted a hollow and rehearsed laugh. "I guess Tessa wants to share my secret. I've only been in the wine world for ten years, although truthfully I've been in it nearly all my life—drinking it, that is." He chuckled to himself, his shoulders convulsing. "You could say it's the only thing that has ever truly won my heart." He looked down at my legs and then at my chest before meeting my eyes again.

"Garrett is a businessman," said Tessa as her smile shifted into a smirk. "One day, about ten years ago, he woke up and decided to buy a winery." She turned to him. "Tell me, Garrett, do you actually pick any of the grapes?"

"Oh please, Tessa. That's what employees are for." He tugged at the right side of his mustache.

I pointed to his glass. "You make Chardonnay, am I right?"

"Yes, along with other ones that are eloquent, marvelous, and great for everything. In fact, the other day, I decided to add a few table-spoons of Chardonnay to my salad dressing and it was divine. You'll have to come over and try it sometime." Garrett stepped closer to me.

"Well, Katie is looking for a boyfriend," said Tessa.

Garrett raised his eyebrows. "Oh really? You know, I have some fabulous bottles that I've been hoping to share with someone special."

"Yes," said Tessa. "She likes men her own age. So maybe you have a son or a nephew for her?"

"I'll keep it in mind," he said, his voice clipped. "I must go, I'm out of wine." He shook his glass, the ice cubes jingling. "It was a delight meeting you, Katie, let's chat again later." He winked. "Nice to see you, Tessa." His voice wasn't as jovial. He sauntered toward a small group of people nearby.

"He's an interesting character."

Tessa laughed. "I know, weird, right? Watch yourself, he gets super flirty the more he drinks. But he's harmless and actually a nice guy when he's sober, the rare occasions. I'll have to take you to see his winery sometime. He's loaded, so it's super modern."

"I'm surprised. I didn't think you'd care." I sipped some more of my wine, the Merlot virtually dancing on my tongue.

"And they give out free truffles in the tasting room."

"There's the Tessa I know."

"Yes, and the Katie I know would love to see all the high-tech wine equipment."

"That would be nice." I looked up at the stone building illuminated by the party lights strung high above us. "But I also love the romance of the older wineries. So full of character."

"You're so poetic about wine." Tessa took another gulp from her glass as an electric chime went off in her pocket. She took out her phone, the blue glow illuminating her face. "Now? Like right now? Ugh."

"Everything okay?"

"Yeah, it's fine. Mark. Ugh. I have to go do something. I'll be back in a bit. Here, take my glass." She finished the rest of the wine and handed me the empty glass. "Thanks." Tessa tucked her phone back in her dress pocket and glanced anxiously around at everything but me.

"You sure you're okay?"

"Yeah, I'll be right back, I just wasn't expecting this. Enjoy the food, chat, flirt, that sort of thing." Tessa smiled a tight, closed grimace. "And I can explain this later, but if anyone asks, I've been with you the whole time." She disappeared into the crowd.

FOUR

PAIRING SUGGESTION: RIESLING—MOSEL, GERMANY

A slightly sweet wine that can handle both sweet and spicy situations.

❧

I PUT BOTH WINEGLASSES on a nearby table and started after Tessa. "Wait. I'm coming with you." My tall heels sunk into the dirt, slowing me down.

"Careful," said a male voice. "You look like you're about to trip."

My heel struck a lump of grass and I stumbled forward, a strong arm catching me before I fell. I looked up into green eyes surrounded by golden skin.

"Those shoes aren't the best for lawns." The man, who appeared to be in his late thirties, helped me back to a standing position. "You okay?"

"Yes." I peered into the crowd to find Tessa, but she was lost in the mass of party guests.

"You must be Katie. I've heard a lot about you."

I returned my focus to the stranger as he held out his hand. He was tall, over six feet, with wavy brown hair and a tanned face. His leather jacket rested uncomfortably on his broad shoulders, as if sizable muscles prevented it from fitting properly.

"I'm Jeff Kingman." He smiled, revealing straight white teeth and a twinkle in his green eyes. I politely shook his hand and turned around once more, but Tessa's blond curls were nowhere in sight.

"Looking for someone?" Jeff followed my gaze into the crowd.

"Tessa. She was just here but she ran off."

"Probably a party issue. This is still work for her." Miniature wrinkles formed around Jeff's eyes and a small bead of sweat ran down his temple, but he didn't bother to wipe it away.

"You're right, it's probably something to do with the party." I glanced around but was met by a sea of unfamiliar faces. I returned my attention to Jeff. "Wait, how did you know my name?"

"Tessa told me about you. We work together." His voice carried the slight tinge of a southern accent.

"Ah." The tension in my shoulders released. "It's nice to meet you."

"Yes, I agree, but I see a major problem."

"What's that?"

He motioned to my empty hand. "You're not drinking."

"Oh." I looked around and noticed the two glasses on the table near me, one empty and one half full. "I put it down."

"Here." Jeff picked up a glass and handed it to me. "Is this one yours? Can't waste a drop of this. This is Frontier wine," he whispered and then laughed, in a way that was half joking, half serious.

I nodded as I sipped the Merlot, the liquid sending a wave of relaxation through me. "Yes. And it's good wine."

Jeff watched me, a subtle smile on his lips, his five o'clock shadow highlighted by golden brown stubble that matched his hair. "I can see you like the wine."

"I do. I mean, I've always liked Frontier wine, at least when I've been able to try it. Which was only the Cabernet. But this Merlot, this …" I admired the wine in my hand, swirling it around the glass. "This is exquisite." I stopped and looked up at Jeff. "Sorry, I got carried away." I shifted awkwardly. "What do you do, Jeff? Something outside, right? Maybe in the vineyard?"

"Why do you say that?"

I wanted to say because he was tan, the back of his neck was a little red as if he spent time in the sun, his strong build meant something with heavy lifting, and even though I was sure they were clean, his nails had dirt alongside the cuticles, the kind that's hard to get off after a day in the vineyards. But instead, I replied, "Lucky guess."

"Good guess." He winked. "My job is to make sure every grape is happy and healthy."

"Excuse me?"

"I'm the vineyard manager." He grinned and his green eyes sparkled in the soft lighting.

"That's an admirable job. So much to know and so many different factors."

"Yeah," Jeff agreed, "but I love it. It's thrilling to watch a grape grow from a small bud to maturity so it can be picked and made into great wine. We just picked the Pinot grapes last week and the Merlot and Cab will be next, but I have a feeling it will be a good year for our Pinot." Jeff looked at the glass of wine in his hand. "I love creating something that will be enjoyed by others, you know? That they're enjoying that particular wine because of me."

My mouth opened but nothing came out. I tried again, my voice almost a whisper. "I couldn't agree more." I held my glass to my lips as I watched Jeff take a drink of the wine, his strong throat moving as he swallowed. His eyes focused on me and I gulped my wine, not noticing how much I swallowed until the last drop was gone.

Jeff pointed to my glass. "No empty glasses around here tonight, it's a celebration. What can I get you? Which one was that?"

"It was a special bottle. But maybe I'll try whatever they're serving at this booth. Are my teeth purple yet? Maybe I should have some white wine." I closed my mouth, heat rushing to my cheeks.

"Nah, don't drink that stuff. Tonight's white is from Garrett Winery. People who treat wine as a business make bad wine." He held up his hand, the palm facing me. "Well, not everyone, but definitely next door. I can't respect it if there's no care put into it, you know? Only use Garrett wine if you've spilled red wine and need to clean it up."

"I can see you're his biggest fan."

Jeff brushed his fingers across his brown hair. It fell back perfectly into place. "He's okay, aside from the fake accent. I'm just not a fan of his wine. But then, I've always been partial to red." He glanced in the direction of a wine booth, where servers in white aprons poured glasses of wine.

"Let me get you another glass." Jeff stepped over to the booth, his frame towering over the crowd, as I looked around at the tables. Tessa was still nowhere to be found.

Jeff returned a moment later with two glasses of red wine. "Here you go."

"What is it?"

Jeff smiled. "You tell me."

I looked at the glass and shook my head. "I can't."

"I thought you were the friend who could taste wines really well. Did I hear that wrong?"

"No, I just can't right now."

His face softened. "Sorry, I didn't mean to put the pressure on."

"No, it's fine. It's just that I get nervous and overwhelmed, and then I can't taste the wine. I just … can't."

"Hey." He made eye contact with me. "It's okay. Can I give you a hint though? Before you taste wine, or before you do anything in life, take a deep breath. That will help."

"Thanks." I took a deep breath.

"Better?"

"I guess," I laughed. I held up the glass, the white tablecloth of a nearby table highlighting the red. "This is younger than the one I was just drinking."

"Yes, anything else?"

I shook my head. "Not right now."

"This is the '08 Cabernet. I played a role in this one." He glanced at me. "See, you knew this one was younger."

"Yes." I stood up straighter as a small smile spread across my lips.

He motioned to the tables. "Shall we grab a seat?"

I looked into the crowd in a last-ditch effort to find Tessa. Nothing. "Sure."

We reached a table, vacant except for discarded wineglasses and two small plates. "There are appetizers if you want any." Jeff glanced around in search of a waiter. "Dinner will be out around eight."

My stomach rumbled. "No, I'm okay." I put my wineglass on the table. "I'll wait until Tessa comes back."

"Are you sure? It's always good to eat while drinking. Here, I'll be right back." He stood up from the table and returned a few moments later with a plate loaded with cheese, crackers, and sliced deli meat. "You don't have to eat any of it, but I want you to have the option." He set the plate between us.

My stomach growled as I stared at the slices of Gouda. I reached for one.

"I thought so. Here, I'll join you." Jeff reached for a piece of cheese and tossed it into his mouth.

I did the same, the saltiness of the cheese accenting the wine. I sighed. Wine and cheese. Always my favorite.

"Tessa mentioned you were coming to the party. Said you've been friends for a long time."

"Yes, about twenty years."

"Wow, that really is a long time. Why haven't you been to Frontier before?"

"This place is like Fort Knox."

Jeff laughed. "Even Fort Knox has ways to get in. You just have to know them."

"Well"—I picked up another piece of cheese—"I'm here now."

Jeff leaned back in his chair and took a drink of the '08. He held the glass in front of him. "I love how you can taste Napa in this glass."

I nodded. "The soil, the weather, the sunlight. It all ends up in the wine."

"Yes, especially with the rich soil we have here." He motioned to the ground near my feet. "It's probably good for you to sit. Give you a break from those heels."

I glanced at my shoes, the heels wet with blades of grass. "I don't normally wear these, but Tessa asked me ..."

"I'm sure you can take them off. No one will notice if you're barefoot."

"No," I laughed. "I can't be barefoot. This is a fancy event."

"If Tessa's feet hurt, she'd be the first one to kick off her shoes and parade around, no matter what people thought."

"Yes, well, that's Tessa." I looked around at the crowd. "She likes heels, I prefer running shoes."

"Ah, you're a runner." He crossed his legs, his knee out at a right angle. "Glad to meet another one. I do a three-mile jog every morning along the vineyards."

I scooted closer to the table. "I'd love to do that. Right now I run in Golden Gate Park, but to run in the vineyards every day would be perfect. My life would be so calm, so collected."

Jeff smiled at me, his eyes twinkling in the light. He swirled his glass and pointed to mine. "Hey, you haven't tried the '08 yet. I want to hear what you think."

"Oops, sorry." I laughed as a rush of heat burst through my cheeks. I picked up the wine and took a sip. The tannins gripped the inside of my mouth, erasing all signs of the smooth aged Merlot. I held it over my tongue and waited for it to mellow.

Jeff's smile faded. "You don't like it?"

I swallowed. "No, it's great. It was just a contrast to the '94 Merlot I was drinking earlier."

"A '94 Merlot? I can't say I was involved with that wine. It was about ten years before I got here, but what did you think?"

I nodded and opened my mouth to speak, but a bloodcurdling scream interrupted my evaluation of the wine.

We locked eyes as the scream repeated, longer and louder this time.

Tingles ran up my arms and across my scalp as I spun around to see where the scream had originated. Dozens of party guests turned in the direction of the winery.

"Come on," Jeff jumped up from the table. "Maybe we can help." He ran up the lawn, maneuvering through the crowd of people who stood frozen.

I took one step and nearly fell, my ankles collapsing in the heels. I kicked them off and ran after Jeff, my quick stride catching up to him.

When we reached the stone winery, Jeff took the first step inside the open door as I followed, my heart beating through my chest with adrenaline.

Large wooden fermentation tanks dominated the two-story building. At the far side was a labeling machine and a bottling machine where bottles would line up in the spring, waiting for their chance to be filled with wine. Closer to me was the pneumatic wine press, a substantial silver machine with a rounded top where grapes were pressed. Everything looked ready but paused in time, anticipating the work day to come.

A female caterer with black pants and a white apron stood with her fingers in front of her mouth, her face vacant of color, and her eyes wide. There was an overturned tray at her feet. I followed her gaze to the first fermentation tank, most likely filled with the Pinot Noir that had just been harvested.

There was nothing unique about it. In fact, it looked the same as nearly every other wooden fermentation tank I had seen in numerous wineries over the years, except for a splash of red wine on the concrete beneath the tank. Nothing to make someone scream and drop a tray.

That's when I saw the arm.

It was hard to see at first, caught between the lid and the opening at the top of the tank, but once I noticed it, I couldn't focus on anything else. Jeff must have seen it at the same time, for he sprinted toward the tank. I ran behind him, my eyes focused on the arm as I approached, everything moving in slow motion.

Jeff grabbed the rolling stepladder and pushed it against the tank. I gripped the rails at the bottom as Jeff rushed up the steps.

I stared up at the arm, its white sleeve stained purple halfway down from the juice of the grapes, the strong male fingers slightly curled, a thin gold band on the ring finger.

Jeff tugged at the arm as the back of a man's head popped into view.

"Oh my God," I breathed.

Jeff pulled again, his hands now underneath the shoulders of the man.

I tried to help, but my feet were cemented to the ground. I could only watch as Jeff struggled with the weight.

"Do … Do you need help?" I managed to ask.

Jeff grunted and tried again, lifting the body all the way up as wine and grape skins poured onto the winery floor.

The man's feet were caught in the opening and Jeff nearly tumbled down the steps as he readjusted his grasp. He yanked again and the feet came free.

I stepped back as Jeff brought the man down the stairs and laid him on the floor, red wine spreading like snakes on the concrete.

He leaned over the man's face, forcing his breath into his mouth, before pressing on his chest with sharp, sudden movements.

I kneeled at the man's side. "You breathe, I'll pump." I put my hands on his cold chest and counted as I had done in my long ago CPR class. A chill crept into my fingers, the absence of warmth underneath them.

"He's cold. I don't think he's coming back." I stopped pumping and picked up the man's wrist. The veins were lifeless, the chance of a pulse long gone. "It's no use."

Jeff leaned over the man and breathed into him.

"Jeff, it's no good. There's no pulse and he's cold."

Jeff sat back on his knees and I finally saw the man whose face stared blankly at the ceiling.

It was Mark.

FIVE

PAIRING SUGGESTION: GEWÜRZTRAMINER—ALSACE, FRANCE

A highly aromatic wine to ignite your senses.

ॐ

THE NIGHTTIME NAPA BREEZE added a chill to the air and I rubbed my arms for warmth as I stood guard. The winery door behind me was closed, a preventative measure after Jeff called 911, and all other doors had been locked before he headed to the driveway to wait for the police.

More than once I had to turn away guests who possessed a morbid curiosity. The crime scene needed to remain intact, apart from what we had done in an effort to revive Mark. I winced at the evidence we might have disturbed.

"I guess I should tell any guests still arriving to go home, huh? Not going to be much of a party now."

I turned to the voice, finding Seb next to me. His eyes darted back and forth from the driveway to the lawn, an intense nervous energy that I hadn't noticed when he came to the table earlier. Then again, maybe I had. Everything was distorted.

"No, the party is definitely over. The police should be here any minute and I'm sure they'll want to interview everyone who was here."

The entire winery was masked in a serene calm as caterers, staff, and guests sat at the tables on the lawn, barely moving.

"Some people, um, already left."

"That's not good. But I'm sure Tessa has a list of everyone who was here." I looked at Seb. "Do you know where Tessa is? I haven't seen her since before this whole mess started."

"Um, no." Seb shifted back and forth next to me. "Now is the time to drink, huh? But the caterers aren't pouring anymore."

"You work here, I'm sure you can grab a bottle. If you really need it."

"Not. Worth. It." Seb walked toward the offices, a slight sway to his gait. I wasn't sure how much he had drunk in the short time of the party or beforehand, but the sway could be the situation and not alcohol-induced. Death can do strange things to people.

Two squad cars raced up the driveway, the flashing lights disturbing the static atmosphere, spilling blue and red colors into the night sky.

They illuminated Jeff's silhouette, his arms motioning toward the winery. The cars came to a stop ten feet from me.

A sheriff's deputy exited the first car and said a few words to Jeff before the two of them headed toward me.

"Body in here?" said the deputy as he reached the doorframe.

"Yes." I opened the door and the deputy stepped inside. Jeff followed him and I noticed the wine stains on his clothes had turned dark blue.

Two more sheriff's deputies walked into the winery followed by one in a suit, his blond hair slicked back from his face. He started writing in a notebook as he crouched in front of the body.

"Has it been moved?" he asked as he stood up, only slightly shorter than Jeff, but with a solid stance.

"He was in the fermentation tank and I pulled him out, thinking I could save him. Unfortunately, he was already gone," said Jeff as he rubbed his forehead. His strong shoulders slouched over as if they carried the weight of the world.

I crossed my arms and leaned against the doorframe as the deputies stood over Mark's lifeless body, his arms splayed out to the side, his clothes soaked with purpled wine and dotted with grape skins.

"How was the body found? In here?" The blond deputy motioned to the first tank.

"Yes," I said from the doorway. "With only his arm sticking out."

"Join us," said the deputy as he scribbled on his notepad. "I'm Detective Dean, the officer in charge of this investigation. Why are you barefoot?"

I looked down, my red nail polish contrasting with the blue coldness of my toes as I approached. "I kicked off my shoes when I ran. They're outside."

"Okay," he said. "What brought you in here to find the victim?" He was in his midthirties and wore a gold badge on his belt, which glinted in the winery lights.

"The scream," I replied as two additional officers and a lady whose jacket had CORONER on it walked past me and joined the group. "A caterer screamed."

"Katie and I were together at the party and we heard the scream. We both ran in here and once I saw the arm, I ran up the steps." Jeff re-enacted the scene, climbing up the stepladder. "I grabbed his arm and pulled him up here." He pointed to the top of the tank. "As soon as I got him, I brought him to the floor and attempted to revive him."

"Watch where you're stepping," said Detective Dean.

"My footprints and fingerprints will be all over here anyway. I work here, and in trying to get him out..." His voice trailed off.

Dean kept his focus on Jeff's shoes as Jeff stepped back over to me. My dad had the same intensity when working on a case, the subject occupying every moment of his life, a smile never crossing his face until it was solved.

My attention drifted to Mark's vacant eyes, his open mouth, and his pale white skin. The sight wouldn't have fazed my dad—just another dead body to add to the uncountable list that he had seen in his career—but for me, it was only the second one I had seen. Two more than I ever needed to see. My stomach turned. "Can I go back outside for some fresh air?"

"That sounds like a good idea," said Jeff. "I can answer any questions. We were both in here together."

"Yes, but stay near. I'll want to get your statement later," said Dean, his attention still on his notepad.

I nodded and walked outside to the corner of the lawn, the balls of my feet sinking into the damp grass.

Loud sobs from the offices drifted on the breeze with a sadness that sent chills across my neck. The sounds were hollow, a loved one dealing with the first moments of grief, unable to grasp the situation.

It would only get worse as the night wore on. I knew that people could sometimes live in denial for days, even weeks, but emotions eventually surfaced to hit them like a smack in the face. When my mother passed away, denial wore off more quickly than I would have liked.

It was now eight thirty and Tessa had been gone more than an hour. I needed to find her. And my shoes. I approached the group of tables, glancing at each person as I passed by, but every face in front of me was a stranger.

The black heels I had kicked off lay between two tables. I slipped them back on, the hard leather a surprising comfort and relief from the cold ground.

Alan sat alone at the last table, cowboy hat in his hands and his face expressionless as he stared at the lawn near his feet.

I approached him with a wobble as the heels sunk into the grass. "Alan? Have you seen Tessa?"

Alan looked up at me, his eyes full of sadness. He shook his head and returned his gaze to the ground in front of him.

I needed to reach Tessa. I needed to call her. I headed across the lawn to the driveway, frustrated that I hadn't thought of phoning Tessa sooner. Maybe that's why I had failed my exam. I ignored obvious answers.

A black Jaguar had parked too close to my car but I managed to squeeze through and get my door open a few inches to grab my cell.

I returned to the edge of the lawn and called Tessa as one of the deputies gathered the caterers together in a group.

The phone rang three times. "You've reached Tessa. Leave a message and maybe I'll call you back."

"Tessa, where are you? Something happened and I can't find you. Call me back." I hung up and tried again. The result was the same. I cancelled the call before the message ended and sent a text. CALL ME. ASAP.

"Attention," demanded Dean, now standing outside the winery door. He was flanked by two additional deputies.

I approached the back of the crowd.

"I need to have everyone's name and if you saw anything that seemed strange or off tonight. You can tell me or Deputy Peters or Deputy Blake, but no one leaves until you've checked in with us."

Several lines formed with caterers and guests eager to leave the winery. I joined the back of one line as I scanned the property in search of Tessa. I tried her again, knowing it wouldn't work but needing to do something.

"Next."

I looked up to see a large gap between me and Dean. I stepped forward.

"Name?" Dean stared at the notebook in his hands, ready to write.

"Katie Stillwell, I'm a guest ..."

"Stillwell," Dean interrupted as his blue eyes rose from his notes and met mine. "Any relation to LAPD Chief Gary Stillwell?"

"Yes. He's my father."

"Well, what do you know. You a cop as well?" His demeanor softened, as did my father's when he met another member of law enforcement.

"No, a sommelier."

"What?"

"A sommelier. Basically, a wine expert."

Dean's rigid posture returned and his left hand scribbled notes. "Were you working this event?"

"No, I'm here as a guest. My friend—"

He cut me off. "What's her name?"

"Tessa Blakely."

More scribbling, his eyes never leaving the paper. "Where is she?"

"That's the thing, I don't know where she is." My stomach tensed.

"When did you last see her?" Small creases formed in his cheeks as he talked.

"During the party, but a while ago. Before everything happened here."

"Do you think she's still on the property?"

"I don't know what to think. She's been gone a long time, it's not like her." I motioned to the sheriff's cars. "Especially with all this.

I'm sure she'd be out here watching." I kept back the fact that Tessa had a thing for cops and wouldn't miss an opportunity to flirt.

"We'll find her. What is her affiliation with the victim?"

"She works here, in charge of the wine club."

"Let us know if you hear from her and we'll keep an eye out." He continued to write. "Did you notice anything else tonight, aside from your missing friend, that seemed strange?"

I shook my head.

"Address and phone number?"

When I finished giving Dean my contact information, he looked past me, his attention focused on the next person. "Name?"

I stepped away from the group and tried Tessa's cell phone again. It went straight to voicemail this time. I needed somewhere quiet where I could gather my thoughts away from all the commotion. My car would be ideal.

I returned to the driveway but stopped several feet away from my car. It hadn't registered before, but when I first arrived at Frontier, Tessa's silver Nissan had been in the space next to mine; now it was occupied by the black Jaguar. A tingling sensation shot across my scalp.

"Dean, we found something," a deputy echoed from the winery door.

"You okay?" said a voice close to me, causing me to jump. Jeff stood nearby, his brown jacket pulled together, hiding his stained shirt.

"No." My voice was weak.

"Are you cold?" He slipped off his jacket and put it around my shoulders.

I moved my head in a diagonal manner, neither up and down nor side to side. "Tessa's missing. I haven't seen her since I talked with you earlier and I don't know where she is."

"I'm sure she's fine." Jeff rubbed the sides of my arms in an effort to warm me up, but the cold chill remained. "She's probably getting more wine from the cellar."

"No. Her car's gone. It was parked right there."

"Are you sure? Maybe she moved it? Or maybe valet took care of it?"

I looked across at the three valet attendants on the far curve of the driveway. "I don't know. That doesn't seem right."

"Here, let me check for you. She drives a silver Sentra, right?"

"I think so. Yes."

"Okay, I'll be right back." Jeff jogged down to the attendants and spoke with them, his hands motioning back at me.

The attendant inspected the tag of each key on the white valet key board and shook his head.

Jeff ran back to me. "They haven't seen her car."

"Katie Stillwell," Dean's booming voice came across the lawn.

"Yes?" My voice came out as a whisper. "Yes?" This time it had more confidence.

"Come here, please."

"I'll go with you," said Jeff.

"No, it's okay." I approached the winery, meeting Dean at the door.

"There's something we want you to see." Dean lifted up the yellow crime scene tape that had been placed across the entrance.

I ducked under it and entered the winery. Officials milled around inside, dusting for fingerprints, taking photos, and making notes.

Mark's body had been covered with a white sheet but the fingers of his right hand stuck out from underneath in a deathly curl.

"Flip him over again," said Dean.

Deputy Peters pulled off the sheet and turned over the body. "Recognize it?"

I stepped forward, swallowing hard. "Recognize what?"

"Look closer," he pressed.

Firmly placed in Mark's back was a small knife attached to a wine opener.

"It's a wine opener."

Detective Dean kept his focus on the body. "Yes, but you can identify its owner."

"Me?" I tried to meet Dean's eyes but he wouldn't make eye contact. "Why?"

"Take a closer look."

I crouched down. My eyes traced the polished wood of the opener until I reached the engraved name of Tessa B. "Yes." I stood up and faced Dean. "It's Tessa's."

Dean removed his black notebook from his pocket. "When exactly did you last see Tessa?"

"Around seven thirty. Or maybe it was just after. She said she had to run an errand or something and that she would be back." I twisted my hands around each other.

"Where were you?"

"Near the tables and she headed up the lawn, but then I was distracted and when I looked back, she was gone." My eyes drifted to Mark's body as the deputy covered it back up with the sheet. "Also, her car is missing. I mean, she might have moved it, but—"

"But?" he interrupted, his eyes still on his notebook.

"She's not answering her cell phone." The words tasted dry as I said them.

"Describe Tessa." Dean's pen started moving before I even had the chance to speak.

"She's about five-five, shoulder length blond hair, hazel eyes. She was wearing a navy blue dress."

Dean nodded and grabbed his radio from his belt. He put it to his mouth as he read out his notes. "We're on the lookout for a female, approximately five-five, blond, hazel eyes, wearing a navy blue dress." He clipped the radio back on his belt. "Your friend, was she unhappy with her job?"

"Wait, no. Tessa wouldn't do this." I motioned to Mark's body on the floor. "She loved her boss. They got along great. I sat with both of them tonight, everything was fine." I readjusted my position until I stood directly in front of Dean and looked straight into his eyes, a trick I had learned to do with my father when I wanted his attention. "I've known her for twenty years, this isn't her."

"Okay ..." His eyes showed a human side, a kindness deep beneath the badge.

I wanted to use that to my advantage. "Maybe," I interrupted. "the person that did this took her, too. What if she's in danger?"

"Ms. Stillwell ..."

"Katie," I corrected.

"Katie, we will do everything we can to find her. Now"—he returned to writing on his notepad—"what did she say about this errand?"

"She said she would be right back and ..." My voice tapered off as Tessa's request went through my mind: to say that I was with her the whole night.

"And?"

"Nothing," I murmured. "That was it."

"Would anyone else know her whereabouts? Friends? Possibly family?"

"She doesn't have any family. Her parents died when she was in middle school. She only has ... me." I stepped back as the floor no longer felt solid.

Dean's hand rested on my back. "Why don't you go outside and get some air? We'll keep you updated. Peters, can you escort her?"

Deputy Peters led me outside the winery, the night air feeling colder than before.

"What has she gotten herself into?" I whispered under my breath.

"Has your friend had trouble with the law before?" asked Deputy Peters, standing at the winery door.

"Yes, but ..." I pulled Jeff's coat tighter around me. "That was different. Very different."

SIX

PAIRING SUGGESTION: GRÜNER VELTLINER—KREMSTAL, AUSTRIA

A dry white wine with a hint of spiciness.

I TRIED TO STARE across the winery to the vineyards, but it was too dark to see the calmness of their organized rows.

Jeff approached me from the driveway. "Is everything okay?"

I shook my head. "No, I need to find Tessa. Now. This is all my fault."

"What do you mean?"

I shook my head. "It doesn't matter, I need to find her."

"Here, I'll help."

"No, I don't need help—" I stopped. "I'm sorry, I'm used to doing things on my own." I looked up at him. "Listen, I'll let you know if I need you, but right now I need some time alone."

"Okay." The twinkle was gone from Jeff's eyes. He took a business card from his wallet and a pen from his shirt pocket. He wrote a number on the back of the card and handed it to me. "Here's my cell number. If you decide you need help, call me. I'm really good in these situations."

"Thanks." I took the card before I pulled his jacket off my shoulders. "Here. Thanks for this."

"Keep it. It will give us a reason to see each other again." He placed his hand on my arm. "I really liked meeting you tonight." Jeff ducked under the tape and headed into the winery.

I turned to the lawn, the advice from my tasting group floating around in my mind. "Don't leave points on the table," Jackson, a member of my tasting group and an Advanced Sommelier, would always say in reference to my exam. "Point out everything you can." Clearly I hadn't listened, but I was listening now.

I glanced around the area. I was close to the vine-covered walkway that led to the offices. The walkway lights, if there were any, were out and the vines prevented exterior light from illuminating the path.

I took a deep breath and started down the walkway, the darkness enveloping me. I focused on the small beam of light ahead of me and quickened my pace.

The distinct sound of heels came toward me.

I paused. "Tessa?"

"Hardly," said a voice as a shadow approached. A break in the hanging vines allowed the lawn lights to highlight the face of Lisa, Mark and Vanessa's assistant. "That's a first," said Lisa as she stepped fully into the light. She was in her midtwenties, her bright red lipstick a stark contrast to her pale white skin. "We're nothing alike."

"Sorry, I'm looking for Tessa."

Lisa flipped her long dark hair and stood in the middle of the walkway, her gaze searching the winery. "Isn't it interesting," she remarked, "how one minute everything is fine and the next, it's complete chaos? Like a board game turned over halfway through someone's turn. All the silly pawns ..." Her attention shifted to me. "I'm sorry, have we met?" Lisa's solemn face stared back at me.

"No, not yet. I'm Katie, Tessa's friend."

"Oh yes. The one that Tessa begged Mark to invite, even though it was an event only for the wine club." Although her voice appeared emotionless, the trace of resentment was hard to miss. "We don't allow strangers into our mix here. We need to protect ourselves from things." She waved her hand toward the flashing lights from the sheriff's cars. "Like this happening."

"Wait, are you accusing me of being involved? I didn't have anything to do with this."

"Are you sure?" Her eyes narrowed. "You're the only person here I don't know."

"Yes. And I was with Jeff for a while before Mark was found. You can ask him yourself."

A thin smile formed on Lisa's lips. "Don't be so quick to judge where someone's loyalty lies. What you see here is not always what you get. Besides, you're friends with Tessa. That says a lot."

"What's that supposed to mean?" I stepped forward, my stance casting a shadow on Lisa's face.

"All I mean is that this isn't surprising," said Lisa. "She has a record, doesn't she? I told Mark not to hire her. Now look what she's done."

I shook my head. "The record wasn't … Listen, I need to find her."

"But weren't you with her at the party? Weren't you her guest?"

"Yes, but I haven't seen her since … this."

"Then, Katie, you know as much as I do." Lisa flipped her hair as she forced a smile. "If you don't mind, I must be on my way. I have to put out some fires. The owner of the winery is dead, you know."

"Wait, one last question."

Lisa glared at me. "What?"

"Tessa said she had to do something tonight, like an errand. Do you know where she could have gone?"

"An errand? Tonight?" Lisa emitted a snicker. "What on earth would we need tonight? We have everything here. It sounds like she wasn't being honest with you, either. Now excuse me, I have to get back to the deputies. They want the guest list." Lisa took a few steps forward but turned around. "However," she said with a small smile on her lips, a shadow from the vines across her face, "since you're new around here, I'll give you a little hint. You might want to check out the lodge on Mount Veeder. Your friend is most likely there."

I mentally retraced all of my conversations with Tessa, but I couldn't recall any mention of a lodge. "Why would she go there?"

"She tended to run errands there during her coffee breaks and lunches. As if we didn't know. Your friend"—Lisa waved her hand horizontally—"she's not too bright. You can't keep secrets here at Frontier. Not from anyone." She pulled her hair over her shoulder, turned on her heels, and made her way to the winery.

I paused for a moment as I retreated into the shadows of the walkway, my eyes staring through the vines to the activity on the lawn. In my tasting group, I was constantly reminded that the key is to ask what is there, what you can find. Even though I didn't know where the lodge was located, I knew where I could find out.

I slipped off my heels and held them in my hand as I continued along the rest of the walkway. It ended in front of the offices at a solid door with an ornate looped handle. Which was locked.

My eyes drifted along the gravel to the corner of the building where I had met Tessa when I first arrived.

The sharp edges of the gravel dug into my feet and I crept along in pain until I reached the three steps, the wood a soothing relief to my feet.

I turned around to face the rest of the property as I wrapped my fingers around the handle. There was no one around this side of the building.

I opened the door and stepped inside.

SEVEN

PAIRING SUGGESTION: VIOGNIER—LODI, CA

A white wine with bold peach and apricot flavors,
meant to be consumed young—don't wait.

❧

THE DIM HALLWAY WAS void of activity except for a thin band of
light under one door at the far end, the same office that Tessa had
identified as Mark's. I focused on the light as it flickered with movement from inside. I stepped toward it but stopped when I noticed
the unopened doors to the right. *Don't leave points on the table.*

I opened the first door. The break room again. I silently closed
the door and opened the next door in the hallway. The room was
small with a wood desk and a placard bearing the name Lisa Warner.
I pulled at the desk drawers but each one was locked. I glanced
around the room. There was nothing else in the office that would
suggest an address of the lodge.

I continued down the hallway, moving closer to the door with
the light. Distant voices came from behind the door, their volume
increasing as I approached.

"No..." said a female voice.

"We need to talk about this," a male voice replied.

"Not now. This isn't the time. Please."

"Nessie…"

"No, stop … It's barely been an hour."

I leaned toward the door, straining to hear more clearly.

"Why now? Why can't you wait?" said the female voice. "I don't understand the urgency."

"You know why," replied the male voice. "I would still be asking even if this night hadn't happened, but it did. Now I'm here for you. To help."

The voices became muffled. I pressed my ear to the door as the heels in my hand collided with the wood frame.

"Shh," said the female voice. "Someone's outside."

I jumped back. My heartbeat echoed in my ears as I frantically searched for a place to hide, realizing that I would never make it down to another office or the break room. My only chance was the narrow door to my left. I reached for it, my hand slipping on the handle as the footsteps approached, the heels swaying in my other hand.

I tried again and the door opened. Several thick coats hung together in the small space with no extra room. I pushed into the coats and ended up sitting underneath them on several pairs of shoes, including the ones that Tessa had stowed away for me. I pulled at the door, only managing to partially close it. Through the inch-wide gap, I watched as Garrett and Vanessa stepped into the hall.

"I swear someone was out here. I saw a pair of feet under the door." Vanessa looked down the hall.

"I'm with you, my dear. Someone was listening. That's not good," Garrett said, his speech slightly slurred. "I'm going to find them. They have to be nearby." He approached the closet door, the ice cubes in his glass clinking.

I stopped breathing, a pair of boots digging into my bare legs.

He stood outside the closet door and reached for the handle. "Come out, come out, wherever you are." He pulled the door open a few inches.

"There you are." Dean's booming voice filled the hallway, matched only by my pounding heartbeat. "I need to talk to you about tonight. Can we step outside?"

"Will this take long?" asked Vanessa as she sniffled. "I can't take much else tonight."

"Of course, Mrs. Plueger. We'll make this as quick as we can."

"Thank you," she sniffed and clomped down the hall.

Garrett stayed at the opening to the closet. I closed my eyes, afraid to look in case he stared right at me.

He paused for a few more seconds and then his footsteps echoed down the hall. I leaned back and let all of my breath out. A small bead of perspiration ran down my cheek.

I checked the hallway from a kneeling position. It was empty. I stood up, shoe imprints dotting the back of my legs. I stepped toward the office where Garrett and Vanessa had been.

The curdling scream of a cat shattered the silence. The fright took me down, the shock from hitting the floor delaying for a split second the pain that then emanated through my body. The cat hissed at me before scampering down the hall.

I jumped to my feet as I debated diving back in the closet. I waited, my back pressed against the wall, listening for someone to come in the main door. No one did.

I relaxed and looked in the direction the cat had run. "Cat, you'll give me a heart attack."

I ducked into the office. I wouldn't have much time to find the lodge's address before Vanessa or Garrett, or both, returned.

A grand desk filled the center of the room with two file cabinets behind it, each with four drawers. The desk was clean except for a small stack of papers next to a pad of paper with Mark's name embossed near the corner.

Needle in a haystack. Not a problem. I flipped through the loose papers. Bills, invoices, shipping orders, and general correspondence.

The desk drawers were locked, so I turned my attention to the first filing cabinet. I ran my finger across all the file tabs in the top drawer. Nothing mentioned a lodge, Mount Veeder, or additional property.

I moved to the next drawer down, but again, there was nothing. The third and fourth drawers returned the same result.

In the second filing cabinet, the heavy top drawer contained a folder labeled *Property Tax*. I pulled out the file and flipped through the papers until I found a tax form for 1829 Mount Veeder Road. Bingo.

I scribbled down the address on the desk notepad and ripped off the paper, folding it into my right hand. I returned the file to the cabinet, closed the drawer, and reopened the office door. The hallway was empty.

I grabbed both pairs of shoes from the closet and kept an eye out for the cat as I headed for the exit. I stood up straight, trying to seem nonchalant, giving the appearance that I had a legitimate reason to be there.

The cold night air greeted me as I stepped outside and closed the door behind me.

"Katie, there you are." The sound of Detective Dean's voice made me jump. "What were you doing inside?"

"Getting my shoes," I calmly replied, my game face on. I held both pairs in my left hand, my right hand behind my back.

"Okay." He studied me like my father did when he was trying to figure out if I had been in trouble. "You wear two pairs?"

I kept my position steady, my face unmoving. "Tessa lent me a pair for tonight and the other pair is mine. Is that a problem?"

"No. That's fine." Dean paused, the overhead light above the door casting a soft glow on his face. "Have you heard from Tessa yet?"

I shook my head. "No."

"We'll find her, don't worry. I'll let you know as soon as we hear anything."

"Thanks." I gripped the piece of folded paper. "Are we free to go? I mean, can I go? It's been a long night."

"Yes, we have your information if we need to contact you. Be safe out there."

"I will." I passed by Dean and headed to my car. I couldn't shake the feeling that Dean watched me as I walked, but I didn't turn back to check.

EIGHT

PAIRING SUGGESTION: VOUVRAY—VOUVRAY, FRANCE

*Made from the Chenin Blanc grape,
this wine can hold up through the ages.*

❧

I WAITED UNTIL THE winery was out of sight before pulling to the side of the road. I unfolded the piece of paper and typed the address into my phone. It came up with an estimated drive of thirty minutes.

If the party had continued as planned, I would be eating dinner and possibly dancing by now. But that was life with Tessa. Things never seemed to go as planned.

The Mount Veeder area became dark and winding as it climbed in elevation. I passed two residences, wineries I assumed, as I drove up Mount Veeder Road until I came to a mailbox with the number 1829. I slowed and turned into the driveway, my headlights illuminating a one-story wooden building.

My heart fell as I parked my car, the only car, in the driveway. Darkness consumed the area as I turned off my headlights, the only remaining light a soft glow from the curtained window of the lodge.

My ears strained for the slightest noise—aside from my pounding heart—as I took one step at a time up the path that curved across what appeared to be a lawn. I wasn't sure if I would run toward the lodge or back to my car if I heard something, but I held my keys pointed in my hand, ready to attack.

I reached the front door and grasped the handle, expecting it to be locked. Instead the handle depressed and the door opened to a scream.

I jumped back, holding the keys in front of my face, but I lowered them when I recognized Tessa standing in the living room, her hand to her chest. "Tessa?"

"Katie? You scared me to death!" Tessa leaned against boxes of Frontier wine stacked against the wall. "I'm about to have a heart attack. Don't you know what stress does to the heart!"

"I'm sorry, but I've been looking for you!" I stepped inside the small living room. It was covered in yellow carpeting with two doorways leading off it and a thick smell of cardboard and wine in the air. "What are you doing here?" Boxes of wine lined the floor around the edge of the room.

"I'm running an errand for Mark. I'm about to go to the party now. Want to head back? Hey, whose jacket are you wearing? Did you meet a boy?"

I studied Tessa. Her smile seemed bright as ever and her blond curls bobbed on her shoulders as she moved a box of wine into the corner.

"Tessa, why are you really here tonight?"

"I had to bring wine here. It's a long story."

I glanced at the boxes around Tessa. "Tell me."

"Later."

"Now." My voice was stern.

"Mark texted that I needed to take more wine to the lodge. Vanessa isn't supposed to know and since the party was going on, the timing was perfect. It's not a big deal, Katie. I was coming right back."

"Coming back?" I glanced at my watch. "It's nearly ten o'clock. You've been gone over two hours."

"Oh, is it that late? I really should start wearing a watch again. This whole phone deal doesn't quite cut it. Come on, let's go."

"Tessa, why did you invite me to the party tonight?"

"What do you mean?" Tessa brushed her hair away from her shoulders. "I wanted you to enjoy Frontier."

"But what about when you left the party, you said I needed to say I was with you the whole time."

"I can't let anyone know I'm doing this errand. You were my cover. Why? What's going on?" Tessa tilted her head.

I waited for Tessa's tell, the way she pulled her mouth to the side when she was lying. But Tessa's mouth remained in a half smile with no evidence of a lie.

"Tessa, the party's over."

"Over? Don't be silly. The band is booked to play until eleven. What, did someone get super drunk and do something stupid?"

"It's Mark. He's … He's dead."

Tessa's mouth dropped open as her eyes drained of emotion. "Please tell me you are kidding. This isn't funny, Katie."

"It gets worse. The deputies found your wine opener in his back. They want to talk with you."

"My wine opener?" Tessa reached into her pocket but came back empty. "I must have dropped it." She put her hand to her head. "I need to think. Give me a few minutes. I need to be able to explain."

"Explain what? Just tell the truth."

A spray of headlights flashed on the wall.

"Who is that?" Tessa ran to the window as a car door slammed. "Katie, you brought the sheriff with you? Are you trying to be like your father? I'm sure he'd really love that, finally be proud of his daughter." Her eyes narrowed as she shook her head. "I can't believe you're doing this. I covered for you. I took the fall for you. And this is how you repay me?"

"Tessa, I didn't! I came here to find you and to help you. He must have followed me."

Tessa's eyes softened. "No, that's not it. You're giving up on me. That's your new thing, isn't it? You've given up on taking the Certified test and now you're giving up on me." She flinched as a loud knock sounded on the door.

I shook my head. "I'll never give up on you. Tell the truth, Tessa, and you'll be fine. You didn't do anything, right?"

"No. I didn't do anything."

"Then you have nothing to worry about." I opened the door.

"Katie. Tessa, I assume." Dean stepped inside, his eyes flicking to me. "Did you know she was here the whole time?"

"No, I found out about the lodge and on a hunch, came to see if she was here. I'm glad I found her and she's okay."

"Yes, she is." Dean looked around the room, staring at the stacks of wine boxes. "What's all this?"

"I can't tell you," Tessa whispered, her face growing pale.

"Looks like stolen property to me," said Dean. "You're racking up quite a list tonight."

"This wine belongs to Mark." Tessa crossed her arms.

"Yes, it belongs to Mark. Not you."

Tessa glared at Dean. "He told me to bring it here."

"Interesting. We'll find out more about that soon. You're coming with me back to the station. We need to ask you some questions."

"I didn't do anything wrong." Tessa stood straighter as her voice level increased. "I didn't kill him. I didn't kill anyone."

"Detective, I believe her," I interjected.

"Then let her come down to the station and prove it. At this point, we're only asking her questions."

I extended my hand toward Tessa. "He's right. Let's go down there and get this figured out."

Tessa hesitated, a drawn look on her face, before taking my hand with a cold and clammy palm. I gave it a reassuring squeeze as we walked outside and down the path toward my car.

"Where do you think you guys are going?" Dean's loud voice followed us. "She can't go with you."

I looked at Dean. "What?"

"She has to ride with me." He motioned to his squad car.

"We'll follow you."

"No can-do. Tessa's a suspect in this investigation and I can't let her out of my sight." Dean opened the rear door of the sheriff's car.

"Katie, no. Don't let me go with him. I don't want to go back to jail." Tears formed in Tessa's eyes as her shoulders crumpled.

I couldn't remember the last time I had seen Tessa cry. Not even when police stormed the house years ago and Tessa stood in the living room after pushing me out of the officer's sight. Tessa had bravely held out her hands, waiting to be cuffed, as I watched from the safety of the bushes. Not a word from her lips, only a small nod to me before she was put in the back of the squad car. I had let her go without a fight. Without any assurance. I wouldn't let that happen this time.

"Tessa, it will all be okay. I'll be waiting for you when you're done and then we'll get this whole thing figured out."

Tessa paused. "But what about my car?"

"Where is your car?"

"Around back."

"I'll drive you back here and we can pick it up. It's not a problem."

Tessa sank into the back seat of the sheriff's car as Dean closed the door.

"Wait," Tessa banged on the window, her eyes wide with fear at me. "Wait, I can prove it. Ask Seb."

"What?" I stared at Tessa, not understanding as the car's engine muffled her message. "Why, Tessa?"

The car drove away as I stood in front of the lodge, the glowing red brake lights creating a trail down the dark driveway. I jumped in my car and followed, but instead of continuing to the sheriff's station, I turned toward Frontier Winery.

NINE

PAIRING SUGGESTION: ALBARIÑO—RÍAS BAIXAS, SPAIN

*A white wine with low alcohol and floral flavors
while you think things over.*

☙

GRAVEL FLEW UP FROM the driveway as I reached the Frontier offices and parked in the same spot. Aside from the absence of the catering van and only one sheriff's car instead of two, the scene at the winery hadn't changed in the hour I had been away. A few chairs were tipped over and the floral arrangements seemed to droop, saddened by a celebration that never happened.

"You came back, huh?" Seb stood near the winery, his left knee shaking as he tapped his fingers.

"Yeah, I needed to find you."

"Me?" Seb's eyebrows went up and his eyes held a look I couldn't quite place. Terror or curiosity, I wasn't sure.

"Tessa's in trouble. They think she had something to do with tonight."

The frequency of Seb's tapping increased. "You mean with Mark, huh?"

"Yes. I know that's not true, but when she was arrested…"

"She was arrested?" Seb interrupted, his brown eyes wide open.

"Well, yes. I mean no. I mean, they took her down to the station for questioning. But she told me to come find you and ask you."

Seb's face returned to normal, his surprise masked by what seemed like an eerie and rehearsed calm. "Ask me what, huh?"

"That's the thing, I don't know."

Seb shrugged. "Um, I don't know either."

"Did you see anything tonight? Anything with Tessa? Or see Tessa with Mark?"

He shook his head. "Um, I saw her with you at the table and that was it. I didn't see her again."

"Are you sure?" I stared at him. "Why would Tessa tell me to come ask you then?"

"I have no idea, huh. I've only known her for a few months, right? I don't know why she does stuff."

"Sebastian." Jeff appeared at the side of the winery. "Lisa's asking for you."

"Gotta go." Seb disappeared into the darkness near the offices.

"Hey, I thought you'd left," said Jeff. "Are you still looking for Tessa?"

"No, I found her. But I needed to come back. I needed to ask Seb something."

"Did you get what you needed?"

I stared at the damp grass below my feet. "No. Not really."

"Can I answer it for you?"

I looked up at Jeff. "I don't think so." My palm touched the base of his jacket, which I still wore from earlier. I took it off. "Here, thank you for this."

"Keep it, it's cold out."

"No, it's okay. I want to give it back. I don't know the next time I'll be out here and I'd hate to think of you without your coat."

Jeff leaned closer. "Then come back sooner. Hey, come back here and go running with me."

I placed the jacket into his hands. "I don't have time for … I mean, I don't know. Maybe. But thanks." The last thing I needed right now was a relationship or even a date.

"Okay," said Jeff as he slung the jacket over his shoulder. "But give me a call sometime, okay? I can at least give you the tour here."

"Thanks." I gave a brief smile and walked toward my car.

A shadow crossed the driveway from the offices as the sound of soft cries reached me. Vanessa's profile came into view under the lights, a tissue held to her mouth and the slight fragrance of jasmine in the air.

My heart ached for the new widow, even though I had heard the argument between her and Garrett. It didn't matter at that moment, as I identified with the beginning of her painful journey. I approached her, but she looked up at me without any sense of recognition. "Vanessa, I'm so sorry."

Vanessa blinked, her face blank.

"It's Katie, Tessa's friend. We only met tonight but I wanted you to know that I'm so sorry for your loss."

"Thank you," she replied, her voice quiet and strained. "I feel so lost. Nothing is making sense right now." Vanessa ran her fingers across her purple scar, all the foundation rubbed off as she mindlessly outlined it.

I placed my hand on her shoulder. I wasn't sure what to say. When I lost my own mom, people said sorry to me so I repeated it. "I'm so sorry."

Vanessa's shoulders convulsed under my hand. "The vipers are already moving in and decisions will need to be made. I can't—" Her words became lost under the heavy sobs.

"I'm so sorry," I repeated. "So sorry. Please let me know if there is anything I can do."

"I don't know who I can trust," Vanessa sputtered through the tears. "I feel like I have no friends."

"No, that's not true. You have friends."

"I don't."

I reached into my purse and pulled out my business card. "Here, my number's at the bottom. If you need to talk to someone, call me. I've been in your shoes."

Vanessa clutched the card. "Stillwell? That's familiar. I did Junior League with a Silvia Stillwell, back in the day."

I took a step back. "That's my mom."

"Really?" Vanessa's blue eyes opened wide. "What are the chances? How is she?"

I swallowed hard. "She passed away."

"I'm sorry to hear that." Her gaze fell to the card. "Thank you for this. I may end up calling you."

"Please do. Will you be okay tonight?"

"No, but I'll make it." Vanessa stared into my eyes, all remnants of composure seen at the party earlier, now shattered.

"Can I help you somewhere?"

"No, I'm fine. I'm going for a walk. I don't want, I can't, be in the house right now."

"I understand." I stood motionless as Vanessa continued across the lawn, her blond head hanging down as she walked.

I was about to follow her but stopped. Vanessa shouldn't be alone, but first I needed to be a friend to Tessa.

I glanced around the property. Jeff stood near the walkway. "Jeff," I called out as I approached him, "I'm worried about Vanessa. Can you make sure she's okay?"

His eyes shifted to the lawn and back to me. "She's a tough lady, I'm sure she'll be fine."

"But she just lost her husband."

Jeff shook his head. "Katie, there's so much you don't know around here. Vanessa is a lot stronger than you think. I'm certain she doesn't want my help right now."

"But Jeff..."

He put his hand on my arm. "Okay. I'll go check on her. But do me a favor. Don't get too involved here. There's a lot more going on than you realize."

I nodded. Because that's the thing with a wine during the blind tasting process. You might get a clear indication right away, but you can't judge too quickly. Every element is a clue, but you have to wait until you put them all together in order to see the story.

TEN

PAIRING SUGGESTION: SANCERRE—SANCERRE, FRANCE

*Made from the Sauvignon Blanc grape,
this wine has high acidity and pairs well with tartness.*

❧

THE STARK WHITE LOBBY and steel benches of the sheriff's station provided little comfort as I sat outside the counter that separated the desks from the public area.

I wasn't sure how long I had been there, but it was long enough for my foot to fall asleep. My mind was the opposite, repeatedly going over the events of the night as I tried to ignore the smell of disinfectant and coffee, which mixed together in the air. A deputy had offered me coffee, but the Styrofoam cup sat untouched on the bench next to me.

The door swung open from the back room and I sat up. Instead of Tessa, Dean appeared.

"Is she almost done? Can I take her home?"

Dean came through the swinging gate and sat on the bench next to me. "You know we can hold her for forty-eight hours."

"I know, but you don't have any evidence or you would have charged her."

"I forgot that you're a cop's daughter," he said, his eyes softening. "It shouldn't be too much longer. Peters is wrapping up his questions and then he'll bring her up here."

I scratched my forehead. "I hope she doesn't make any jokes." Or flirt, but I kept that to myself.

"She's lucky to have you. You're a good friend." His voice was calm but emotionless, as if he had been taught specific phrases to say.

"If I was a good friend, I would have gone with her tonight. If I was a good friend, I would have been by her side. If I was a good friend, I wouldn't have let her take the blame ..." I took a deep breath. "Doesn't matter."

The back door opened and Deputy Peters walked out with Tessa, a clear smirk on her face.

A wave of unease swelled through me. "Tessa, are you okay?"

Tessa nodded. "Sure. Isn't this fun? I mean, I got arrested. Isn't that crazy! What a story I'll have to tell!"

"You weren't arrested, you were questioned."

"Well, whatever. Quite the Friday night, don't you think?"

I pointed to my watch. "It's past midnight. It's already Saturday."

"Fine," Tessa sighed. "Then, what a weekend."

I stood up. "Come on, let's get you home."

Dean stepped forward. "I think this goes without saying, but stay in the area. We may need to be in touch."

Tessa snapped her fingers and gave him a thumbs up before walking out the door.

I turned to Dean. "Thanks. Night." I followed Tessa outside.

Tessa skipped down the steps. "Interrogation questions are so boring. They repeat themselves so often, it's annoying. Come on, slowpoke. Let's get this show on the road." She leaned against my Jeep Cherokee.

I unlocked the car and Tessa got in. I slowly sat down as she closed the door behind her. I put the keys in the ignition but didn't start the engine. "Tessa, what is going on?"

"What do you mean?"

"I mean, you don't seem to be taking any of this seriously."

"Sure I am. I'm serious that I want to go home and go to bed."

"No, Tessa. I mean the snapping, thumbs-up, saying this is cool."

"Lighten up, Katie. I didn't kill him, so stop worrying."

"But they don't know that. And your wine opener was found in his back."

"Yeah, that was weird wasn't it?" Tessa raised her eyebrows. "But it's a wine opener. They're all over the place."

"This one had your initials. It was yours. Do you know how it got there?"

Tessa lowered her head and glared at me from under her eyebrows. "Are you seriously asking me if I killed my boss, Katie?"

"No, I'm trying to get you to talk to me. How did your wine opener get there?"

"I have no idea." Tessa leaned back in the seat. "That's what they kept asking me inside, too. The last time I remember having it was at the table with you. I probably dropped it or something." She shrugged. "Can we go?"

I started the car and pulled out of the station. "Why do you have to smuggle wine to the lodge? Why can't you just sell it?"

Tessa tapped her empty ring finger. "Vanessa. She's real big on money. I think she used to be poor or something. She didn't want him selling that wine, even though it was his winery before she came into the picture eight years ago. Says the wine will be worth more money later on, but Mark knows the wine is peaking right now."

"How long have you been doing this?"

Tessa stretched her neck and shoulders. "Um … Two months, maybe?"

I stopped at the light. "How often?"

"Can't remember." Tessa cracked her knuckles. "Do you think we can pick up fast food? I'm hungry."

"Tessa, focus!" I slammed my hands on the steering wheel, causing Tessa to jump. "This is important. How often were you taking the wine to the lodge?"

"About every week or so," said Tessa. "When Vanessa was busy or out of town, or something like that. We could never let her see. I didn't do anything wrong, you know. Selling the wine was completely legal. It was Mark's wine to do what he wanted with. There's no law to say you can't do something without your wife knowing."

"Yes, but you're not under suspicion for stealing. They're looking at you for Mark's murder."

"Mark …" Tessa's eyes watered. "He's really gone." She started to cry.

"Tessa, tell me what happened with the text. What did it say?"

She took a break from her sobs. "It said *aerate the wine*. That was our code to take the next shipment to the lodge, so I pulled my car up to the wine cellar and loaded three cases of wine into the trunk. Then I drove to the lodge."

I drummed my fingers on the steering wheel. "What about the winery, did you go in there?"

"Why would I go in there? I was taking bottles of wine to the lodge, not Dixie Cups of unfermented grape juice."

I pulled into the parking lot of Tessa's apartment and turned off the car. "But why did you tell me to ask Seb? You said 'ask Seb' as you got in the patrol car."

"Because he saw me drive away. Did you ask him? He was in the back driveway as I drove past and he saw me. And that proves that I was off the property before anything happened. Ask him."

I slowly nodded. "I did. I went back to the winery tonight after you left the lodge with Detective Dean. I found Seb and asked him if he had seen you tonight. He said the only time he saw you was when we were drinking the Merlot."

Tessa jerked up in her seat. "But that's not true. He was there when I left."

I looked at Tessa. "Are you sure it was Seb? I mean, if it was dark, how could you tell? What did you see?"

"A tall lanky kid with brown hair named Seb."

"Well, if he was there, he doesn't remember. Did you tell the deputies that Seb saw you leave?"

Tessa put her finger to her cheek and tapped it. "I think so. Maybe. Hmm ... Maybe not. I can't remember. You've never been interrogated, Katie. It's intimidating."

"Okay, but it still doesn't prove to them that you're innocent. Eye witness testimony can be incredibly inaccurate."

"Wait, no, it does work." Tessa sat forward in her seat. "Because Mark was talking with Lisa when I left you."

"I thought you said you hadn't seen him."

"Well, I'd forgotten until right now." Tessa pulled her mouth to the side. "But I did see him. With Lisa. They were talking near the winery. So that proves that I'm innocent." She wiped her hands together. "Easy peasy. I wonder if your dad solves cases this fast? Maybe I should have been a cop. Officer Blakely. Has a nice ring to it."

I sighed and got out of the car but Tessa didn't move from the front seat. I knocked on the passenger window. "You coming?"

Tessa slowly got out of the Jeep. "I'm hungry. We didn't get any fast food."

"Seriously?"

She nodded, her hair bouncing. "I want a burger."

"Come on." I motioned up the stairs. "I'll make you something. Plan on having an easy day tomorrow. They're going to be watching everything you do. Stay at your apartment or only go nearby, around here. No big movements, okay?"

"If I'd only ignored that text from Mark, I wouldn't be in this mess."

"Was the code he texted always the same code? *Aerate the wine?*"

"No, we changed it every week so that no one would catch on." Tessa fumbled with her front door key.

"When did you choose this one?"

"Two days ago."

The door swung open and Tessa headed straight to the couch, throwing her body down on the cushions.

"Two days ago where?"

"Um...In the winery. Behind the two large vats next to the wine press. We didn't want anyone to hear us and we knew we'd be alone there." Tessa pulled a cushion to her chest and snuggled into the couch. It was one of only two pieces of furniture in the living room, complemented by a small coffee table and boxes in the corner. Tessa still wasn't fully unpacked from when she had moved in four months ago.

"Anything else you want to tell me about tonight?"

"Yes," replied Tessa. "Definitely not enough drinking."

I shook my head and sat down on the couch next to her.

"Katie?"

"Yes, Tessa?"

"Can you make me mac and cheese?"

I exhaled. This was just like Tessa. Nothing was ever serious. Her emotions flared up and died out just as quickly. "Fine, I'll make you mac and cheese."

"Thank you." Tessa's voice was muffled voice from the cushions. "And Katie?"

"Yes?"

"Can you stay with me tonight?" She turned over and looked up at me. "Like a sleepover, like we used to do."

I looked at Tessa, her curls crushed by the pillows. "But I have work tomorrow, Tee."

"I know, but please. For me?"

I hesitated, the events of so many years ago going through my mind. "Give me a sec." I grabbed my phone and texted my coworker.

CAN YOU DO INVENTORY TOMORROW? I'LL BE BACK IN TIME FOR MY SHIFT.

NERD, Darius texted back.

THXS. SO CAN YOU COVER INVENTORY?

There was no response. I watched the phone, waiting for it to light up. "Come on, Darius, come on."

The phone lit up with another text. I'LL DO IT FOR A BOTTLE OF OBAN.

SERIOUSLY? OBAN.

YES.

Darius and his love of whisky. FINE, A BOTTLE OF OBAN.

COOL. YOU'RE COVERED.

"Okay." I removed a metal pot from the kitchen cabinet. "I have inventory covered for tomorrow. I'll stay here with you."

"Thanks, Katie," said Tessa as she curled up on the couch. "I owe you one."

I looked back at her and shook my head. "No, you don't." The playing field was far from even. It was time for me to repay the favor that Tessa had done for me. "I'm going to make everything okay." My voice lowered to a whisper. "At least, I hope I can."

ELEVEN

PAIRING SUGGESTION: CHABLIS—CHABLIS, FRANCE

A dry Chardonnay with lots of minerality and rigid character.

⤶

WHEN I ENTERED THE sheriff's station the next morning, it had the same static atmosphere as hours earlier but the coffee smell was stronger. I was almost tempted to try a cup, but coffee always seemed to smell better than it tasted. The black suit I wore—one that I kept in the trunk of my car in case I was called into work at a moment's notice—smelled stale and I shifted uncomfortably as I approached the counter.

An unfamiliar deputy was on duty, his eyes focused on the paperwork in front of him.

"Excuse me. I'm looking for Detective Dean."

"He's not in," he said without looking up. "Can I help you?"

"I wanted to talk to him about the murder at Frontier Winery?"

The deputy raised his head, his brown eyes staring directly into mine. "The one from last night? What do you need?"

I adjusted my stance. "Well, I wanted to ask about the wine opener that was found at the scene. Were there fingerprints on it?"

"Fingerprints on what?" said Dean as he walked in from the back room.

"Thought you weren't coming in till ten, buddy," said the desk deputy.

"Active murder investigation. Who needs rest?" Dean nodded at me. "Good morning. You're here for the case? Or to see me?" A smile spread across his lips, creating dimples on both cheeks. He looked like a regular person, no longer a figure of authority.

"Ah, actually"—I hesitated—"about the case."

"Just teasing." Dean put his arms on the counter, his toned muscles showing through his dress shirt.

"I didn't know you were funny."

Dean laughed, his demeanor softer than the night before. My dad never softened, at least not when he was in a work capacity. They were different after all. "So let's hear about these fingerprints."

"On the wine opener. Did you check it for fingerprints? I mean, I know Tessa's will be on there, but were there anyone else's fingerprints?"

"You're really invested in this, aren't you?"

"I know in my heart that she's innocent. I'll do everything in my power to clear her name."

"Investigations take time. Surely you know that from your dad."

"Yes, but that doesn't mean I can't wish for a quick resolution."

"True." Dean leaned forward. "The only fingerprints they found on the wine opener were Tessa's."

I could read something deeper in his eyes. "There's something you're not telling me."

"You're perceptive. Some of her fingerprints were smudged. As if someone used gloves or a towel to hold it."

A wave of relief swept through my body. "See? I told you."

"It doesn't clear her or implicate her, it's simply a fact of the investigation." Dean let out a deep breath as he stood back up. "Katie, your friend hasn't been arrested. She was only brought in for questioning."

"But that doesn't mean you're not filing the paperwork to charge her right now. I want to make sure she's going to be okay. If she's innocent, I'm going to prove it."

Dean stared at me. "Interesting that you said *if*."

I stopped. I had a habit of using the word *if* in my blind tasting group. *If this wine is a Chardonnay, if this wine has high acidity*. My group constantly reminded me to only speak with certainty. No wonder I had failed. I straightened my posture and pulled my shoulders back. "She's innocent."

"Great. Then we'll see where this case goes, shall we?"

I studied Dean for a moment. If he was like my father, a little kindness could go a long way. I needed to get on his good side. "You're right. Hey, where can you go around here to get a decent cup of coffee? I've had a heck of a twenty-four hours and could use some caffeine."

Dean motioned to a side desk. "We have some here, I'll get you a cup."

"Ah, no thanks. I'm looking for something bet…" My voice trailed off. "Something different."

"Grandma's is a block away. They serve good coffee."

"Nice." I leaned on the counter. "You don't start till ten, right? Want to join me?"

Dean moved back. "Um, what are you exactly… I mean, coffee?"

"Yes, coffee."

"But you're Tessa's…"

I put my hand to my chest and dropped my head. "What do you think I am doing?" I almost laughed inside. Drama had never been my strong suit, but I was certain this was coming off perfectly. "I just

want a cup of coffee. I'm not hitting on you, I'm trying to be polite."
I shook my head. "Anyway, a block away? Thanks."

I turned and walked toward the door. Even though my dad was all business, he couldn't stand it if he hurt someone. I hoped Dean would be the same.

"Katie, wait," replied Dean from behind the counter. "I'm sorry. I didn't mean to be rude."

"You weren't rude. You were blunt. There's a difference." I stepped outside the station. As I headed down the steps, I heard the station door open.

"Wait, Katie."

I hid my smile before I turned around. "Yes?"

Dean hesitated at the top of the steps. "I'd like to join you."

"Even if I'm Tessa's friend?"

"Even if you're Tessa's friend." He reached my side as he slipped on his suit jacket.

"Great." I motioned to the street. "Which direction is the coffee shop?"

"Up here to the right."

I glanced at Dean as we walked along the sidewalk. He seemed to be on the lean side, but his suit made it hard to tell.

We reached Grandma's Coffee Shop, a white wooden building with red trim.

"Have you ever been here?" Dean held the door open for me.

"No. I'm not in this area too often."

"That's right. You're a San Francisco girl."

The noise of plates clanging together and jumbled conversations met us along with the scent of cinnamon rolls and strong coffee.

Dean put up two fingers to the waitress, who pointed to a red booth next to the window. Dean waited for me to sit down before he slid onto the seat across from me.

"What can I get'cha?" The waitress held a small pad of paper in front of her pale blue and white uniform.

Dean motioned to me.

"Oh, I don't know yet." I scanned the menu, but a cup of coffee didn't seem to fit the bill anymore. "Can you give me a second?"

"Sure thing," said the waitress as she stepped away.

Dean raised his eyebrows. "I thought you wanted coffee."

"Yes, I did want coffee." I paused. "But that's because I was thinking only of coffee and wasn't exploring any of the other options."

"You know," said Dean, "you're not as stealth as you think you are."

I grinned. "I never said I was."

The waitress returned. "Ready?"

"Yes, I'll have a hot chocolate with whipped cream."

"Coffee," said Dean. The waitress left and Dean winked at me. "A sweet tooth, huh?"

"A little." I put my hand on the table. "Tessa—"

"So you do want to talk about her. Or did you want to keep talking about coffee?"

"Funny. Obviously she's on my mind."

"Understandable."

"And you're here. So maybe we could talk about her. Nothing to it, just two people talking about Tessa."

The waitress placed the cup of coffee in front of Dean and the hot chocolate with a generous dollop of whipped cream in front of me.

"Obviously my goal is to get her free of suspicion." I took a sip of the hot chocolate.

"If she's innocent."

"Correct. Which she is." I licked whipped cream off of my lips.

Dean stirred sugar and milk into his coffee. "Okay, so let's say she is innocent. Who killed Mark?"

"That's what I want to find out. Do you have any other suspects besides Tessa?"

"I can't share that, you know that."

"Okay." I nodded. "If you can't share, then let me say this. I heard Vanessa and Jim Garrett arguing last night, after the murder. It sounded pretty heated."

"Why didn't you tell me this before?"

I gave a mild shrug. "I'm telling you now."

Dean took his black notepad out of his pocket and started writing. "What were they arguing about?"

"I don't know, I couldn't exactly hear. Something about decisions."

"But you know they were arguing?"

I nodded. "The tone wasn't two people talking. It was tense."

Dean flipped through his notebook. "Let's see. Vanessa and Lisa were together when they heard the caterer scream at seven forty-eight. We assume the approximate time of death was between seven fifteen and seven forty, as Seb was the last one to see him around seven fifteen." Dean turned a few more pages in his book. "Jim Garrett said he was talking to different groups of people until he ended up sitting at a table."

"With anyone?"

Dean looked at the notes. "Nope. Apparently he's quite the drinker and from what I heard from other guests, they know to avoid him."

"That's it?"

"What do you mean?"

I sat back in the booth and crossed my arms. "Garrett doesn't have someone that can account for him during the murder?"

Dean looked again at his notes. "No, I guess he doesn't. With Tessa missing from the party, all the attention was on finding her. But Garrett doesn't have a motive."

"Neither does Tessa." I met Dean's gaze.

"Not that we know of yet."

"Yes, but Garrett could also have a motive that we don't know about yet."

"Good point," said Dean. "Okay, I'll look into Garrett and his whereabouts during the party."

"Also"—I took another drink of my hot chocolate, the warmth burning my throat as I swallowed too fast—"Tessa said that Seb saw her drive away last night while Mark was still alive."

Dean tapped his pen on his notebook. "Why didn't she say that during questioning last night?"

I shook my head. "Tessa doesn't always think of the right thing at the right time. It's one of her, well, characteristics."

"Okay, so Tessa said she saw him. Did Seb confirm that?"

"No, Seb said he didn't remember when I asked him. But I believe her."

"So we have Tessa, who says that Seb saw her, and we have Seb, who says he didn't see her." Dean's light blond hair swept over his face. I hadn't noticed how attractive he was before. Perhaps the situation last night had clouded my judgment.

"Yes."

"Katie," Dean said, putting down his pen, "you're too close to this case."

"Maybe, but I also learned a lot about investigating from my dad. I know that the most obvious suspect can be the wrong one and while everyone is focused on that one, the guilty one gets away."

"You're talking about the O'Reily case, aren't you? The one that put your dad on the map?"

I shrugged. "My dad looked beyond the obvious clues, which pointed to the father-in-law, and he found the real murderer."

"I know. That was a national case."

"Exactly. So don't you think it's worth looking at everyone?"

Dean nodded, his eyes on his notebook. "You make a good point." He looked up at me. "Why aren't you a cop? Isn't your whole family in law enforcement?"

"Yeah, my dad, my two uncles, and my grandfather." I forced a smile. "But that's a story that takes longer than a cup of coffee."

"I'd like to hear it." Dean's eyes locked on mine and then he sat up, as if remembering where he was. "Anyway, I'm heading back to the winery this morning to go over the details of the case and review potential evidence. I'll find Seb and see what he can tell me about Tessa last night." Dean tipped his mug back and downed the rest of his coffee before putting his empty cup on the table.

I looked at the hot chocolate left in my mug. I could feel Dean's eyes fixated on me so I took my time, waiting a few more seconds before slowly drinking the last few sips.

When I was done, I carefully placed the cup in front of me. "Thanks for joining me. I don't often meet people for coffee. Or hot chocolate."

"No?" said Dean, his eyebrows raised. "No boyfriend?"

I laughed. "That's a leading question."

"Sorry." Dean's cheeks flushed a light shade of pink. "That's not what I meant."

"No, I know. Don't worry about it. I meant with my line of work, nights and weekends, it doesn't really leave time for a cup of coffee. Wine, yes, but coffee, no. This was nice." I motioned to the waitress for the bill.

"Same," said Dean. "I appreciate your info about the argument with Vanessa and Garrett and also about Seb."

"I'm happy to help. And not just because of Tessa." I cringed at the last statement. What was I doing? This wasn't like me. I never flirted. Ever.

90

The waitress slipped the check onto the table. I reached for my purse, but Dean held up his hand. "No, please. Let me."

"Thank you. That's very nice of you."

"My pleasure." Dean put a ten-dollar bill on the table.

I stood up. "So are you heading back to the winery right now?"

"Yep." Dean held the door open for me.

"You know," I said as we walked out of the coffee shop, "it might be helpful if I came along."

"This is an investigation."

"I know. But I've picked up a few tips from my dad. You never know, I might notice some clues that could help."

"You're Tessa's friend."

I stopped walking and faced him. "Detective Dean."

"People mostly just call me Dean."

"Okay, Dean, this is important." I stared straight into his blue eyes. "I'm not going to jeopardize the case. I want to help."

Dean broke the eye contact and focused on the street behind me. "I can't."

"Yes, you can," I inserted. "There's no law against taking someone along with you. Civilians join officers on ride-alongs all the time."

He slowly shook his head. "I shouldn't."

"But?" I waited.

"Fine. But if anyone asks, you only wanted a ride, okay? You don't ask any questions, you don't touch anything, and you don't make suggestions in front of other people. You're not involved. Got it?"

"Got it." I did my best to hide my smile as we approached the station.

Dean pointed to a sheriff's car in front. "We'll take that one. I'll be right back." He ran up the steps of the station as I waited by the car.

When he returned, he opened the driver's door and pointed to the passenger side. "You can get in, you know."

"Just wanted to make sure I can ride in front."

"Of course."

I slid into the front seat. "Thanks, Dean."

"Don't mention it," he said. "Like really, don't mention it."

TWELVE

PAIRING SUGGESTION:

PINOT GRIGIO—FRIULI-VENEZIA GIULIA, ITALY

*Subtlety is key in this unoaked white wine
with flavors of lemon and peanut shells.*

❧

ALTHOUGH WE PASSED BY vineyards as we drove, Dean kept all the windows up in the car, the scent of Napa replaced by pine air freshener. My eyes drifted along the perpendicular rows covering the hillsides and I did my best to imagine the familiar aroma missing from our drive.

"You're very quiet. You okay?" asked Dean.

"Oh, sorry. I was watching the vineyards."

"Watching the vineyards?"

"Yeah." I glanced at Dean. "I love the organization and the magic that is happening on those vines at this very moment, everything coming together in order to create a great bottle of wine in the future."

"Bet you don't see a lot of vines in Los Angeles, right?" Dean remarked.

"Not too many. How do you know I'm from Los Angeles?"

He shrugged. "Your father is the police chief there. I just figured."

"Yeah. Born and raised there, now I'm in San Francisco."

"Didn't want to stay close to home?"

I sighed. "It's complicated."

"Isn't everything? I remember meeting your father years ago at a law enforcement convention in San Diego. He's very respected." Dean turned down the Silverado Trail. "Why didn't you want to go into the same profession?"

I leaned back in the seat and watched the vineyards go by. "As I said, it's a long story." Tightness filled my chest as the memory of flunking out of the Police Academy went through my mind. I replaced it with an image of my mother holding a glass of wine. "But let's say the wine world was calling."

"The wine world is good, too," said Dean. "I have some friends who work in it. In fact, one says he can tell what the wine is only by tasting it."

I bit my lip to stop from smiling. After a pause, I added, "I can do that."

"Really?"

"Yeah, blind tasting. I mean, I'm not excellent at it, but I'm pretty good. At least I thought I was." I shook off the sentence. "I meet with a group twice a week to practice. We bring bottles in paper bags to hide the labels and we each have to identify a wine only by sight, smell, and taste."

"Can I come watch?"

I laughed. "It's not like that. It's a group of somms studying for the sommelier exams. There's no audience." I glanced at Dean. "How about you? How long have you been with the sheriff's department?"

Dean straightened his posture and held the wheel with his right hand, the other hand on the side of the door. "It will be eleven years this fall and I've been a detective for two. But I've only been in Napa about six months. Transferred here from Sacramento."

"You like it? Being a detective, I mean."

"Love it. Righting the wrong, looking out for the little guy."

"The little guy. You mean the innocent? I think Tessa falls into that category."

"Possibly."

I could almost see a small smile appear on his face, but I wasn't sure. "Watch, she'll be proven innocent and then you're going to have to make it up to me."

"Oh really?" Dean looked over at me. "And how will I do that?"

"I haven't decided yet." My smile grew larger. "But I know it's coming."

Dean slowed down as he turned into the driveway of Garrett Winery.

"We're going here?"

"I have a couple of questions for him, then we'll head over to Frontier."

A modern beige building with a pointed roof and intricate wood-work came into view, a stark contrast to the one-hundred-year-old neighbor next door. The driveway stopped at a vast parking lot next to an area with picnic tables and white umbrellas. Two men rolled barrels into the courtyard as a third man, Jim Garrett, stood nearby.

I looked at Dean as I motioned to Garrett. "Don't tell him it was me, I don't want him to know I was listening."

Dean nodded as he turned off the engine. "I'm very discreet and I never reveal my sources. You're welcome to stay in the car while I talk to him."

An SUV pulled up next to us.

"Yeah, right," I said as the SUV's occupants headed toward the sign for the tasting room. "It's just past ten and they're open for tastings." I glanced at Dean. "Besides, who says I can't blend?" I got out of the car as the two men in the courtyard started to steam the barrels, the sweet smell of toasted oak, cinnamon, and nutmeg in the air.

I followed the path to the tasting room, passing the outline of an old concrete foundation filled with flowers. The scents of different varietals greeted me as I entered the tasting room, which was combined with the gift shop. Shelves of glasses, mugs, books, and gift baskets covered the light wood walls. A broad wooden bar sat in the middle with a silver-haired lady behind it, helping two people at one end. I pulled up one of the polished wood stools and took a seat, watching as she poured white wine into the tasting glasses.

Her eyes met mine as she finished pouring and she walked over. "Are you here for a tasting?"

"At the moment, I'm just looking."

"Okay, darling, you let me know if there's anything you want to try. We have a flight of four wines for forty dollars and we offer a few wines by the glass." She placed a laminated wine list on the bar in front of me. "There's also truffles if you would like one." She motioned to a bowl full of chocolate truffles dusted with powdered sugar.

"Will do." I glanced at the list of Chardonnay, Sauvignon Blanc, Viognier, Pinot Noir, Cabernet Sauvignon, and two dessert wines. I was tempted to try at least one of the wines, but I didn't know how long Dean would be. I leaned back on my stool and glanced outside the door. Dean stood in the courtyard, writing as Garrett talked. This could take a while.

I motioned to the lady, who came right over. "Did you want to try something?" Wrinkles formed around her eyes as she smiled.

"Yes, I'd love to try your Sauvignon Blanc. Just a single tasting, please."

"Not a problem." The lady placed a glass in front of me and pulled a bottle of Garrett Sauvignon Blanc from under the counter. She poured approximately one ounce into the glass, the golden liquid swirling around. "This is our 2014 Sauvignon Blanc. We age it for five months in French oak." She returned to the couple at the other side of the bar as I lifted up the glass. Amber droplets ran down the side.

I held it to my nose and took four short sniffs. I raised my eyebrows and looked at the glass. It was void of the ammonia smell I tended to detect in many Sauvignon Blancs, a characteristic which usually turned me off of the varietal.

I sniffed it again and identified yellow apple, Meyer lemon, white flowers, butterscotch, and oak. It was clearly Sauvignon Blanc. I felt my confidence in my blind tasting slowly returning.

I took a sip, swishing the wine around my mouth. Flavors of apple, lemon, grapefruit, pineapple, and mango filled my palate before I spit in the nearby bucket, the crisp acidity still on my lips, the flavors lingering on my tongue. Nicely done, Garrett. I wasn't sure why Jeff hadn't been a fan of Garrett wine. Maybe it was the use of oak, which wasn't discernible in Frontier wine, but here, jumped out of the glass.

I stared at the Sauvignon Blanc. My way of figuring out the alcohol level was to swallow the wine, but I didn't want to smell like alcohol in front of Dean.

I shrugged and took another sip and swallowed. The heat of the alcohol flared up in my throat and it was clear that this wine was at least 14 percent, if not more.

I continued tasting, this time letting the wine fall over my tongue before spitting in the bucket. When the glass was empty, I placed it on the counter.

The lady returned. "Did you like it?"

"Delicious. I really like the acidity in this one. Would pair well with a white flaky fish."

"I'm glad you like it. Garrett makes a great Sauv Blanc." She lifted up a different bottle. "Want another one?"

"No, thank you." I paused. "What was this winery before it was Garrett?"

The lady hesitated, as if enjoying a memory. "Chateau Fleur de lys. It was all wood and it was beautiful. It had been around about thirty years. But when Garrett came in, he wanted everything new." She motioned to the room. "So here we are."

I motioned outside. "Was that the foundation out there, the one with flowers?"

She nodded as she picked up a different bottle. "That was our old tasting room." She poured another ounce into my glass. "This one's on the house. Let me know what you think."

I picked up the glass and sniffed, immediately identifying floral notes and a lot of honeysuckle. I took another breath. Peaches and apricots. I tasted the wine. Bold flavors of tangerine and peach captivated my mouth and I delayed spitting it out for longer than usual. When I finally did, I remarked to the lady, "Almost a shame to spit it out."

She winked. "I can see by your smile that you like that one. Thought you might. That's our Viognier. We have a vineyard up in St. Helena."

"Do you grow all your own grapes or do you source?"

"Both," said the lady as she polished a glass with a blue towel. "We grow a lot of our grapes in our vineyards around Napa, but we also source from other vineyards. We have certain Chardonnays that are estate bottled, but we don't offer those in the regular tastings."

I swirled the wine left in my glass before looking up at the lady. "Have you worked here long?"

"Twenty years, give or take."

"So before Garrett?"

The lady smiled politely. "Yes, before we were Garrett Winery."

I stared at my glass and tilted it sideways, the light coming through the wine in amber waves. "Tell me, how do you ferment the grapes? Steel, oak, or concrete?"

"We have stainless-steel tanks."

The wine splashed up the sides of the glass as I brought it back down to the counter. "Does Garrett help with the process? Maybe loading the grapes?"

She laughed. "Garrett doesn't know how to do any of that. He bought new presses, new tanks, new everything when he took over, but he can't operate a thing. Between you and me, I miss the old winery."

"Would he be able to open the top of the tank?"

"Honey"—she titled forward, an amused look on her face—"he wouldn't even know what the top looks like. Besides, he threw his back out a few years ago and can't lift more than a few pounds." She motioned to my glass. "You all done?"

I nodded and reached into my purse. "How much do I owe you for the tasting?"

"Ten dollars."

I opened my wallet and pulled out twelve dollars to incorporate a tip. "Thanks, this was fun. You make great wine."

"Thank you. We're offering fifteen percent off all cases this week if you want to place an order."

"I'll keep that in mind."

"There you are," said Dean as he stood at the entrance to the tasting room. "Ready to go?"

"Yep." I took the last swig of the wine, swished it around in my mouth, and spat it into the bucket.

"I wondered about that," Dean whispered as I walked past him and out the door. "Is it bad wine?"

"No, it was delicious." I took the steps two at a time and waited for Dean. "It's polite to spit it out. That way you taste the wine but don't get intoxicated."

"Hmm …" said Dean. "Interesting. I can still smell it on you though."

"Figures. I have been tasting wine, you know. Should I worry about your detective skills?" I winked as I reached his car and opened the door. I had a feeling of elation, but it wasn't from the alcohol. It was the happiness I experienced whenever I tasted excellent wine.

"What are you smiling about?"

I turned to him. "Good wine, my friend. It's good for the soul." I faced the front and stared at the nearby vines as Dean started the car. He paused at the exit of Garrett Winery, waiting for a car to pass before he pulled onto the road.

"So …?" My comment broke the silence. "What did you find out? Can you fill me in on what Garrett said? You talked to him for a little while."

Dean turned into the driveway of Frontier Winery, a sheriff's car stationed at the gates. Dean waved as we drove past. "Yeah, that didn't go exactly as I had planned, but it's to be expected."

"Did you ask him about the argument?"

Dean nodded.

"And?"

"He said it's none of my business. Actually, his exact words were, 'Sir, that is none of your business. Now good day.'"

I leaned back in the seat. "Wow."

"Murder brings out an interesting side of people." Dean parked in front of the Frontier offices.

"That's okay, I'm glad I had better luck."

"What do you mean?"

"I don't think Garrett had anything to do with it."

Dean turned to me. "Please explain."

"Apparently he can't lift more than a few pounds. Has a bad back. Also, from what I just heard, he wouldn't know the slightest thing about any of the equipment. I guess Tessa was right; he really is just a businessman." I could see Dean out of the corner of my eye as he stared at me. I looked at the scenery in front of me instead of meeting his gaze. Eventually he turned off the engine.

"See, I told you I would be helpful." I started to open the car door. "Let's see what we can find out here. It's like my group reminds me during blind tasting—everything is a clue."

THIRTEEN

PAIRING SUGGESTION: CHARDONNAY—SONOMA COAST, CA

An oaked and buttery wine as things start to get rich.

༈

THE YELLOW CRIME SCENE tape flapped in the wind around the doorway of the winery, but Dean motioned to the offices.

"We'll go here first." He headed up the steps toward the side door and held it open for me.

The heavy pounding of a keyboard echoed in the hall. Dean walked past me to the second door, where Lisa sat typing furiously in front of her computer.

"Can I help you?" she asked without looking up.

"Detective Dean."

She stopped typing and formed her bright red lips into a clearly rehearsed smile. "Why Detective Dean, how nice of you to stop by." Her focus drifted to me. "And Tessa's little friend. What can I help you with?"

"I have a few questions for Sebastian Hain. Is he working today?"

Lisa shrugged. "After the mess last night, I'm not sure who's working and who's not. Technically he should be here. But is he? I don't know. You'd have to go the winery and look for him."

"What about Vanessa? Is she around?"

"No, I'm afraid not. She's visiting her mother in the city. It was a rough night, as you can well imagine."

"Yes." Dean opened his notepad. "Since I have you here, I'd like to ask you some questions."

"I'm very happy to help our members of law enforcement." She straightened up in the chair and folded her hands on the desk in front of her. "What can I tell you?"

"I'd like to know about Mark and Vanessa's relationship. Did they get along?"

Lisa put her hand to her chest, the red nail polish contrasting with her white blouse. "Is Vanessa a suspect? Because I'd heard that you already arrested Tessa for the murder."

"Tessa is a person of interest, I will tell you that, but we're exploring every lead."

"You're so thorough." Lisa placed her chin on her hand, her elbow on the desk. "I like it."

I shifted uncomfortably.

"As you know, all relationships have their issues." Lisa's eyes fell to his left hand and then back up to his face. "Or maybe you don't know. But overall they were a happy couple. Of course, every relationship is like a bottle of wine. Sometimes it improves with age and sometimes it goes sour."

"Can you explain?"

"I think it's self-explanatory." Lisa's eyes were emotionless as she smiled with her lips closed.

"Okay." Dean looked at his notepad. "To your knowledge, has Mark received any threats from anyone? Maybe an ex-employee or a rival?"

"We're all friends here in Napa," said Lisa. "There's always a little friendly competition, however I don't know of anyone that would want to hurt Mark. He was a nice guy. Maybe too nice, if you get my drift."

"Care to explain?"

"Nice people get walked on, Detective Dean. I think he let himself be controlled too much by others."

"Can you tell me who?"

Lisa's eyes flashed at me and then back at Dean. "No, I think I'm done here. I've said enough. If you'll excuse me, I have a lot of work to do. One of our owners died, you know." She returned her focus to the computer screen and started typing.

"Ms. Warner," Dean started, but Lisa put her hand up without looking away from the computer screen.

"Any additional questions will have to go through my lawyer. If everyone's a suspect, then I need to protect myself. However, I will say this, which could help you. Be wary of grapes that shouldn't be growing together. That's the best I can do." Lisa looked up and forced a smile. "Be a dear and close the door on your way out." She returned to typing.

We exited the office and I closed the door behind me.

"Sour grapes," I whispered.

"The usual." Dean looked down the dark hallway, the open doors vacant of activity. "Let's go find Sebastian." He opened the door and I stepped through.

"When someone refuses to talk anymore and wants their lawyer, what can you do with that?"

Dean shook his head. "Nothing at the moment. If I need more information from her, I'll get in touch with her lawyer. It's the way some people want to play. It doesn't always mean they have something to hide. Sometimes they don't want to get involved and other times they want to make it difficult."

"I wonder what set her off?" We started walking across the lawn. "One second she was sharing, the next she wasn't."

"I don't know exactly, but it was when she looked at you. I don't think that was a coincidence. Did Tessa get along with her?"

"I'm not sure. I know last night she made a comment about Lisa wanting to take credit for everything. Oh, and she said Lisa doesn't play nice. Other than that, I don't know any specifics. What a mess."

"Don't worry. Things always seem to come out of the blue when you least expect them." Dean pointed around the winery toward the hillside. "Anything back here? I didn't get around here last night."

"The wine cellar. I'll show you." I motioned to the concrete entrance set into the hill. "It's there."

"Would anyone be inside?" Dean approached the wooden doors.

"You ask a lot of questions of me, it's pretty interesting. How would I know?"

"Your best friend works here. I figure you would know more than me."

"But I don't. I have no idea how things work around here. Like you, my first time on the property was yesterday."

Dean pulled open one door and stuck his head in. He stayed there for a few seconds before stepping back outside and closing the door. "It's cold in there."

"Keeps the wine safe at a steady temperature. Anyone in there?"

"Not that I could see. Let's head over to the winery," said Dean. The hill sloped down to our left as we walked by rows of vines, each branch dripping with full, ripe grapes.

"Even living here, I don't know much about wine," said Dean. "But I like having a glass now and then."

I smiled. "Me too. The having a glass now and then part."

Dean pointed to the large clusters of red grapes hanging next to the light green leaves. "I guess these will be ready soon."

"Pretty soon." I cradled a bunch of grapes before gently letting them return to their place on the vine. "Probably next month. The thicker-skinned grapes always get picked last." I noticed Dean watching me. "What?"

"Nothing. But I can see you really care about this. Both the grapes and the wine. You clearly love it."

I nodded. "I do. I started working in restaurants when I was twenty-three and then gradually gained sommelier duties until I became a full-time sommelier three years ago."

"And you started right out of college?"

"Not quite ..." My voice trailed off. "I had a small detour first, but then I knew wine was the right choice for me. I've always loved the idea of wine since I was little."

"Wine, even when you were a kid?" Dean raised his eyebrows.

I laughed. "Not exactly. My mom would come home from a long day at work and have a glass of red wine. I'd sit next to her and have cranberry juice in a smaller version of a glass like hers. I guess that's where it all started. Add in a couple of summers on my uncle's winery in France and here I am."

"I bet your mom's proud." Dean's arm brushed up against my shoulder as we walked.

"She passed away."

"Oh, I'm sorry."

"It was a long time ago." I glanced at Dean as heat flushed my cheeks. "I don't share that wine story a lot. Usually I give the generic story of watching the *I Love Lucy* episode when she squashed the grapes."

Dean gave a hearty laugh. "I've seen that one."

"Yeah." I rested my hand on the trellis wire of the last row before the dirt road separated one vineyard from the next. "I've always wanted to stomp grapes, but there hasn't been an opportunity yet. But one day." I looked across the rows and then back to the winery, where a tall man wearing a cowboy hat entered through one of the back doors. "There's Alan. I met him at the party. He's the head winemaker."

"Let's go talk to him."

"Good luck with that. He's a man of few words."

"We'll see."

I nudged Dean. "I'll be impressed if you get more than five words."

Dean looked at me with a smile on his face. "Is that a dare?"

"No, it's just a prediction."

"Interesting."

The smell of fermenting grapes became thick in the air as we walked through the winery door. The crime scene tape cordoned off the area around the first fermentation tank, but work had recommenced around it, bringing life and activity to the winery, a stark contrast to the emptiness of the night before.

Alan crouched in front of a machine with bottles lined up in a long white channel. He maneuvered a screwdriver into the middle of a round mechanism that didn't seem to want to turn.

"Sir, I'm Detective Dean. I'm investigating the murder of Mark Plueger."

Alan murmured an affirmative noise and continued working on the machine.

"Can I ask you some questions?"

Alan repeated the same noise.

Dean looked at me and I winked. "Alan, what's wrong with the labeling machine?"

"Labeling machine?" asked Dean.

"It sends the bottles through and puts the labels on them," I replied. "Are you tuning it?" I asked Alan.

"Broken," his gravelly voice replied. "Again."

Dean crouched down next to Alan and looked at the mechanism, which finally turned with the screwdriver. "Does it break a lot?"

"Hm hm," Alan repeated.

I stepped closer to the machine. "Why not get a new one?"

"No money." Alan removed a spring-loaded contraption from the machine and held it up to the light.

I nodded. "I can understand that. They're probably expensive."

"Nope," said Alan. "No money."

"Wait," said Dean. "You have no money or the winery has no money?"

Alan adjusted one of the springs on the contraption in his hand. "Winery."

Dean pulled out his notepad and started writing. "Interesting. Is it bankrupt?"

Alan put the contraption back into the machine. He used the screwdriver to tighten the screw next to the contraption and stood up. "We'll see about the offers." Alan plugged the machine into the wall.

"What offers?" Dean stood next to Alan, trying to make eye contact. Alan looked solely at the machine, making Dean's efforts futile.

Dean looked at me. I shrugged.

Alan clicked the red button and the machine whirled to life. Bottles moved along the line, labels stuck firmly to their fronts.

"Alan?" Dean tried, but the loud noise of the machine was a clear indication that the conversation was over. Dean motioned to me and we stepped away.

"I'm impressed. He actually talked."

"Yep." Dean leaned over as if to say something to me, but Seb's entrance into the winery interrupted his effort.

Seb wiped his purple-stained hands on a white cloth. He threw the cloth in a wooden crate against the wall, looked at the both of us, turned around, and walked out.

"Seb, wait." I rushed through the door to outside. Seb's mop of brown hair bounced as he walked alongside the winery toward the vineyards. "Seb!"

He turned around with a feigned look of surprise. "Oh, um, hey." His eyes drifted over my shoulder to Dean.

"We were looking for you," said Dean. "Wanted to ask you some more questions about the party."

"Sure," said Seb as his body rocked slightly back and forth and he tapped his fingers against each other. "What can I help you with?"

"When was the last time you saw Tessa last night?"

"Tessa?" He rocked again. "I'm not sure."

"Think," said Dean.

"Um, I don't know. Somewhere around the tables, I think. Maybe seven o'clock?"

"Really?" I replied as Dean shot me a look.

"Where were you at around seven thirty last night?"

Seb looked over his shoulder and then back at Dean. "What do you mean? I was at the party. Wasn't everyone?"

Dean repositioned his stance. "I know you were at the party, but I want to know exactly where you were."

"That's a little tough to pinpoint. I don't wear a watch." Seb held up his bare left arm. His fingers shook and he lowered his arm when he noticed me watching.

"Okay, if you don't remember where you were, at least answer me this. Do you remember seeing anyone leaving the party last night? Prior to the discovery of Mark's body?"

Seb looked slightly to the left and then back at Dean. "Um, no, I don't think so. People were supposed to be arriving, not leaving."

"Are you sure?" asked Dean. "Think hard. You didn't see anyone leave?"

"Detective, it was a party with, um, free alcohol. Do you honestly think people would leave?"

"Seb," I interjected, "Tessa said that you were standing in the driveway and saw her drive away. Before Mark's murder."

Seb tilted his head and looked at me, as if studying me for a moment. He glanced over his shoulder before returning his focus to me, staring straight into my eyes. "Huh, I don't recall that at all."

"You don't remember seeing her leave?"

"Nope." His eyes darted back and forth. "Actually, I, um, don't remember her at the party except when I saw you two at the table at the beginning. Drinking the '94 Merlot."

Dean looked at his notepad. "Tessa said she saw you in the driveway as she drove away."

"Huh, must've been someone else." Seb tapped his fingers on his jeans.

"You were the last one to see Mark alive at seven fifteen," Dean said. "Where was he when you saw him?"

Seb motioned to the winery wall near us. "Here. Talking to Vanessa."

I looked at Dean and back to Seb. Tessa's comment went through my mind. "Are you sure it wasn't Lisa?"

Seb cocked his head. "Um, no, it was Vanessa. I'm sure of it."

"So Vanessa was the last one to see him alive?" I asked.

"I guess," Seb said.

"Why were you watching him?"

Seb's eyes went from me to Dean and back again. "I'm an observer, huh. I wasn't watching him. I happened to notice. Do you, um, have any other questions? Because it's still work time around here. I could get in a lot of trouble talking to you." He paused. "People, uh, might not look too kindly on the fact that I'm standing around when there's work to be done."

"The owner of the winery was murdered." I motioned around the area. "Who would get upset at you talking to us?"

"You'd be surprised." Seb looked over his shoulder. "Huh, I gotta go. Am I dismissed?"

"Yes," replied Dean. "For now."

Seb turned on his heels and disappeared around the winery.

Dean's cell phone rang and he answered it with a sturdy sounding, "Dean." He motioned to me to give him a minute and he stepped to the side.

I wandered alongside the winery to another row of vines whose light green leaves danced in the breeze. The dark purple grapes were plump with juice as the sunlight highlighted them. I lightly placed my hand on a cluster, the skins still cold from the nighttime.

"Beautiful, aren't they?"

I turned to see Jeff standing only a few feet away, his face shadowed by a straw sunhat.

"Sorry, I didn't mean to intrude on your work."

"No, it's fine." Jeff's jeans were covered with dirt and grape stains, and he held a small pair of clippers in his left hand. He leaned over to the bunch I had touched and picked from it. He opened his palm toward me, three purple marble-sized grapes rolling around. "Here, try one."

I took one from his hand. "Thanks." I wiped the dust off and popped it in my mouth, squishing it with my tongue. The tart juice ran down my throat.

"Can you tell what grape it is?"

I chewed the rest of the grape skin and swallowed. "I'm going to guess Merlot. Am I right?"

"Nicely done." Jeff smiled as he pushed the hat away from his face. "Not everyone can do that. I gave one to someone once and asked them what type of grape it was and after a few seconds, they replied 'red.'"

"Ha," I laughed. "Bonus points for creativity."

"Yeah." Jeff popped the remaining two grapes in his mouth. He pointed to the bunches of grapes swaying in the breeze. "Nearly harvest time. We'll be picking these over the next few weeks."

"That sounds fun. My job is serving the wine, but I'd love to be involved in the whole process of where the wine came from. Picking the grapes, stuff like that."

Jeff looked surprised. "Really? You'd want to do that?"

"Yes."

"It's hard work."

I shrugged. "So is everything in life."

Jeff studied me for a second. "If you want to, you should come help us here. You can do one day, or even a few days if you want."

"Seriously? I'd love to help." I waved my hand in the air toward the entire property. "The morning fog, the grapes waiting patiently on the vine until I pick them and place them in the basket, on their way to become wine. There's a whole romantic side to it, you know?"

"I love the way you talk about wine. Most of the people here treat it as a job. You're unique. Then again, maybe you'd feel the same way after doing it for a little while. Once it becomes routine, it loses its magic."

"No, I don't think so." I looked at a large cluster of grapes in front of me, the sunlight bouncing off their skins. "I don't think I would ever get tired of anything that involves wine. I love the whole process."

Jeff leaned on the pole holding up the wires for the vines and stared at me. "You're really something. It's refreshing to meet someone who is so into wine."

Heat rushed to my cheeks. "Thanks. And you? Is this a job for you, or is it more?"

He winked. "It's always something more." He bent down and picked up a fallen grape. He held it between his pointer and thumb. "Alone, this is a grape. No different from any other grape." He pointed to a bunch hanging from the vine. "But together, they create wine. Wine that will be enjoyed by people, families, friends. Wine that will create memories, you know?"

"I do."

Jeff dropped the grape out of his hand and it rolled in the dirt. "One day I'm going to have my own winery. It's going to be really something, you'll see." He smiled. "So tell me, Katie, what was the bottle that did it? What was the bottle that got you into wine?"

I smiled. "How do you know it was a certain bottle? How do you know it wasn't simply a fascination with wine?"

"It's always a bottle. Some special bottle that opened your eyes to the wine world and how unique a glass of fermented grape juice could be. You ask anyone who works with wine and they'll tell you the bottle that did it. Even if you already had a fascination with wine." He winked. "So what was the bottle?"

I hesitated. "I don't think it was a bottle."

"No? Okay then, what bottle do you think of fondly? What bottle brings back a rush of memories? Humor me and share."

I laughed and glanced down at my feet, kicking a small clump of dirt with my shoe. "Okay," I looked back up at Jeff. "My uncle came to visit us when I was fourteen, and he opened a bottle of 1969 Chateau Margaux. As he poured it, he talked about the vineyards in Bordeaux and the history of the area. The consistency of the soil near the banks of the river, the way the morning sun touched the vines. The glass of wine came alive in my hand and I've never looked back."

Jeff nodded slowly, his eyes fixated on me. "I love that. That's … perfect." He moved a step closer to me. "I actually have a bottle of 1969 Chateau Margaux."

My mouth dropped open. "You don't!"

"I do. I have a large collection from over the years and a few bottles from Chateau Margaux, including a '69."

The memories of that first bottle flooded into my mind and I could remember every moment, every taste, every aspect. I was back at the kitchen table with my uncle and mom, carefully holding my glass the same way my uncle held his. I swirled when he did and sipped when he did. My mom had been too sick to drink the wine, but she asked me to describe everything I could taste. I talked about the wine for as long as I could, the smile on my mom's face the brightest I had seen in years. It was one of my last memories of her.

"Hey, you okay?"

"Sorry." I shook my head and looked at Jeff. "Just remembering."

"Listen," Jeff said, "do you want to come over tonight and share the bottle with me? I'd love to open it with someone who would appreciate it."

"I have work tonight."

"After work then?" The breeze shifted direction, sending scents of the neighboring vineyard toward me.

"Um, I can't."

"You have a boyfriend?"

"Ah, no. It's that I need…" I paused, uncertain of how to answer. "I need to take care of Tessa."

Jeff's attention focused behind me. I turned around. Dean was on his cell phone in the distance, pacing back and forth by the car.

"Detective Dean is back," said Jeff in a slow voice.

"Yeah, we came together."

Jeff paused as he studied me. "Why?"

"To investigate the murder."

Jeff looked surprised. "You're helping him with this? I thought you were a sommelier. Does it also stand for detective?"

"Aren't they one and the same?" I let a small laugh escape from my lips, but Jeff didn't react. "No, it's that I need to." I waited. "For Tessa."

"Is she okay?"

"Why wouldn't she be?"

Jeff shrugged. "You were worried last night. I wanted to make sure."

"She'll be fine, I think. Once I get everything sorted out." I took a deep breath. "Once I make sure that they no longer think she was involved."

"Well, if you're as passionate about that as you are about wine, you'll have no problem."

I studied Jeff's face. His attention was solely on me and not on the work he was supposed to be doing. "Thank you."

"For what?"

"For not assuming she's guilty. I wish I could say the same for everyone else."

"People like to get the quick fix," said Jeff. "If there's someone they can blame, they will, so they can get on with their lives." He looked intently at me. "If you want to prove Tessa is innocent, I'm sure that you'll do it."

"Thanks."

Jeff glanced over my shoulder again and then at the vines in front of him. "I think your friend is ready for you, and I should probably get back to work."

I looked back at Dean, who stood at the squad car, driver's door open. "Yeah, that's my ride. Did you need to talk with him about anything before he leaves?"

"Nope. We talked enough last night. Gave me a lot of flack for walking over the crime scene when I tried to get Mark out of the tank. So much for trying to save a life."

"Sorry about that."

"It's fine." Jeff looked at the leaves on the vine closest to him and tapped one with his hand. "Everyone has a job to do." He reached into his back pocket and took out his cell phone. "Wait, let me get your number. I'll call you when we're starting the harvest. Probably in the next two weeks."

"I"—I paused—"don't usually give out my phone number."

"Oh." His eyes met mine and he slowly put his phone back in his pocket. "Okay."

"But wait, I do want to help with the harvest."

"Okay, so what do you want me to do? Should I send you a telegram?" A small smile grew on Jeff's face.

I gave him my cell number.

"Great," said Jeff as he took his phone back out and entered the digits. "I'll call you in a day or so and let you know the exact date. It'll be fun. Then we can run together afterward and maybe drink some good wine." He put his phone back in his pocket. "And let me know if you change your mind about that '69 Chateau Margaux."

A wave of uncertainty flooded through me. "Sounds good. Talk soon." I stepped backward.

"Good luck with the case."

"Thanks. I'll need it."

"Nah. You have a good head on your shoulders. I'm sure you'll do fine."

"I hope so," I replied as I headed to Dean's car. "If I can figure out what I'm missing."

FOURTEEN

PAIRING SUGGESTION: ZINFANDEL—PASO ROBLES, CA

A rich and jammy wine filled with promise and intrigue.

༞

DEAN WAS STILL FOCUSED on Jeff when I reached his squad car.

"Ready?" I said as I smiled at him.

He looked at me, his return smile void of emotion. "Ready."

There was an uncomfortable level of silence as we headed down the gravel driveway.

"Well," I said, "that was productive."

Dean glanced over at me. "How so? Seb didn't see Tessa."

"Yeah, that part wasn't good." I took a deep breath. "But I think Alan gave us an Easter egg there with the financial status of the winery."

"I'll look into the money more," said Dean. "A winery on the verge of bankruptcy could give a lot of people a motive."

"And Vanessa said the vultures are already moving in."

"When did she say that?"

"Oh, sorry. When I saw her late last night."

Dean stopped the car in the middle of the driveway and looked at me. "When last night?"

"After you took Tessa to the station, I went back to the winery."

"You didn't tell me this."

"Sorry, I forgot. Although I kind of did at the coffee shop, because I said I went to find Seb to see if he had seen Tessa leave, but he hadn't."

Dean leaned on the steering wheel. "Wait, why did you want to find Seb last night?"

"As you took Tessa away, she yelled through the window to ask Seb."

"Yes, I remember that."

"So I went to ask Seb, but when I found him, he had no idea what she meant. Same as today. Didn't give any additional information. When I was leaving, that's when I saw Vanessa."

"Tell me more about that." He put the car in park and stared at me.

"She was crying—understandable given the situation."

"Where was she crying?"

I motioned toward the lawn. "Over there. I saw her and I offered my condolences. That's when she said the vultures were already moving in."

"Interesting." Dean returned his focus straight ahead and started driving. "Alan said there were offers. Maybe people made offers last night, once they found out Mark was dead."

I sat up. "The fight. That had to have been what the fight was about last night with Vanessa and Garrett. Because she said something about not understanding the need for urgency and he said that he would be asking even if Mark wasn't dead, or something like that. I bet he was trying to get her to sell the winery to him."

Dean nodded. "That could be more of a motive for Garrett. It's easier to cheat a widow than a solid couple."

"This is good. Other possibilities are coming to light. I mean, possibilities other than Tessa."

"There's still a lot more to figure out, Katie."

I shrugged. "Yes, but it will happen. I know it." I stared at the passing vineyards until Dean eventually pulled into the station and parked the car. "Thanks for letting me come with you."

"You're welcome. You sticking around?"

"No, I've got to get back to the city for work."

"Wait," said Dean as I reached for the door handle.

I stopped. "What?"

He shifted in his seat before meeting my eyes. "I don't know how to say this so I'm just going to say it. I didn't get a good feeling when you were talking to Jeff."

"What do you mean? We talked about grapes and wine. You were on your phone."

"I know, I know," said Dean. "But I get a weird vibe from him. I think he's up to no good."

"Jeff? He's nice." I shook my head. "Is this a weird guy thing? Did you see him taking my number? It was about helping with the harvest, which would be good for my career. You know, getting to know more about the grape-growing process, getting hands-on experience with a harvest."

Dean's face grew softer as he looked at me. "I'm saying I want you to be careful."

"Okay. I'll be careful." I paused for a moment. "But keep in mind that I was talking to Jeff at the party when the murder happened. He's not part of this."

"Okay, but I've been on the force for eleven years and sometimes you get a gut feeling that you have to trust."

"I'm a cop's daughter. I get gut feelings, too." I kept back the fact that my gut had been giving me a bad sign since the moment I first arrived at Frontier.

My journey back to San Francisco began the same as my other drives, but as I continued on Highway 29, I noticed a black truck rapidly approaching from behind. I waited for it to pass me, but it stayed a moderate length in the distance. I watched it for a few more seconds and then turned up the music, a deep sense of melancholy overcoming me as vineyards no longer graced my view.

When I turned onto I-80, the truck trailed behind me in the same lane. A wave of unease began in my stomach. I changed lanes and the truck did as well. What was going on?

I transitioned back to the slow lane and the truck didn't follow. I started to relax.

The truck pulled up beside me and I glanced at the driver, but the dark-tinted windows hid its occupant.

I increased my speed, but the truck kept its pace with me. That's when I felt the impact.

My Jeep swerved to the right as the noise of metal against metal permeated my car, followed by the high-pitched squeal of tires and other vehicles honking. I yanked the wheel to the left to avoid going off the highway as the truck moved away. My heart raced and I shuddered as my ears replayed the intense crushing sound so loudly, I wasn't sure if it was still going on.

I took my foot off the gas to prepare to pull to the side, but the truck slammed into me again. The force jolted my hands and the car shook as the Jeep's passenger side tires edged onto the dirt shoulder. My breath caught in my throat and I pulled the wheel to get back on the pavement. Still the truck pushed, my hands vibrating with every bump.

Dirt flew in the air as all four tires were shoved off the road. I tried to brake, but that only allowed the truck to maneuver my car closer to the embankment.

Adrenaline riveted through me and I jammed my foot on the gas pedal, trying to get ahead of the truck. The truck matched my speed.

I had one last chance.

I slammed on the brakes as hard as I could.

The force of the sudden stop threw me forward, my face lunging toward the steering wheel. The seatbelt yanked me back, my head banging back against the seat as the truck broke free, its black body careening into the distance.

Although my head was spinning, I looked for the license plate as the truck sped away. There was a blank space where the white square should have been.

Cars flew past but no one stopped to check on the damaged Jeep on the side of the road. My hand shook as I turned off the Jeep's engine, the eerie silence broken only by my pounding heartbeat.

When I felt I could stand without collapsing, I forced my door open and inspected the damage. The entire left side of my vehicle was crunched, and the dark green paint was down to the metal in several sections. Perfectly drivable, but cosmetically pathetic.

My first hit and run. Lovely.

I returned to the driver's seat and closed the door, grateful that it still worked. My breathing was rapid and I tried to take bigger breaths, each one deeper and calmer, until both my air intake and my pulse were at acceptable levels. When I was calm enough to safely drive, I restarted the car.

My hands were still trembling when I reached my two-story apartment building in the Inner Sunset area, only a few blocks away from Golden Gate Park.

As usual, every parking space in the area was already taken and although there was a garage on the right-hand side of the building reserved for the one tenant who paid more, I was not that tenant. I circled the block twice, but the only curb missing a car was the section in front of the stairs and it was painted red.

I stared up at the building as I debated what to do. The two-story art deco building hadn't been touched since the 1940s except for a lick of cream paint about fifteen years ago, which was now starting to peel.

My eyes drifted back to the empty curb. I knew that if I left my car there for even a few minutes, parking enforcement would be ready with a ticket. Whenever I parked at an expired meter or double parked on my block, the enforcement arrived minutes later even if I hadn't seen them for days. It was as if they sensed me thinking about it. We had played this game repeatedly over the last four years but I was currently winning—although there had been numerous close calls where I managed to get into my car and drive away before the officer was able to start the citation process, I had only been ticketed twice.

I drove around the block once more, but it was clear that the curb was my only option. I needed to shower and change before I headed to work and I was running out of time.

I parked at the red curb with my emergency flashers on and ran up the stairs. Within fifteen minutes, I had showered and pulled my wet hair back into a bun for work. I ran back out to the curb, a small piece of paper flapping in the wind on the car. Great, a ticket. The parking enforcement had won after all.

I removed it from the window and got into my car, unfolding the paper before I started the engine. My heart started to pound.

Stop looking into Frontier, or next time you drive the road to Napa, it won't be a warning.

FIFTEEN

PAIRING SUGGESTION: BEAUJOLAIS—MORGON, FRANCE

A light red wine that is best when chilled.

I ARRIVED AT THE parking lot of Trentino Restaurant with a few minutes to spare before my 3:00 p.m. clock-in time. I smoothed my white blouse and buttoned the coat of my fitted black suit, then adjusted my bun to make sure my hair was in place before I opened the door and walked through the restaurant.

"Katie, you made it," said Bill, as he stood near the kitchen.

"Did you think I wouldn't?" I stopped in front of him.

"You missed inventory. Everything okay?" He raised his eyebrows, his brown eyes deep with concern.

I took a deep breath. "Yeah, I'm fine. Something came up with Tessa and I had to handle it. Darius covered for me, right?"

"Yes, he was here. But I want to make sure you're okay."

"Yeah," I said as I ignored the fact that my car was damaged and my nerves were rattled. "I'm fine."

"Are you still thinking about the test?"

"Not exactly."

"Okay." Bill paused. "Even if you fall off the horse once, doesn't mean you can't get back on. It doesn't matter that you didn't pass. You'll pass next time."

I sighed. "Thanks."

Bill leaned on the partition that divided the restaurant into two main sections. "Hey, how was Frontier last night? Which wines did you try?" His mouth formed a half smile. "Did they make you sign an NDA?"

"Hasn't the news…" I stopped as I remembered the secrecy that surrounded Frontier Winery. Even the sheriff had managed to keep it out of the media. "No NDA." I shifted my feet. "The experience was interesting to say the least."

"I look forward to hearing all about it. I'm going to assume they brought out some of their prized wines from over the years."

"Yes, they did. But there was a lot going on." I took a deep breath. "I'll fill you in as soon I get everything figured out."

Bill nodded. "Now get to work. We have two hundred covers tonight."

I saluted. "Yes, sir."

I headed to the time clock, my posture straightening as I adapted a work zone attitude and started my pre-shift duties. When five o'clock rolled around, I waited near the bar as the main doors of the restaurant opened.

"Inventory sucks," said Darius as he arrived at my side.

"Yeah, not exactly the most fun. Thanks for covering."

Darius shrugged. "It's fine. Did you bring my Oban?"

"It's coming. I didn't have a chance to get it today."

"Don't flake on me."

"I won't."

He leaned on the bar. "Hey, I heard about the test. Bummer."

"I know, right?"

"I think the next one's in Texas. Means you'll have to fly this time."

"Maybe." My eyes drifted across the bottles of wine. "I don't know yet."

The host motioned to me. "We have a walk-in asking about the wine list. I sat him at table forty-two."

I glanced through the restaurant to a gentleman at table forty-two, a corner booth. "Gotta go."

"Yep," said Darius. "The work games have begun."

I smoothed out my jacket, adjusted my collar, and approached the table.

"Good evening, welcome to Trentino." I stopped in the middle of my speech. "Seb?" Seb's familiar face stared back at me. "What are you doing here?"

"Oh, huh." Seb paused as his eyes darted back and forth. "I didn't know you worked here." He looked around nervously. "I'm meeting a friend for dinner."

"It's a long drive from the winery."

He shrugged his shoulders. "Maybe. But I've heard a lot about this place and figured I should check it out. It has a good reputation, huh." He drummed his fingers on the table as his focus shifted from me to the restaurant and back again.

"Wait, what kind of car do you drive?"

Seb squinted his eyes. "Huh? A blue Ford Escort."

"And it's outside?"

"With valet. Why?"

"Who drives a black truck?"

"Huh? A black truck? Um, I have no idea."

"Never mind." I stood up straighter. "Did you have a question about the wine list or do you want to wait to order until your guest arrives?"

"Oh, um, no. Let me look." Seb picked up the wine menu from the table and skimmed the list. "I'll take the Windjammer Chardonnay, 2014. A glass."

"Excellent choice. I'll be right back." I headed to the bar and poured a glass of the golden wine. I placed it on the tray held firmly in my left hand and returned to the table.

I stood to the right of Seb and put the glass down in front of him. "Is there anything else I can get you at the moment or should I come back when your guest is here?"

"Actually, since you're here, huh." Seb looked over his shoulder and then back at me. "And we're alone, huh, there's something I should probably tell you." He lowered his voice. "It's about Tessa."

An elderly gentleman at a nearby table of four motioned to me.

"Hold on, let me take care of this other table and I'll be right back." I approached the table and went through my normal greeting a little quicker than usual. I explained the wines on the list, answered questions, and took four drink orders. I walked to the bar and filled my tray with three glasses of Cabernet and one glass of whisky.

My eyes flicked up to Seb as I approached the table with their drink orders. He didn't look at the menu, like most guests who arrive prior to their date, but instead watched my every move. My hand shook and a glass on my tray wobbled and fell over. I never spilled a tray. Ever.

Get it together, I reminded myself as I returned to the bar. I cleaned the tray, wiped down the other glasses, and refilled the glass of Cabernet.

I focused on the tray as I delivered it to the waiting table. My eyes remained only on the guests as I quietly and calmly placed a glass in front of each of them. "Is there anything else you need at this time?"

"This is fine," said the gentleman as he raised his whisky glass for a taste.

I stepped back and watched the group for a second before I returned to Seb's table. The seat across from him was still empty.

"What were you saying about Tessa?" I stood across from him, my eyes monitoring the door of the restaurant.

"Can you talk? You have time, huh?"

Six guests entered through the front door and waited at the host stand.

"I only have a few seconds. It gets busy in here very quickly."

"That's okay. I want you to know"—his fingers tapped on the table—"that your friend might not have been on the up and up, if you know what I mean, huh."

"What?"

"I know you're close to Tessa, but, um, I don't know if you know your friend as well as you think, huh. She wasn't exactly a straight shooter."

"Seb, I only have a few more seconds, so what are you trying to say?" I held my notepad up to look as though I was taking an order. "Tessa is my best friend. I know she's not a murderer."

"I know, I know." His fingers tapped, their beat increasing. "But she is a thief. There's been money, huh ... missing."

"What money?"

"From the winery accounts. For a while now. Someone's been taking money from them, huh. I think you should take a good look at Tessa. You might be surprised at what you find."

"Seb, please. I'm not going to buy that."

"No, it's the truth, huh. Ask Detective Dean to look into it. She's been taking money. Maybe she's in debt? I don't know. But, um, I thought you should know. If she goes down, I don't want you to go down, too."

I shook my head. "I don't believe it."

"Listen, um, look into it."

"Okay. I'll look into it." I noticed Bill looking in my direction. "I have to do my rounds, I'll be back."

"One more thing, huh?" He looked up at me, his face solemn. "Um, I know you're looking into everything, um, about last night. But I know something that others don't."

"About the accounts?"

"No, about…" The tapping of his fingers got louder. "About Mark."

I glanced at the other tables. "Tell me in a few seconds, I have to go. I'll be right back."

"No, wait. Listen. Mark wasn't, huh, faithful."

"Oh, that makes sense, from what Lisa said."

Seb's eyebrows went up. The tapping stopped. "What Lisa said?"

"I think so. It's all getting muddled right now. I have to go grab this table. I'll be back."

"Huh. I'm surprised Lisa said something."

I paused before leaving his table. "Why?"

"Because Mark was having an affair with Lisa."

Bill coughed and I looked up. "Give me five minutes," I said to Seb. "I want to hear more."

Seb stared at me but didn't reply.

I visited the rest of the tables in my section, taking and delivering drink orders as I went. I was eager to get back to Seb, but I didn't want to spill again, so every movement I made was calm and calculated.

The fourth table had multiple questions about the wine list. If the circumstances had been different, I would have treasured questions of that nature, providing details about each wine and sharing its story. Instead, dread filled me after my short answers while I waited to be asked another question or be dismissed.

The table decided on a bottle of Champagne and I retrieved it from the refrigerated wine cellar, presented the bottle, opened it silently as I controlled the pop, and poured it for each guest. I placed the bottle into the ice bucket, covered it with a towel, and returned to Seb's table. His seat was vacant and a twenty-dollar bill was stuck under the empty glass of wine. I looked toward the front of the restaurant, but Seb was gone.

SIXTEEN

PAIRING SUGGESTION: CHINON—CHINON, FRANCE

*Made from the Cabernet Franc grape,
it pairs well with most dishes and situations.*

∞

I HAD TROUBLE CONCENTRATING during the rest of my shift as my mind was focused on Seb's comments. I had noticed Tessa's brand-new shoes at the winery and her apartment coffee table seemed to be nicer than the one I had seen on my previous visit.

Things had been rough financially before Tessa started the job at Frontier. Although I didn't know how well her wine club position paid, I wasn't sure it was enough to pay off her mounting credit cards. Perhaps the wine smuggling with Mark gave her kickbacks, some cash under the table. I wasn't sure, but I couldn't shake it from my mind.

When the last two tables in my section had full glasses of wine, I stepped to the back of the restaurant and called Tessa's cell phone. It rang several times and went to her voicemail.

I cancelled the call and returned to the dining area. The patrons at my tables were happily drinking and eating. I waited a few moments and called again. It rang and went to voicemail.

The only time Tessa didn't pick up her phone was when she was in a movie theatre or out of cell range. She didn't have a car since it was still at the lodge and I hadn't given her a ride yet to get it. She should be keeping a low profile at her apartment where she had full reception.

I waited a few more minutes in case Tessa was in the shower and tried again. No answer.

The minutes crawled by until the two last tables finished their meals and paid the checks. It was 11:37 p.m. by the time I clocked out and got into my car. I tried Tessa's phone again with no luck. A sinking feeling flooded over me. I drove past the turn for my apartment and started the drive to Napa, my foot pressing harder on the gas pedal than legally allowed.

The streets were relatively empty, only a few passing cars with people on their way home from dinner or parties, and within forty minutes I was in the city of Napa, home to over 75,000 residents, including Tessa.

I parked in her apartment's lot and ran up the stairs of her building. "Tessa?" I knocked. "Are you there? Wake up."

No answer.

I knocked again. "Tessa, answer the door." There was a tremor in my voice.

The window next to Tessa's apartment opened. "She's not there."

"Where is she?"

The streetlight illuminated a teenager with dark hair sitting in the window, the blue glow of a television screen behind her. "I heard her saying she was going to Matteo's."

"Matteo's?"

"Head to Lincoln. You'll see the restaurant once you turn right, about a block away."

"Thanks."

"No worries." The window closed shut, the girl watching me as I headed down the stairs.

I left my Jeep in the parking lot and walked toward the main drag, the moon casting a soft silvery light, coating the hedges with a colorless shroud. When I reached Lincoln, I turned right, a few cars passing as I walked.

For the time of night, Matteo's was anything but quiet. People flowed in and out, and I waited for a couple in their midthirties to exit, catching the door before it closed behind them. A roar of noise greeted me as I entered the restaurant. Nearly every table was occupied and the bar was packed at least three people deep at every section.

A jazz band played music from the corner and the host, wearing horn-rimmed glasses, stood at the dais, a waterfall cascading down the wall behind him. I scanned the crowd for Tessa's familiar blond curls.

It didn't take me long.

Tessa stood on a table in the corner of the bar, dancing to the music as three guys at the table watched her every move. The sway of her dance was a clear indication that she was having a good time and an even clearer indication that she was inebriated.

I made my way through the crowd and reached Tessa in the middle of a drunken ballet turn on the table.

"Tessa," I yelled. "Tessa, what are you doing?"

Tessa looked down at me and opened her arms. "Katie, you came!" she said in a slurred voice. "Come on, get up on the table with me, we're having a party!"

"Tessa, get down from there."

"No, I like being up here."

I pulled Tessa's arm. With her drunken sway, Tessa collapsed on the legs of a man sitting in the booth, her elbow narrowly missing the face of the gentleman next to him.

"Aw, you're no fun. You took away my stage." Tessa turned to the man whose lap she occupied. "And you're comfy. Have we met? I'm Tessa."

"Tessa, this is ridiculous!" I snapped. "What are you doing?"

"I'm having fun. Living it up. Enjoying the moment." Tessa closed her eyes. "Wait, now I'm a little tired."

The man moved from underneath her and Tessa sank into the seat, her head falling back against the cushioned booth.

"Tessa, come on, get up. I'm taking you home."

"No, I want to stay. The night is young."

"It's nearly one o'clock."

"And there's more to drink, right, boys?" Tessa opened her eyes and looked at the three men at the table, but their attention had turned to a nearby girl in a short red dress.

"I can't believe this," I whispered loudly in her ear. "Your boss was killed last night and here you are partying? Do you have any idea how that looks?"

Tessa looked up at me. "I think it looks like a party. I'm celebrating life."

"You look guilty. Come on, I'm taking you home." I stood and pulled Tessa's limp body from the booth. "Let's go. Stand up."

"Do you ladies need help?" said a young man from a nearby table. "Can I call you a cab?"

"No, we're fine." I heaved Tessa up to a standing position. "The walk will do her good." I put my arm around Tessa's waist and pulled her close to me. "Walk with me, Tessa. Keep your head up. Let's leave with some dignity."

Tessa lifted her head and we made it to the door, which someone opened for us.

The cold night air was a blast of sobriety for Tessa and she managed to propel herself forward as we made our way down the street. The walk wasn't pretty, similar to a newborn giraffe with her legs going in every direction, but at least she was moving. My arm ached from the weight of holding her up, but I focused on getting her home.

The stairs up to her apartment turned out to be a little more tricky. Tessa fell on the first step and I caught her right before her face hit the concrete edge.

"You okay?"

"Yeah." Tessa sat on the step, catching her breath. "I'd be better if you'd left me there. I was having fun."

"I'm looking after you."

"No, you're ruining the fun," Tessa slurred. "Hey, is that your car? What did you do?"

I glanced at the damaged driver's side of my Jeep. "Yeah, about that…"

"Katie," Tessa interrupted, "you should drive better."

"Okay, thank you. Come on, stand back up."

Using a pathetic amount of effort, Tessa slowly stood up. I put my arm around her waist and we took the stairs together, turning along the walkway when we reached the top.

I leaned Tessa against her door. "Tessa, where's your key?"

"Huh?"

"Your key? To your apartment."

The window next to the apartment opened and once again the neighbor put her face against the screen. "She keeps it on her wrist. Like a bracelet."

"Thank you." I reached for Tessa's arm where I found a green curly bracelet with a gold key attached. I took off the bracelet and opened the door as Tessa slumped against me. "Almost there. Just a few more feet."

Tessa took two steps inside and collapsed cross-legged on the floor.

"Nope, not yet. Come on, let's get you to the couch." I grabbed Tessa under her arms. The memory of Jeff doing the same for Mark flashed through my mind. I shook the image out of my head and tried again, this time getting one arm under her shoulder and the other arm under her knees, lifting her up like a baby.

The dead weight seemed much more than Tessa's one hundred and ten pounds and my body trembled as I carried her to the couch, heaving her onto the cushions a little harder than planned. I shook out my arms as I walked into the kitchen and filled a glass with water.

I put it on the coffee table in front of Tessa. "Drink this."

"No ... No more drink."

"It's water, Tee. Not alcohol."

"I don't want water."

"Yes, you do. Now drink." My tone was forceful, unusual for me but effective in this kind of situation.

Tessa picked her head up from the couch cushion and with my help, sipped at the glass of water. "The room is starting to spin." Tessa lay back down.

"I bet it is. You have a lot to drink?"

"No," said Tessa, her hand draped across her forehead. "One, no two, maybe three. I don't know. Counting is hard."

I grabbed the small trash can from the bathroom and brought it back to the couch, placing it on the floor next to Tessa. "Tee, this is here in case you need it, okay?"

"Okay," she mumbled.

"I thought you were going to stay in your apartment, lay low. Why did you go out?"

"Geez, can't a girl have a little fun?" asked Tessa.

"You're a suspect in a murder investigation and you go out and party?"

"Not party. I was working."

"How was that work?"

"I mean"—Tessa turned onto her side and closed her eyes—"going to work. Those guys were going to get me a job. Networking is important." Her voice grew softer.

"Tessa, don't fall asleep, we need to talk." I sat down on the cushion next to her and tapped her cheek with my hand. "Tessa, focus. Listen to me. Do you know anything about money disappearing from the winery accounts?"

Tessa's eyes opened, glassy and unfocused. "Money? Money is bling bling." Her voice was a whisper and I knew I only had a few more minutes before sleep took over.

"Yes, money."

"It's not about the money, honey, bunny," Tessa sang, then laughed.

"Tessa, this is important. Focus."

She readjusted her head on the couch cushion. "It's sleepy time, you talk too much." Her eyes fluttered as they always did when she was falling asleep, followed by the heavy breathing that signaled she was out for the night.

I sat back and watched her. Tessa tended to be straightforward, sometimes a little too much, while inebriated, but my questions had provided little information. Maybe I didn't know my friend as well as I thought.

I glanced at my watch. It was 1:37 in the morning. There was no point in driving back to my apartment, and I needed to have a serious talk with Tessa in the morning.

I covered Tessa with her comforter and grabbed a blanket and a pillow for myself, curling up on the end of the L-shaped couch so I could be within earshot if she needed me. I stared at Tessa's brand-new shoes, which were on the floor beside her. Navy blue Manolo Blahniks. At least five-hundred-dollar shoes.

SEVENTEEN

PAIRING SUGGESTION: RIOJA—RIOJA, SPAIN

*Made from the Tempranillo grape,
it creates a slight sweetness on the palate.*

❧

THE MORNING LIGHT STREAMED through the blinds, stirring me awake. I looked at the ceiling, then at the walls around me. This wasn't my apartment.

My eyes drifted to Tessa asleep on the couch, her legs and arms sticking out at awkward angles from under the comforter. The memory of last night flooded back to me.

I sat up, leaned against the couch, and rubbed my eyes, making sure I was fully awake before I stood up. My stomach rumbled, a reminder that I had missed my post-shift meal at work.

The floor creaked as I walked into the kitchen. Tessa stirred and flipped over but remained asleep.

I opened the fridge to find a jar of pickles, mustard, and a package of store-bought cupcakes. No surprise there. It was one of the few things we really had in common, not stocking the fridge.

I closed the door and turned to the cabinets, a second grumble from my stomach as I picked up a box of Cornflakes, which I put right back after remembering Tessa didn't have any milk.

I wrote a note, *Gone to get food. When I come back, we can go get your car*, and put it next to the coffee maker as I knew it was a place where Tessa would see it. Tessa would definitely need coffee after a night like last night.

Only after I closed the door to the apartment did I realize that I had left Tessa's key inside. When I returned, there would be a lot of pounding on the door to wake Tessa up, I was certain.

The cool morning mist still floated in the air as I made my way to the main street. A couple walked past me, their eyes focused on my hair. I put my hand to my head, my fingers combing over the tangles, and I did my best to scrape my hair into a ponytail.

I retraced my steps from the night before and approached Matteo's. A restaurant like Matteo's, which thrived on nightlife, wouldn't be open for breakfast, but there might be one nearby that would.

I was in luck. One block down from Matteo's was a small boutique coffee shop, its door propped open beneath a white awning as a line of people stood waiting to order. I reached for my sunglasses but they weren't in my purse. They were still in the car. I joined the line and kept my head down to avoid being noticed by anyone I knew. I had slept in my black pants and white shirt from work and the extensive creases across the front indicated as such. I tried to smooth them out but my efforts did nothing. I gave up and focused on the chalkboard menu above the counter.

The line moved forward and a cheerful server behind the counter greeted me with a smile. "Morning. What can I get for you?"

I looked up at the menu again. "I'll take a croissant, an egg and cheese bagel, and two orange juices. All to go."

He typed up the order. I handed over cash and waited for my change, placing a few dollars in the tip jar on the counter.

More people had arrived and the line snaked into the courtyard. I stood with my back to the wall as I waited for my order. The wine industry was actually pretty small and I prided myself on a clean appearance. A morning in Napa looking like I had slept in a barn would not be good for my career.

"Egg and cheese bagel, croissant, and two OJ," said another counter attendant as he hit the small bell next to him.

"Thank you." I gathered up the items and headed into the courtyard, my eyes to the ground as I passed the line of people. No one recognized me, or if they did, they didn't acknowledge me.

By the time I returned to Tessa's apartment, the fog had lifted from the area, revealing the blue Napa sky. I knocked on the door, but there was no reply.

"Tessa? It's me, open up."

I tried again, this time using my fist to pound on the door.

Several seconds later, Tessa opened the door, still in her dress from the night before, her tangled hair falling onto her half-awake face.

"Good morning, sunshine." I walked into the apartment. "I'm glad you're awake."

"Yes, I don't sleep when someone's breaking down my door."

"Thankfully."

Tessa flopped back onto the couch.

"How ya feeling?"

"Peachy."

"Hung over?"

"Don't know," said Tessa as she looked around. "Too early to tell. What's that smell?"

"I went to a coffee shop and bought you orange juice and a croissant."

Tessa put her hand to her head. "Don't mention food. You'll make me throw up."

"Yep, definitely hung over. Take a few bites, it will make you feel better."

"Not a chance." She waved her hand in front of her face. "I'm so tired." She maneuvered to the edge of the couch and put her face in her hands. "Stop the pounding in my head."

"Orange juice will help that."

"Shut it, no it won't," said Tessa, her voice muffled. "But coffee will." She stood up, red marks on her face from her hands, her body swaying as she walked into the kitchen. "Thanks for your note," she said as the coffee maker started to percolate.

"Clearly it worked."

"Clearly."

My stomach grumbled in increased anticipation as I unwrapped the egg and cheese bagel and started eating. I pushed one of Tessa's Manolos with my toe. "When did you buy these shoes?"

She stuck her head out of the kitchen. "I know, they're cute, right? I got them last week."

"Very cute."

"Do you want to borrow them? You can."

"No, I think I've had enough of an adventure with heels for a while." I glanced around the apartment. "I like what you've done with the place. Especially the boxes, that's a nice touch."

"Katie," Tessa said in a strained voice as she returned to the couch with a cup of coffee. "I'll get to unpacking one day, but that day is not today." She closed her eyes.

"Is this table new? I don't remember it from my visit last month."

"What?" Tessa opened her eyes.

"Nothing."

"What table? I think that was here the last time you came. I don't know." Tessa put her coffee cup down. "I think I need to go to bed."

"Are you sure you don't want orange juice?"

"Ugh. Why are you so awake?"

"I didn't drink last night."

"Shame." Tessa stood up and walked toward the bedroom, dragging the comforter behind her.

"Hey, Tee, what about work?"

"What work? I don't have a job."

"But do you know that for sure?"

Tessa paused at the entrance to the bedroom. "Too many questions, Katie. I've already been interrogated once this weekend."

"All I'm saying is that maybe you should call Frontier."

"Hell no." She closed the bedroom door.

"Or at least Vanessa," I yelled. "To offer sympathy?"

Tessa cracked open the door and looked at me, her eyes half open. "Katie, you're my best friend, but really? You don't have a clue." The door closed and I continued eating, finishing my bagel.

The muffled ringing of my phone came from my purse at the foot of the couch. I pulled it onto the seat next to me, the noise increasing in volume. The phone number was one I didn't recognize.

"Hello?"

"Katie? It's Dean. Detective Dean. Hope I didn't wake you."

I looked at my watch. "It's ten forty, and I never sleep late anyway." My stomach dropped. "Is everything okay? Did something else come up with the case?"

"We received the coroner's report."

"And?" The egg and cheese bagel churned in my stomach and I regretted eating it so fast.

"Mark's time of death was prior to seven thirty."

I stood up. "Which means?"

"Which means he was dead before Tessa got the text at seven forty as her phone records show. She was with you until then so she has an alibi. You."

I put both arms in the air in a Rocky Balboa pose. "Thank you!"

"Thank me? I didn't do anything."

"I know, I know." I did a little dance. "But thank you so much for calling me! This makes me so happy!"

"I'm glad."

I took a deep breath, my neck and shoulders completely loose. "You've made my day." I touched the red button to end the call and placed it on the coffee table. I opened the door to Tessa's room. "Tessa, you're free, you didn't kill Mark."

Tessa sat up in bed, her blond hair falling over her face. "Huh?"

"You're free. You didn't kill Mark."

"I know I didn't kill Mark."

"I mean they've cleared you. The coroner's report came back and he was dead before you got the text."

"Yay," Tessa mumbled and lay back down.

"Don't you want to celebrate?"

"Katie," Tessa said dryly, "you just told me I didn't do something, which I knew I hadn't done. This news isn't exactly shocking. We can celebrate later. After sleep." She pulled the comforter over her head.

"If we go get your car, you can sleep the rest of the day." I grabbed my orange juice off the table and took a long drink, washing away any remaining stress.

My phone rang again.

I picked it up from the table. "Did you forget to tell me something?" I waited for Dean's deep voice.

"Uh," said an unfamiliar female voice. "I'm calling for Katie?"

I readjusted the phone. "Sorry, I didn't look at the number and I thought it was someone else. Who's this?"

There was hesitation on the other end of the line. "Katie, this is Vanessa."

I swallowed hard. "How are you?" The reality was most likely setting in. The hard days of realization. I closed my eyes, my breathing shallow as I waited for Vanessa to speak.

"I'm … I'm hanging in there. I guess. I wouldn't have called you on a Sunday, but I saw you walking this morning. At least I think it was you."

I took a breath. "Yes, that was me. I was getting food for Tessa."

"Oh…" Another pause. "Are you still in the area? Can we meet?"

I felt my head roll to the side as the invitation played in my mind.

Vanessa continued, "I need someone to talk to and I remember all the times with your mother in Junior League. She was trustworthy and I need someone like that. Someone I can trust. Or at least I hope I can."

"You can trust me."

"Then can we meet?"

I ran my hands through my hair and looked down at my wrinkled shirt. "When did you want to meet?"

"This afternoon?" her voice wavered. "I don't want to disturb you if you're busy, it's just that—"

I interrupted. "I'm free."

"There's a cafe, Cafe DaMissio, in downtown Napa. Can we meet there? Maybe three o'clock?"

"Sure."

"Thank you," Vanessa said in a tone flooded with relief.

"Of course." I put down the phone and stared straight ahead.

"Who was on the phone?" Tessa stood at the entrance to her bedroom.

I hesitated. "Just someone who needed a friend. We can talk about it later."

Tessa stared at me. "Was it a boy? 'Cause you're not allowed to get lucky. Not after the weekend I've had."

"Shut it, Tee, and get dressed. Let's go get your car and we can grab lunch on the way." I reached into my purse and took out the note that had been left on my car. "Hey, Tessa, whose handwriting is this?"

"Huh?" said Tessa.

"This." I handed her the note.

"*Stop looking into Frontier, or next time you drive along the road to Napa, it won't be a warning?*" Tessa looked up at me. "Katie! Is this what I think it is?" Her eyes lit up. "You got an actual threat! That's crazy! What are you going to do?"

I shrugged. "Keep looking into it. I'm not going to let this bother me. But do you recognize the writing?"

Tessa stared at the note and handed it back to me. "No clue. Doesn't ring a bell for me. Everyone I know uses computers anyway."

———

The daytime drive to the lodge highlighted the California oak trees and sparse sections of vineyards that had been hidden on my nighttime visit to Mount Veeder.

"Tessa, what's your opinion of Seb?"

"Seb, why?"

"I'm trying to figure something out. How well do you know him?"

Tessa shrugged. "I don't know. Nice guy. Always nervous."

"Do you trust him?"

"Trust him?" Tessa looked at me. "Why do you ask that?"

I turned into the driveway of 1829. "Because he said he didn't see you that night in the driveway and now he's telling people that you've been stealing from the accounts."

"What?! What a jerk. I'll kill him!"

"Tessa, watch your language."

"We're in the car, Katie. No one can hear us."

"Still. Not a good habit to say you're going to kill someone, especially when there's been a murder. So tell me." I pulled up at the lodge and turned off the car. "What do you know about him?"

"I don't know. Now I think he's a jerk."

"No, I want serious facts. Tell me everything you know about Seb."

Tessa leaned back in the seat. "I think he's divorced, has a kid somewhere. With the ex-wife."

"Anything else?"

"He's a good worker. I guess he used to pick up some of the wine club duties on the weekend, before I came along." Tessa opened the door of the car.

"Did he get along with Mark?" I asked.

"I think so." She got out of the car.

I leaned toward her open door to keep eye contact. "No, really think about it."

Tessa looked around at the trees. "I never saw them argue, but I know that Seb got in trouble a while ago."

"For what?"

"He ruined a batch of wine. Added too much yeast. The whole thing had to be dumped."

"That's a pretty big deal for a winery."

Tessa shrugged. "I guess. I know that Mark laid into him pretty bad for it. Seb's been careful ever since, trying not to make a bad move. Didn't want to lose his job, you know?"

"Hmm. And it was Seb's fault?"

"Yes." Tessa looked over her shoulder. "Can I get my car now?"

"Just a sec." I paused. "Seb also told me something else."

"When?"

"It doesn't matter, but listen. Do you know why he would want to tell me something about Lisa?"

Tessa raised her eyebrows. "About Lisa? Katie, what are you getting at? I'm tired, I'm hung over, and I'm not in the mood for games."

"He told me that Mark was having an affair with Lisa."

"Affair with Lisa? Ha!" Tessa laughed. "Why on earth would Seb tell you that? That's too funny."

"Why?"

"Because Lisa wasn't having an affair with Mark. She was sleeping with Seb! They've had a little romance over the past few months, but I'm pretty sure it's done now. I haven't seen them together the last few weeks."

"Wait. Why didn't you say something? When I asked you about Seb?"

"I'd forgotten until you mentioned it. Like I said, it's done now, so it wasn't exactly at the front of my mind. Besides, they're both single. Nothing taboo about it. By the way, you look good in my sweater. It suits you."

"Thanks for letting me borrow it."

"Of course. Can I get my car now?"

I nodded. "Go ahead."

Tessa shut the passenger door but then knocked on the glass. I lowered her window.

"Hey, can you swing by Matteo's and get my credit card? I had a tab going there last night and I'm going to assume you didn't close it for me."

"You have your car now, you can go pick it up."

"Are you kidding, Katie? After you dragged me out of there? No way. I'm not showing my face there."

I sighed. "Yes, I'll get it for you."

"Good, I want to go shopping tomorrow."

I tilted my head to the side. "Are you sure you should be shopping now?"

"What do you mean?"

"You might be between jobs. Time to save up."

"Nah," said Tessa as she started walking around the lodge. "I checked my account this morning," she yelled, waving her phone in the air. "Looks like I just got paid."

Less than a minute later, Tessa's silver Nissan passed by.

I followed her down the driveway as thoughts of Seb crossed through my mind. I mulled over the details of the case, similar to the initial conclusion in the blind tasting process before announcing the final decision. That was the key with blind tasting. If you try too hard, things get cloudy. You have to sit back and let the pieces fall into place.

EIGHTEEN

PAIRING SUGGESTION: PINOT NOIR—WILLAMETTE VALLEY, OR

Pairs well with most dishes and has a slight peppery note.

❧

DOWNTOWN NAPA WAS BUZZING with residents and visitors out for Sunday strolls, brunch, or wine tasting, and there was no available parking in front of Cafe DaMissio. I circled the block and found a space flanked by large pots overflowing with flowers.

I walked in the direction of the cafe, the neighboring buildings with a historic air to them and the foothills in the distance adding a poetic note. A woman stood next to Cafe DaMissio's brick patio, but even with a floppy beige hat and large sunglasses hiding her face, there was no mistaking Vanessa's strong jawline. I stopped about twenty feet away, Vanessa's attention focused on each passing car.

Her beige dress seemed to hang off her, as if she had lost weight since the murder, a withered look on her formerly rigid frame. Pain rose in my heart as the sudden temptation to leave formed in my stomach. I tried to remember what I should say to a newly grieving person. All I could remember was to listen and be there for them. Don't offer advice and don't ask too many questions.

I approached Vanessa, whose face brightened when she noticed me. "You came, I'm so glad."

"Of course. As I said, if you need a friend, I'm here."

"Thank you. It really means a lot." Vanessa motioned to the glass door behind her. "This is the cafe. I used to come here..." her voice fell away.

"Let me." I opened the door and Vanessa walked in. I was only a step behind, the aroma of freshly baked bread greeting me as I entered.

The bakery was spacious, more than three times the size of the one I had been in earlier that morning, with people milling around, sitting at tables, or standing at the counter. Staff in crisp white aprons took orders from all areas of the wooden counter, which was decorated with small towers of stacked scones and chocolate croissants on cake stands.

Underneath the counter, glass displays contained cookies, fruit tarts, biscotti, and donuts, while the wall behind the attendants had more baskets of freshly baked bread than I had ever seen.

"Good afternoon, Mrs. Plueger," said a girl who stood behind the counter, her dark hair pulled into a ponytail. "What can we get for you today?"

"A café latte and a croissant." Vanessa motioned to me. "I'll pay for her order as well."

"Oh, that's not necessary."

"I insist."

"Thank you." I grabbed a paper menu and scanned it. "I'll have a chai tea latte."

"Anything to eat?" asked Vanessa.

"No, I ate before I came. Just the tea will be great, thank you."

"Please have something with me. I don't want to feel guilty eating a croissant if you're having nothing." Vanessa took off her sunglasses and put them in her purse. Her eyes were red and puffy, makeup failing to hide the effects of hours of crying.

I scanned the contents of the glass display. "I'll have a madeleine. Maybe two."

"That's more like it." Strands of hair fell from under Vanessa's hat as she handed over a credit card. Her eyes met mine and she gave me a weak smile, the scar visible through the foundation.

"Your order, Mrs. Plueger." The girl placed a tray filled with coffee, tea, a croissant, and two madeleine cookies on the counter.

"Here, I'll get that." I reached for the tray.

"Is the corner okay with you?" Vanessa asked.

"Of course."

She maneuvered through the tables to an empty one in the corner and sat down with her back to the wall.

I put the coffee and croissant on the table and sat across from her, my chair only giving me a view of her and the wall.

Vanessa's eyes drifted around the cafe and finally to me, her face draining of emotion. "Thank you again for coming. I need someone I can talk to. Someone outside the winery."

"Are you doing okay?" I held my cup of tea in both hands, the warmth emanating from its sides.

Vanessa leaned over her coffee and lowered her head. "No, not really. I feel so alone and I don't know who I can trust. Mark was my everything. I loved him so much. We were so happy." She lifted her head and focused on the other side of the cafe. She held her cup to her lips but didn't drink. "He tended to stray, but he always came back to me." She sipped her coffee and placed it down on the table, the cup lipstick free.

"I never worried that he would leave me. He wouldn't. But he got distracted and I was okay with that because in the end, he was my husband and would be coming home to me." Vanessa let out a small laugh and waved her polished nails at me. "I bet you think that's crazy. That I knew he was cheating and didn't mind."

"I'm not judging. In fact, I try to never judge." *Unless it's wine*, I thought.

"Thank you." Vanessa took another drink of her coffee. "We had something very special together. He understood me more than anyone else. Have you ever had that? Someone who understood you, perhaps even more than you understood yourself?"

Tessa had known me the longest, but even though we had a history, she didn't always understand everything I did and she constantly questioned my choices. Then again, I questioned Tessa's choices, too. But Vanessa had asked about the romantic side, which I clearly didn't have. I didn't have someone who laughed with me and loved me even with all of my quirks. Instead I had spent all of my dating years explaining myself to people who didn't care to listen.

"No, I don't have that. I don't think I've ever had that."

"I was so lucky to have him for eight years." Her fingers outlined her scar as she spoke. "Mr. Mark Plueger, my husband. But now he's gone." She rustled through her purse and took out a handkerchief, holding it to her eyes as she sniffed.

"I'm so sorry." I paused. "It sounds like you had something very special."

Vanessa put down the handkerchief. "Are you married?"

"No."

"Why not? A pretty young vixen like you? I'm surprised."

"There's not much time for me to date. I mean, I'd like to find someone, but it's difficult with work and studying."

Vanessa nodded. "Mark and I had both been married before. It was a breath of fresh air when we found each other. Suddenly you find what you've been missing in your life, you know?"

I nodded. I took a sip of my tea. The hot liquid scalded my tongue but I didn't react.

"I can't believe I'm talking about him without crying. I guess I'm all cried out." Vanessa put the handkerchief away. "It feels so good to talk about this. To talk about him. I don't want him to become a lost memory. I want to keep him alive." She leaned back in her chair and looked around the cafe as she drank her coffee.

I decided to take advantage of the pause in the conversation. "How are things at the winery? Are you going to be okay?"

Vanessa smiled—not the plastic smile I had seen on Friday night, but a real one. "I think so. Mark handled most of it, but I have a great team underneath me. Lisa has already stepped up and is taking over a lot of the stuff Mark used to do. I think we're going to be fine."

I hesitated. "You had mentioned that the vipers were already moving in. Was that about the winery?"

Vanessa put her coffee cup back down and took a deep breath before she spoke. "Offers on the winery. We've been getting them for years, but now he's pushing more since Mark is gone. He wants to buy it and I'm not ready to sell. Not yet. What if I can make it on my own? I need to give myself the chance."

"Is he…" I paused and readjusted my statement. "Who is he?"

"Jim Garrett. From next door. He's been wanting to buy Frontier for years," continued Vanessa. "Mark refused to sell. Didn't want it to leave the family." She took another sip of her coffee. "Now that he's gone, I don't know. Maybe it would be easier. There are reminders of Mark everywhere. He was the life and soul of that place. Maybe I should sell so I keep the memory of him intact."

"You don't want to keep the winery?"

"I do, but life isn't always that easy." Vanessa's gaze met mine. "We…" Her eyes glistened. "I guess it's not *we* anymore." She removed the handkerchief from her purse and dabbed at her eyes. "Listen to me, I'm ridiculous." Her mouth formed into a half smile. "I mean, it's only money. But I love the winery. I don't want to lose everything."

"You won't, I'm sure. You can get things figured out, it will just take a little time."

Vanessa muttered a nervous laugh as she looked down at the table. "It would be so easy to let Garrett buy it all, but then what would I do? He's eager for sure. I mean, he didn't even wait an hour after the murder before putting in another offer."

"That night. In your office." The words came out of my mouth before I could stop them. I didn't want Vanessa to know that I had been there.

Vanessa showed no surprise. "Yes. Can you believe that? That night! Who does that?"

"From what I hear, he was really drunk. Tessa said that he gets that way."

Vanessa's eyes narrowed. "Oh yes, Tessa." She shook her head. "They've released her, haven't they?"

"They only held her for questioning and as of this morning, she alibied out."

"What?" Vanessa's mouth dropped open. "How?"

I hesitated. "I'm not sure. But I know that she's no longer a suspect."

Vanessa put down her cup of coffee and stared at it. "I'm glad to hear that," she said. "I didn't like to think that she was the one who did it." She looked up at me. "Do they know who did?"

I shook my head. "Not yet, but I'm sure they'll find out soon."

"I agree." Vanessa sighed. "I think someone close to us was to blame."

"Do you think it was an employee?"

"Maybe. Someone who had motive and opportunity. Someone who had something to hide."

I stared at Vanessa and carefully lifted my cup of tea as I waited for her to give a name, but she stayed silent. I put down my tea. "Who had motive and opportunity?"

"Katie," Vanessa smiled, "I can't answer. But at my winery, people know more than they appear. In situations like these, someone always slips up."

I swallowed hard. "I'm sorry for all that you're going through and that it was done by someone you know."

Vanessa nodded.

"And I'm glad that Tessa is no longer a suspect and can regain your trust. May I assume she still has a job?"

Vanessa stared straight into my eyes for several seconds. She robotically shook her head. "No. Tessa is no longer welcome at Frontier."

I stiffened. "What do you mean?"

"I know you two are friends, but I don't think she's all wine and roses, so to speak. I think she was up to much more."

"Vanessa, I've known Tessa for twenty years. She's a good person. And up until the night of the murder, you felt the same." I paused. "At least, I thought you did."

Vanessa looked up at the ceiling and then back at me. "Don't jump to conclusions, Katie. Because she is innocent of one crime, doesn't mean she is innocent of another. I don't know if I should be telling you this."

I leaned forward. "I want to know."

"I've heard that she was stealing money from me." Vanessa drank the rest of her coffee and put the cup on the table. She looked at her watch. "Oh, I didn't realize we'd been here so long already. I have to go."

"Wait. Where did you hear she was stealing?"

"Katie, dear, I'm not about to reveal my source. But let's say I'm looking into it. If it turns out to be true, I won't hesitate to turn her over to the police."

NINETEEN

PAIRING SUGGESTION: CHIANTI CLASSICO—CHIANTI, ITALY

An Italian wine made from the Sangiovese grape, pairs well with game.

THE CONVERSATION WITH VANESSA still played in my head when I parked outside Matteo's. The glass door of the restaurant was locked, but I put my hands on the window and leaned forward to look inside. Workers milled about in the back, yet they were unresponsive to my knocks. Like everyone else, I would have to wait an hour and a half until the restaurant opened at six.

"Are you trying to break in?" said a voice from behind.

I turned around to see Detective Dean standing close to the street. He wore jeans and a loose collared shirt. The air around him was less dramatic without his suit, but a new charm had emerged.

He smiled. "I didn't figure you to be one for daylight robbery."

"Funny. I'm here to get Tessa's credit card, but they're closed."

"How's she doing?"

"She's doing good. Hoping for a new job, you know, that kind of thing. Hey, thanks for your call about her this morning. I really appreciate it."

"You're welcome. I'm glad it worked out."

I motioned to Dean's outfit. "I like this look. New dress code?"

"I don't start work for another hour, I was just grabbing a late lunch."

I shifted and moved my purse to my other hand, the threatening note from my car barely tucked inside, burning a hole through the leather as well as my conscience.

"Everything okay?"

I zipped the purse closed. "Fine. So I've been thinking a lot about the case and I might have an idea of who killed Mark."

"Really?" Dean wore a bemused look on his face. His hair wasn't slicked back, and I liked the softer side he displayed.

"Yes. I think Seb killed Mark."

"How so?"

"Wasn't he the last one to see Mark alive? That would be the opportunity and I'm pretty sure he had motive. It's still a little hazy, but there's something right there on the tip of my tongue, and I can't quite place it."

"Interesting," said Dean. "Let me know when you think of it."

"Okay, I'll call you. I think I have the station number." I took my phone out of my purse, glad that I had brought it with me instead of leaving it back in the car. It slipped out of my hand and tumbled to the ground.

Dean picked it up and dusted it off. He handed it to me. "I think it's okay."

I stared at the phone.

"You okay?"

"Yes…" I looked up at Dean. "You said that Mark was killed before the text was sent to Tessa, right?"

"Right."

"So who sent the text?"

159

Dean shook his head. "What?"

"Mark didn't send the text, since he was dead, so who did?"

"We don't know yet."

"What about Seb? Where was he during the party? What was his alibi?"

"He was with Lisa. Why?"

I stared at the ground. "Seb saw us at the table, which means he could have grabbed Tessa's wine opener, and he could have sent the text." I shook my head. "But I'm still missing something if he has an alibi. What points am I leaving on the table?"

"What?"

"Nothing. If it's not Seb, someone was still trying to set up Tessa. She was the most recent hire, she already had a record, she's the perfect suspect." I looked up. "I need to start eliminating choices. Like Vanessa. It wasn't her."

Dean's brow furrowed. "How do you know?"

"I met her for coffee this afternoon and we had a nice talk."

"Wait a minute." Dean crossed his arms. "You met her today?"

"Yes. She wanted a friend and I was there. Besides, she provided some helpful information. She knew Mark was having affairs, but she loved him so she stayed with him. And I believe her."

"Who was Mark having the affair with?"

"She didn't say, she only said she knew he strayed. But Vanessa said she always stood by him. I didn't get the sense that she would kill him."

Dean gave a slight nod. "Okay, then who?"

"It still comes back to Seb. He says he didn't see Tessa leaving that night, but she said he did." I stared at the hills in the distance.

"Eyewitness testimony can be flawed, Katie."

"Yes, but I have years of friendship to back me up. Besides, leaving Tessa out of this, where was Seb prior to the scream? You said he was the last person to see Mark alive, isn't that a little strange? And it was really weird, he came to my restaurant, said something about money, and then left."

"Wait, what?" asked Dean, the soft emotion gone from his eyes. He was back to work mode. "You met with both Vanessa and Seb? Katie, what are you doing?"

"Nothing, Seb came to my work. I didn't arrange to meet him."

"Okay, what did he say?"

"He said that I shouldn't trust my friend." I held up my hand to Dean. "Don't say a thing. That's only his opinion. And then he was gone."

Dean put his hands on his hips. "Did he say why you shouldn't trust Tessa?"

I stayed silent.

"Katie?"

I closed my eyes. "He said she's been stealing from the winery. He said money's missing from the accounts." I opened my eyes and looked at Dean. "I tried to ask her about it last night, but I didn't get much out of her. Then Vanessa also said she heard that Tessa was stealing money. It has to be Seb spreading these rumors. He had to have been the one to set her up for the murder, too. He knew she was off property since he saw her drive away. It was the perfect opportunity for him." *And maybe he was the one who ran me off the road,* though I kept that thought to myself.

Dean stood staring at me. I couldn't read his emotions and it caused me to keep talking. "I mean, you already had Tessa in the suspect category, so if you were guilty, wouldn't you want to throw more suspicion on the one who is already a suspect?"

"Maybe," Dean replied.

"Do me a favor. Look into it. There may be more to him than we know. And check with Lisa about the alibi. Tessa said that Lisa and Seb used to be romantically involved. It has to be Seb. He's the murderer."

"I'll look into all of it, but let me know when you're meeting with people involved in this whole thing. I don't want anything to happen to you. Okay?"

I met Dean's blue eyes. "You got it. I'll let you know next time I'm meeting with someone." I smiled. "Do I have to tell you every time I meet with Tessa, too? 'Cause I'll probably see her a lot."

"No," said Dean as he returned the smile. "I think that will be fine."

A lady in a white blouse and a black skirt walked up to the door of Matteo's as she rattled keys.

"Oh, I'll get Tessa's credit card. It was nice talking to you, Dean." I looked at him. "Dean is your last name, right?"

"Yes, but everyone calls me Dean."

"What's your first name?"

"James."

"Seriously?"

Dean laughed. "No, it's John. But I secretly always wished it was James. Would go well with the last name Dean." His cell phone rang.

"See you later."

I stepped inside and approached the lady. "My friend Tessa Blakely left her credit card here last night. She had a tab at the bar."

"Not a problem, let me go check for it."

I watched Dean pace outside the entrance as he spoke on his phone.

"Here you go," said the lady. "Do you want to sign for her?"

"Sure." I took the pen and looked at the tab. $387. I shook my head. Tessa knew how to spend money. I signed the receipt and put the copy in my purse along with the credit card. I texted Tessa. I GOT YOUR CREDIT CARD. MET DEAN :)

I exited the restaurant as Dean ended his phone call, a solemn look on his face. "You okay?"

His eyes met mine. "It's Seb. He's been murdered."

"*What?*"

"They've found his body. I'm heading there now."

"I'm coming with you."

TWENTY

PAIRING SUGGESTION: CABERNET SAUVIGNON—NAPA VALLEY, CA

A bold wine with tannins and high alcohol to smooth tense moments.

❧

DEAN TURNED INTO GARRETT Winery.

"Seb was found here? At Garrett?"

"You know as much as I do about the situation. I only know that we got a call about a body in the vineyard and Garrett identified him as Seb."

Dean stopped the car in front of the vineyard, where two squad cars were already parked next to the coroner's van. "Stay back here," said Dean. "I don't want you traumatized by seeing Seb. It won't be pretty."

"Thanks, but I'll come along. This isn't the first dead body I've seen, remember?"

"Fine, but still stay back. I don't want the scene disturbed by your footprints. The last thing I need is for you to be under suspicion." He looked at me for longer than usual before heading into the vineyard.

I followed a few feet behind. Even though I prepared myself for the sight, Seb's pale white face caught me by surprise. His body dangled from a trellis wire full of vines, his hands impaled by poles, his body weight hanging from them as his legs slumped below his lifeless body.

His jeans were frayed and covered with mud where he had clearly been dragged, either alive or dead, and his shirt was dark, drenched with the blood that had poured from his neck.

My stomach flipped and I turned away. At the restaurant, Seb had been so full of energy. His incessant tapping. His constant looking around. The contrast stunned me and I looked at the vineyards on the hill as I took deep breaths. The calm and order on the hillside worked and when I was able to cope with the sight of Seb again, I turned back around.

Dean looked up and saw me watching. He passed by the other deputies and approached me. "You doing okay?"

"Just fine." I took another breath. "Except the person I was convinced was the murderer is now dead."

"I know," said Dean as he focused on the photographer documenting the crime scene.

"I guess Seb didn't kill Mark after all."

"Why do you say that?"

"I don't know, I would think that the same person who killed Mark, killed Seb."

"I wouldn't assume that."

"Oh?" I looked at Dean.

He motioned to the body. "He could still be guilty."

I looked at Seb's lifeless body, his head angled to the right from the pull of the poles, grape leaves swaying in the breeze near his cheek. "Then who killed him?"

Dean paused. "I guess we'll find out." He took out his notepad. "Seb was last seen around three at Frontier." He glanced up at me. "Where were you this afternoon?"

"I was at coffee with Vanessa. People saw me there."

"I was kidding."

"Funny."

"Detective Dean." Deputy Peters approached from the edge of the vineyard. "Garrett has cameras around the winery. Keeps them rolling to prevent theft and the record stays for forty-eight hours." He stopped in front of Dean. "He's setting up the playback now."

"Great," said Dean. "Let's go." The two men walked toward the buildings.

I followed a few steps behind, keeping a low profile so that Dean and Peters wouldn't see me.

The two men entered the main office, leaving the door open behind them. I stepped inside the doorframe and stopped as soon as the screens were visible.

The office was cold and stark, the row of camera screens with images of the winery staring back at me. I pressed my back against the wall and waited.

Garrett sat in front of the first screen, wearing the same red ascot he wore at the party. "Gentlemen, I don't have a camera in the vineyard, but I have cameras at every building on the property."

"Do you have one that points toward the vineyard?"

"Not quite, but I have one that focuses on the parking lot. That should be your top choice, as it's the closest proximity to the vineyard."

"Let's see that one."

"Good choice, my man, what time do you want to see? I have footage from all day." Garrett tugged at the right side of his mustache.

Dean glanced at his notepad. "Let's see, start it at three o'clock. We think the time of death was between three and four thirty."

Garrett pressed two buttons below the screen and the footage of the parking lot blurred as it rewound, the time stamp still readable in the corner.

"Garrett, did you know Seb was on property?" said Dean.

"Had no idea. Although I'd like to know what the dear chap was doing in my vineyard. Possibly checking out the competition, so to speak. How do I put this? We're friends with Frontier, but it's not acceptable to go to each other's property without an invitation."

"You've gone past it," said Peters.

"Oh, look at that." Garrett fast-forwarded the footage until the numbers read 3:01 p.m. "Shall I press play?"

"Go ahead."

He hit play on the machine and used a remote to skip through the minutes. The room was silent as everyone stared at the screen.

At 3:17, two couples got into two separate cars in the parking lot. They both drove out of the lot at the same time.

"Who was leaving there?" asked Dean.

"Guests from our tasting room."

When the time stamp read 3:19, a silver car pulled up and parked in front of the winery.

"Oh," came out of my mouth as my breathing stopped and a chill shot down my spine.

Dean turned around. "Katie, you okay?"

I shook my head. "No." My eyes never left the screen. At 3:20, a person exited the car and walked toward the vineyard. A female with curly hair. Tessa.

Dean stared at me. "What is Tessa doing there?"

"I have no idea," I muttered. "The last I saw her, I had just dropped her off at her car."

"Did she tell you she was coming here?" Dean's eyes were hard and focused.

"No." I shook my head. "I had no idea. I thought she was heading to her apartment."

Dean looked at Garrett. "Did you know she was here?"

"Not at all, my friend. I was with a group in the cellar doing barrel tastings for most of the afternoon." His fingers rested on his chin. "I only came out when my secretary told me a body had been discovered. That's when we phoned you."

"Had Tessa been here a lot?" asked Dean. "I mean, did she have a habit of coming over unannounced?"

"Hardly. In fact, I was under the impression that she wasn't too fond of me." Garrett rewound the tape and played the section again. Tessa clearly headed toward the vineyard.

"Shame," said Garrett as he turned to Dean. "I understand that we're not Frontier, and therefore not privy to the same secrecy, but could there be a possibility of keeping this out of the media?" He tugged on his mustache. "As I'm sure you gentlemen can understand, no one will want to drink wine made from grapes where someone met their demise. It would be devastating for business."

"We can't promise anything, but we'll do the best we can." Dean's face was stern and unmoving as he focused on me. "Katie," he said. "I need to know where Tessa is right now."

"I have no idea, I was with you. I would assume her apartment, but I don't know. You want me to call her?"

"No. In fact, do not call her under any circumstances."

"Fine. But I'm coming with you."

"With me?" Dean stepped back. "What do you mean?"

"To go pick up Tessa."

"I can't let you do that. Peters, can you please drive Katie back to Matteo's to get her car?"

"No, I want to come with you."

"Katie, you can't." His voice was harsh, a different man than the one who had chatted with me outside of the restaurant.

"But I need—"

"No, you don't. You need to go home. This doesn't involve you right now." Dean turned to Peters. "Can you take her?"

Peters ushered me out of the office. I looked back at Dean. His face was serious but there was still a softness in his eyes.

"My squad car is over here," said Peters.

I opened the passenger door and slumped into the seat, my arms crossed over my chest.

"I'm not used to civilians riding in the front with me," said Peters.

"Well, I'm not sitting in the back."

"I'm sorry about your friend," said Peters as he started the engine. "I know this has to be tough."

"Innocent until proven guilty."

"You're absolutely right." Peters drove out of the winery. "But I'm sorry about the way it looks."

"Maybe. But I'm my father's daughter. He says the most obvious solution is not always the right one. I mean, there's still a chance that she could be innocent in all of this." Even though the words came out of my mouth, I didn't know if I believed them.

"You're right, there's a chance." His voice lowered. "Stranger things have happened."

I stared out the window as we drove toward the station. Tessa. In trouble, again, but this time with video proof. Part of me couldn't shake the fact that this might be all my fault again. I had shared that Seb spread rumors about her and now he was dead. It would take a jury all of two seconds to convict her.

I needed help. I needed someone with experience in these situations. I needed someone like my father. I stared at the road ahead, the yellow lines cutting through the black asphalt.

My father, who had never quite forgiven me for not trying the Academy again. My father, who never liked Tessa because he thought she was a bad influence on me. My father, who had solved numerous cases when everyone else had given up hope.

I took a deep breath and reached into my pocket for my phone.

I scrolled through the contacts and pressed Dad. I waited for a moment and then held the phone up to my ear.

Peters drove in silence as I listened to the ringing on the other line. My father's voicemail came on.

"Hey, Dad, it's Katie. I need your help with … with Tessa. It's important. Please call me back." I ended the call and placed the phone in my lap.

"I heard your dad's in law enforcement down south."

"Something like that."

The sun lowered toward the horizon.

"Good to help out where you can." Peters pulled up outside Matteo's. "I'll have Dean call you when he knows more. I'm sure he'll give you an update on the situation."

"Thanks." I stepped out of the car.

When I reached my Jeep, I stopped and leaned against the door, the keys in my hand as I watched other cars go by. I jumped as my phone rang from my pocket. "Hello?"

"Katie, it's Dad. What's going on?"

"Tessa. She's in trouble." I opened the driver side door of my car and sat down, filling my father in on all of Tessa's legal troubles. He listened patiently, never interrupting as I told the story. "And Dean's gone to go pick her up right now."

"Oh, Katie," my dad replied when I was finished. "That girl is trouble. I mean, she first got arrested when she was what, eighteen?"

"Dad, that was the only time she was arrested. And it … doesn't matter now. I need your help. Please."

He let out a sigh. "I knew it had to be something big. I don't think you've ever asked for my help. Ever."

Silence.

"Dad?"

"I'm thinking."

I sat in the front seat and waited. In the distance, orange and pink tinted the fading sky.

My dad's deep voice came through the phone. "You need to take each case as its own. You think Seb committed the first murder. What you need to do is clear Tessa in Seb's murder. That's the most imminent one, then you can prove Seb's involvement in the first murder."

"But, the video footage. She was at Garrett Winery during the time of the murder. How can I disprove video footage?"

My dad was silent for a moment. "Katie, if the killer wanted to frame Tessa for the murder, they would have made sure she was there during that time. Tessa's not exactly straight laced and, to be honest, she's not the smartest friend you've ever had."

"Dad," I interrupted.

"Let me finish. But she does have common sense. She wouldn't have been so obvious at Garrett Winery if she was really going to kill someone. If she was going to do something, no one would have seen her. Like the time she broke into my liquor cabinet."

"Dad, don't."

"Hey, I'm only saying facts."

"Fine." I nodded as I held the phone to my ear. "You're right. She would have kept out of view." I stared straight ahead as the orange and pink in the sky grew deeper.

"You said Tessa had been there before, correct?"

"Yes, she worked next door."

"Then she had to know there were cameras around. She wouldn't let herself get caught if she was going to do the crime. Unless she's gone off the deep end, but I don't think that's Tessa."

I stared at the sky, the colors becoming more pronounced. It only took a moment for it all to change. "Me neither."

"You're a smart girl, Katie, you'll figure it out. Call me if you need me."

"Thanks, Dad."

"Katie?"

I swallowed hard. "Yes?"

"How did the exam go?"

I took a deep breath. "Well, I . . . I didn't pass."

"I'm so sorry. I know you worked really hard. Better luck on the next one, right?"

"Really? No lecture on how I'm wasting my time and should go back to the Police Academy?"

My dad's heavy sigh came through the phone. "Katie, I only want you to be happy. If wine is where you want to be, then that's where you'll be. I know your mom would be proud. I'm proud, too. Keep studying, you'll be wearing that Master's pin in no time."

TWENTY-ONE

PAIRING SUGGESTION: MERLOT—NAPA VALLEY, CA

A red wine with a history of being misunderstood.

❦

WHEN I ARRIVED AT the station, Deputy Peters was behind the counter. Dean and Tessa were nowhere in sight.

"Katie?" asked Peters as I approached. "Everything okay?"

"No, not really. Where's Tessa?"

He glanced at the side door. "I think they're processing her right now."

"That's fine, I'll wait." I took a seat on the bench.

"She'll be here overnight. If you come back tomorrow morning, I'm sure we can work something out."

"It's okay, I'll wait for Dean. I want to talk to him anyway."

Peters straightened papers and walked away. I waited on the bench, the station void of activity. Apparently people didn't get into trouble on Sunday nights.

Dean approached the counter a few minutes later. "Katie? What are you doing here?"

"Tessa," I replied. "Is she okay?"

"Of course, why wouldn't she be?"

I stood up. "Being in a jail cell, accused of another murder. You know, that whole thing."

"She's not super happy, but other than that, she's okay." He paused. "Sorry for being harsh earlier. I can't let anyone think that I'm biased in the investigation. I hope you understand."

"That's fine, but I want to see her."

"Katie." Dean shook his head. "I don't think that's a good idea."

"No, I can help. I need to help. And I'll share everything with you."

Dean studied me but remained silent.

I decided to try another tactic. "Listen, if she's guilty, then so be it. She'll go to jail and that's that. I can accept that. But if she's innocent, she deserves the best shot at being free. Please let me do this. Five minutes is all I ask."

Dean took a deep breath. "Fine. You have five minutes. But I'm going to listen to everything that's said between you two, you understand?"

"Not a problem. Just stay out of her line of sight. I don't want her to know you're there."

"Of course." Dean opened the gate and I stepped through. We passed by three desks covered with stacks of folders. Dean pulled open a door and we entered into a small hallway with a row of cells on the left.

"She's in the second one down." Dean pointed. "I'll be over here." He stood by the door.

I approached the second cell. Tessa lay on the bare green mattress, staring up at the ceiling, her arm across her forehead, her signature curls limp and lifeless.

"Are you counting the ceiling tiles?"

Tessa sat up and looked at me through the bars. "Katie! Have you come to take me home? Am I free to go?"

"I wish, Tee. Unfortunately you're in a lot of trouble. Tell me about today. What happened?"

"I got arrested again. Twice in one weekend. Isn't that ridiculous!"

"Do you know why you're arrested?"

"Murder." Tessa shrugged. "But I didn't do it."

"Do you know whose murder?"

Tessa tilted her head to the left. "Mark's." She frowned, her eyebrows pushing closer together. "This is still about Mark, right? You know I didn't do it. You told me yourself earlier."

"No, Tessa, this is about another murder."

Tessa's eyes grew wide. "Who else died?"

I waited for Tessa to pull her mouth to the side, but she didn't. "They didn't tell you when they cuffed you?"

"No, they said I was being arrested for the murder of Seb, but that doesn't make sense. I figured it was just a mistake and they meant Mark."

"I'll fill you in on everything in a second, but first, what did you do today? After you got your car from the lodge?"

Tessa twisted her mouth and looked up at the ceiling as she counted on her hands. "I went to the winery, then I was at my apartment for a while."

"Which winery? And why did you go there?"

"Frontier. It's my job."

"No, Tessa, you don't have a job. Your boss is dead and the other one wants you fired."

Tessa rolled her eyes. "I meant I went for my old job, to pick up the rest of my stuff."

I shook my head. "Do you think it was a good idea to go back to a crime scene where you were one of the suspects?"

"But, Katie," Tessa replied, "you said this morning I was no longer under suspicion."

"Fine. And what did you do after Frontier Winery?"

Tessa shrugged as she picked at her nails. "Pretty much nothing. Everything else was a waste of time."

"Tee, stop being coy."

"I'm not, I didn't do anything. I stopped by Garrett Winery for a few minutes, but that turned out to be a bust, so I came back to my apartment and ordered Chinese. Then Detective Dean came and picked me up. Fortunately I got to eat some of it before he came, but"—her voice got louder—"I'm still hungry! Don't you feed people in this place?" Her voice echoed down the hall.

"Okay, I'll make sure they get you some food, but why did you go to Garrett Winery?"

"I got a call."

I stared at Tessa. "Who called you from there? What was their name?"

"I didn't get a name. They just said they were calling from Garrett."

"Male or female?"

"Female. No wait, male with a higher voice. Or maybe female. It was hard to tell and I didn't think about it at the time." She shrugged. "I was excited because they were looking to hire someone and asked if I was interested. Which of course I was. They said for me to come right over so I did. It was a quick drive."

"What time was this?"

"The call came in as I was at Frontier. I guess around three?" Tessa motioned with her hands. "I'm not really sure, but if you check my phone, you'll see the time. I went right over to Garrett, but they didn't know anything about a position or the phone call. Probably a prank. What a tease. People can be so mean." She paused. "What is this all about?"

"I'll tell you in a second, just a few more questions."

"Geez, you're a tease as well."

I crouched down in the hallway, now at eye level with Tessa in the cell. "Tell me everything that happened once you arrived at Garrett Winery."

"I just told you."

"No, I mean every detail. Give me a play-by-play."

Tessa leaned back against the wall. "When I got to the winery, I went into the main office."

"Was that the first thing you did?" I asked.

"Yes. Although, first I checked my makeup in my rearview mirror. Is that what you're wondering?"

I rolled my eyes. "Continue."

"I went into the main office and said that I was there about the job. But the secretary was all weird and said that there was no job and that she didn't call me. I asked if anyone else had called me, maybe Garrett, but she said he was with guests and no one else would have called. I don't know, maybe she got confused or something, but I wasn't about to stick around if there wasn't a job. Besides, I was hungry. So I got in my car and went back to my apartment and ordered Chinese food."

"Did you see anyone else at the winery? Think, Tessa, anyone at all?"

Tessa looked up at the ceiling. "I don't think so. I mean, if I did, I don't remember. After my visit turned out to be pointless, I left. I didn't bother to take notes of anyone around there." She looked back at me. "Now can you tell me what's going on?"

"Seb was murdered today. They found his body in the vineyard at Garrett."

"Oh my God. Why? How?"

"Strung up on the vines, his throat slit."

"That's terrible." Tessa's face turned pale. "And they think I did it?"

"You were at the winery during the time he was killed. They have video footage of you there."

"I was there but I didn't kill Seb. I went into the office and I left!"

"And you did nothing else?"

Tessa put her finger to her mouth and stared at the ceiling. "Wait, I did go near the warehouse, but that's cause there was a kitten. Black with white on its chest. It was so cute so I went over to it. It was afraid of me at first, but then it let me pet it."

I leaned forward. "When was this?"

"When I first arrived. Then I went to the office."

"Is the warehouse near the first vineyard?"

"Yes, why?"

"Did you see anything in the vineyard? Anything at all? A movement? A color? Think."

"No." Tessa lowered her head and looked at me. "I don't stare at vineyards like you do."

"Fine. You went to the warehouse, pet the cat, went into the office, and then got into your car and left. That was it?"

"That's it." Tessa breathed out. "Am I going to have to stay here? I don't want to be here."

"I'm working on it. And my dad—"

"Your dad?" Tessa interrupted. "Why did you tell him? He hates me."

"I needed help. I didn't know where to turn, but he's helping me."

Tessa leaned back as her face grew grim. "I'm really in a spot, aren't I? For you to call your dad, for you to ask for help. What if they find me guilty?" Her voice escalated. "What if they really think I did it and they send me to prison? What if my whole life is over?" Her voice was at its highest pitch.

"Tessa, calm down." I wanted to throw cold water on my panicking friend, or at least slap her across the face to get her to calm down, but neither was an option. "Did you kill Seb?"

"No."

"Then don't worry about it. You're going to be fine."

"But innocent people go to jail all the time." Tessa's voice lowered but was still swollen with panic. "This I know."

"I told you, I'm working on it. Now take a few deep breaths, okay?" Tessa nodded as her chest swelled with a full breath.

"One last question and I need to hear the truth. Did you take money from the winery?"

"Katie, I've never taken a dime from anyone." Tessa stared straight into my eyes, her hazel eyes reflecting the florescent lighting in the cell. "Even the money Mark paid me to take the wine to the lodge was all part of my salary. My documented salary." She sank down into the mattress. "This is getting worse and worse."

"We're going to fix this, but tonight I need you to think really hard about what you saw at Garrett Winery. Try to recall every little detail you can because everything is important, okay?"

"Tonight?" Her eyes started to glisten. "But I don't want to stay here."

"You've slept in worse places." I paused for a moment. "In fact, we both have. Remember that hotel room in Paris? We both slept on the floor with a towel as a pillow for a week. At least you have a mattress here."

"When do you think I can go home?"

"They can only hold you for forty-eight hours before they either release you or charge you."

Tessa closed her eyes and leaned against her hand on the bars. "Great, forty-eight hours. What am I supposed to do?"

"Well, Tessa, why not catch up on some sleep. You do party a lot."

"Ha ha, very funny." Tessa stuck out her tongue. "Go on, do something fun so I can live vicariously through you."

"Fun? I'm trying to get you free." I stood from my crouched position.

"Come on, I need stories."

"Tessa. Seriously. One minute you're scared, and now you're getting saucy. I can't keep up."

Tessa readjusted her position on the mattress. "At least come back with a really juicy story. I want to hear about make-out sessions with Dean. It's nice to see you have a crush again."

"What?" Heat flared up my neck and I tried to ignore Dean in the corner. "What are you talking about?"

"I see the way you are when you mention him and text about him. You haven't been like that about someone in a very long time. It's about time you got some action."

Dean silently slipped out of the hallway and back into the offices. I cringed. "Tessa…"

"Nope, I don't want to hear it. I know you and I know when you like someone."

"It's not like that. We're just both trying to figure out what happened to Mark and Seb."

Tessa smiled. "You like him, don't you?"

"Tessa…"

"That's a yes. I want to hear the sordid details when I get out of here." She lay back down on the mattress. "Now go find some evidence to free me from this place."

"And you'll go over every detail from today to see if you remember anything?"

"Yep." Tessa closed her eyes.

"Night, Tee."

"Night."

I took one last look at my friend before I headed down the hall and back into the offices.

Dean sat at the first desk, staring at the large computer screen in front of him. The door closed behind me and he looked up. "All done?"

"Yes."

"Didn't slip her any knives or files?"

"Excuse me?"

"Teasing."

"Not funny. I'm worried about her."

"Understandable." Dean sat back as a smile grew on his face. "So, you haven't acted this way around someone in a long time, huh?"

"Sorry you had to hear that. She didn't know you were there."

"Clearly. Or maybe she wanted to send me the message that you like me. I'm flattered."

I hesitated. "I don't know what to say about that. But I can say that I know I'm going to get Tessa free. I don't think she killed Seb."

"I don't either."

"You don't?" I lowered myself into the chair next to him.

"No. It's too cookie cutter. Also, I checked her phone." Dean pointed to Tessa's purple phone on the desk. "There was a call from Garrett Winery right before three o'clock. She was telling the truth about that. She was still at Garrett during the time of the murder, but at least she was honest about the call that brought her there. Peters is getting me a list of everyone, workers and guests, who were at Garrett Winery today. Then we'll go from there." He held up Tessa's phone. "By the way, interesting text you sent to Tessa, about seeing me."

I wanted to put my head in my hands, but instead I put my game face on. "Just that I got her credit card and ran into you. Nothing to it."

Dean nodded. "Okay then."

"But the murder." I shifted. "We need to find out where Seb was killed."

Dean leaned his head forward and smiled. "How do you know he wasn't killed in the vineyard at Garrett?"

"The soil wasn't full of blood from where he bled out. Which means he was killed somewhere else and taken there. And the mud and wear on his jeans, shows he was dragged."

"You should have been a cop. You're very good at this."

"You should see me with wine."

Dean raised his eyebrows. "I'd like that."

Tessa was right. I was flirting. I tried to focus. "Okay, so what about evidence from today? Does any of it point to Tessa?"

"That's still to be seen, but we're impounding Tessa's car and I'll have a team go to her apartment to check the clothes she wore earlier. If she did kill Seb, there'd be blood found somewhere, either on her clothes or in her car. Things will become clearer once we figure out the exact timeline of Seb's day and a list of possible other suspects."

"Thanks, Dean. I appreciate it."

"For what?"

"For helping my friend."

"I'm not helping anyone, I'm just doing my job."

"Okay." I smiled. "But thanks." I touched his shoulder. "I appreciate it."

"I'll keep you updated." Dean looked around. "You should probably go. People around here are going to start thinking there's something going on between us."

TWENTY-TWO

PAIRING SUGGESTION: MERLOT—YAKIMA VALLEY, WA

This wine has complex flavors, but lower acidity and tannins than its California cousin.

❧

MY PHONE BEEPED WITH a text message as I started my car.

HARVEST NEXT TUESDAY. SEE YOU THEN.

A smile spread across my face as I wrote back. THANKS JEFF, LOOKING FORWARD TO IT. I pulled out of the parking lot and drove down the street as another text beeped in.

LET ME KNOW ABOUT THE '69 CHATEAU MARGAUX. I'D LOVE TO SHARE IT WITH YOU.

I took a deep breath. I would love to revisit the '69 Chateau Margaux, but I didn't want to lead Jeff on. Now was not the time for a boyfriend.

"Wait, boyfriend?" I said out loud as I put my foot down on the brake, the car stopping in the middle of the street.

A car honked from behind and I pulled to the side as it sped by, the sudden silence focusing me.

Tessa had said she had a boyfriend when I first arrived at Frontier Winery on Friday. Where had this boyfriend been the last few days? Why hadn't he been helping Tessa this weekend? Especially with her two trips to jail. What was Tessa not telling me?

I looked over my shoulder. The road was empty. I flipped a U-turn and returned to the station.

Dean's face lit up as I entered through the main door. "Hey, you're back. Did you forget something?"

"No, the opposite. I remembered something. I need to talk to Tessa again."

He shook his head. "I don't think so. It was a push letting you back there the first time, I can't do it again."

"Please. I remembered a comment she said on Friday and I have to ask her about it."

Dean hesitated. "What is it?"

I looked around. "She said she had a boyfriend."

"And?"

"And, where is he? Why hasn't he been there for her this weekend? Please let me see her. It will only take a few minutes."

Dean shook his head. "Katie, it's late. I don't want to feel like you're taking advantage of me."

"I'm not, I promise. This is about the case."

"You have five minutes, no more."

"Thank you." I walked through the swinging gate into the offices.

"I'm going to listen as before, you know," said Dean.

"That's fine."

Dean opened the door to the hallway and I walked through to the second cell.

Tessa lay on the green mattress with her eyes closed.

"Tessa, it's me, I'm back."

"Already? Does this mean I can go home?" She sat up.

"No, it's not that, I need to say something."

"Okay, what?"

I debated how to approach the subject. "Um, when you get out of here tomorrow, as I'm sure you will, can you get a ride from someone else?"

"That's what you came back in to tell me?" Tessa rolled her eyes. "Really?"

"No, I mean if I have to work, can someone else pick you up? Like your boyfriend?"

"Boyfriend?" The word caught Tessa off guard.

"You know, the one you mentioned on Friday."

Tessa whipped her head up, her sparkling hazel eyes filling with tears. She blinked twice before covering her face with her hands. "Katie, there's so much I need to tell you. I couldn't tell you before and then all this craziness happened."

"What, Tessa? What are you talking about?"

"The boyfriend I mentioned, it's complicated," Tessa said through her sobs. She grabbed the corner of her dress and rubbed her eyes with it. "He's married."

I shook my head. "Tessa, we've been over this before. You don't date a married man."

"I know, but it was different. He really cared for me."

"Just like Greg who strung you along for six months and then went back to his wife?"

Tessa wiped another tear away. "No, not like that. This guy was going to leave his wife for me. He's how I got the job at Frontier. I owe him so much."

"Okay, so where is he now?"

Tessa let out a big sigh. "He's dead."

"What?"

"It was Mark. I was having an affair with Mark."

"Tessa!" I put my hand to my head. "You are in serious trouble. I don't think I can get you out of this."

"No, you can. 'Cause I didn't kill him. I loved him and he was going to leave Vanessa. He needed to make sure she wouldn't get everything in the divorce, so he had to wait until the timing was right. The winery was his to start with." Tessa looked up at me. "But he loved me. He really loved me."

Dean coughed from the corner. "Katie, it's late. You can come back and talk to Tessa in the morning."

"Okay, just a second."

The door slammed as Dean returned to the offices.

Tessa's face was blank. "Was he listening the whole time?"

I shrugged. "It's not important. What's important is to get you out of this whole mess. First, I think Seb blamed you for the money, so I'm going to look into the finances. Because you didn't steal any, right?"

"No. I didn't steal any money." Tessa looked down at her hands. "But now Dean heard all of that and he probably thinks I did."

"No, but I need to keep Dean involved so that we can get you out of here. He's on your side."

"Yeah, right."

I took a deep breath. "I don't understand why you're keeping secrets from me. After this whole weekend, you didn't think to mention that you were having an affair with Mark?"

"*Me* keeping secrets?" Tessa stood up. "Me keeping *secrets*? You're right," she said as her face fell empty. "I've been keeping secrets for way too long."

"Tessa, I know I can never repay you, but I'm trying to help."

"Is that why you're here?" Her eyes flashed. "Because you feel guilty?"

"No, it's not that."

"You know, I wouldn't even be locked up if it weren't for you. I wouldn't even be in this mess."

I stepped back. "What do you mean?"

"I have a record." Tessa's eyes narrowed. "I have a record because of you. Do you think they would be locking me up if this was a first offense?" She folded her arms. "No. They wouldn't. I'm here because of something I didn't do back then and something I didn't do now."

The words stung and tears formed in my eyes. "Tessa, listen—"

"No. I took the fall for you back then. It was your idea to break into that house. It was you who should have gone to jail. But you had your father, the cop. Couldn't let him find out what you did. So I covered for you." Tessa pointed to herself. "Me. Because I didn't have family, but I had you. You were my family. That's what you do, you help each other out."

"Tee, please…"

Tessa threw her hands up. "This is the help I get? I get accused of another crime, another one I didn't do, and the only reason you're here is because you feel guilty?"

I shook my head. "I didn't say that."

"No. You never say anything. You keep your mouth shut and out of trouble. Ever since that night, you've been the perfect daughter." She put her face to the bars, only inches away from me. "You stopped being who you were that night. You used to be wild. You used to be fun. I miss the Katie from twelve years ago. The one who lived life so free. The one who didn't play by the rules. You became the good one, and I became…me." Her voice dropped to a guarded whisper. "You're here because you feel guilty? Let me remove that guilt from you, Katie. I don't need your help and I don't want your help. I'm done with being the albatross around your neck. Want to help me? Really want to help me? Then do me a favor and don't come back. Ever."

I tried to keep my game face on, but tears streamed down my cheeks. "Tee, please. It's not like that."

Tessa walked to the other side of the cell and faced the wall.

"Tee." My whole body shook as I spoke.

She didn't move.

"Tessa, please." My cries were met with silence.

TWENTY-THREE

PAIRING SUGGESTION: CARMÉNÈRE—RAPEL VALLEY, CHILE

Due to its similar qualities,
this wine was previously mistaken for Merlot.

❧

I WIPED MY EYES and put on my best game face before walking through the station, relieved that Dean was absent from his desk.

I headed back to San Francisco, no longer worrying about a car trying to run me off the road. In fact, I nearly welcomed it as I drove, but I arrived at my apartment building around ten thirty without incident. All available parking spots were taken but after the events of the night, I wasn't in the mood to gamble. I drove three blocks down and parked in the expired meters that resumed operation at eight in the morning. I set an alarm on my phone and entered my building, the area silent as I climbed the worn stairs to the second level and down the hallway to my studio apartment.

My four-hundred-square-foot studio seemed darker than ever and my overstuffed couch looked the opposite of appealing.

I tossed myself onto the bed and although my eyes were tired, my mind was wide-awake. Sleep would be a long time coming but I knew it would eventually come, and it did.

My phone alarm woke me at ten to eight, the shrill reminder that tickets, and possibly a tow, were on their way. I dressed in my running clothes and after moving my car to a free space on the street, I set off for a run in Golden Gate Park.

My pace was slower than usual, the three-day break affecting my stride. Two young girls, no more than ten years old, kicked a ball around on the grass, one with blond curls, the other with long brown hair. A pit formed in my stomach, but I quickened my pace and pushed harder, even passing the area of the park where I usually turned to head back to my apartment.

The crisp air felt good on my skin and I could see and think clearly for the first time in days. When I finally returned to my street, my thighs ached and my lungs hurt. I bent down to take a deep breath but I found myself smiling. I hadn't run that far in years.

By the time I left for Trentino, it was already 10:57, only a few minutes before the tasting group started, and I still needed to stop by a liquor store on my way.

Trentino was half empty, most patrons choosing to go out to dinner rather than for lunch. I opened the door to the private tasting room, the faces of Jackson, Kurt, Darius, and Bill staring up at me from the oblong table. I had never been late to a tasting session in the two years I had been a part of the group, and the surprise on each of their faces was hard to miss.

"About time you got here," quipped Darius.

"Yeah, sorry. I should have called." I stared at the table set up with five glasses at each place, only one empty chair remaining, the one on the window side of the room. My chair.

"I don't think I've ever seen you in jeans," said Kurt. "Not even when we were…" His voice trailed off as he failed to say the word *dating*.

I shrugged as I looked down at my jeans. "I figured it was time to go comfy."

Jackson motioned to the empty spot. "Sit down. We've only done one wine so far."

"Oh, thanks, but I'm not staying."

"Why not?" asked Bill.

"I have to drive to Napa. I have to clear up something I should have done a long time ago."

"So you'll be here on Wednesday?"

I took a deep breath and shook my head. "I've decided I'm not going to take the next Certified test. I'm going to take a step back and figure some things out. So I won't be here for a little while."

"You're kidding," said Kurt.

"No, actually I'm not." I put my bag on the table and pulled out the bottle of fourteen-year-old Scotch whisky. "Darius, as I promised. Here's your bottle of Oban. Thanks again."

"Sweet!" he said as he took the bottle. "Anytime."

Kurt took the bottle out of Darius's hands. "Wait, you're giving him Oban? Why?"

"He covered my inventory shift on Saturday. I owe him."

"You never bought me scotch," said Kurt. "Call me next time, I'll cover for you."

"You don't work here."

He shrugged. "Small detail."

"Anyway, I have to go. Good luck tasting today."

"Can't you stay for a few minutes?" Bill raised his eyebrows. "One last tasting before you leave us?"

I hesitated. "No. I can't."

"Katie," said Bill.

"I know, I know," I interrupted. "The horse thing. Gotta get right back on. And I'll be back eventually, just not today."

The door opened behind me and the group turned to look.

Alexis, the hostess, stuck her head in the door. "Hey, Bill?" Her eyes moved to me. "Katie, I didn't think you were here. There was a phone call for you about ten minutes ago."

"Oh. From who?"

Alexis moved inside the room. "From a Lisa? At least I think it was for you. She said the call was for 'Tessa's little friend.'"

I nodded. "Yeah, that would be Lisa. Did she say what she wanted?"

"It was a quick call, but she said that Vanessa has a case of wine for you, as a thank you for meeting with her."

"Who's Vanessa?" asked Jackson.

"The owner of Frontier." I picked up my bag from the table.

"What? That would be fantastic. A case of Frontier?"

I sighed. "I don't really want to go back there."

"Don't go, I will," said Jackson. "I'll pick up the case, but don't expect me to bring it here. I'm gonna take it home and cook a steak."

"No, guys, really. I'm done with that place and that wine."

"But you're going to Napa right now anyway, right? At least bring the case back here for us," said Kurt. He winked at me like he used to and my heart softened. It was my only relationship where the guy opened every door, pulled out every chair. I had been the one to break it off after six months, declaring that I needed to study for the exam. That was over a year ago.

"Especially if you're not going to come to the tasting group anymore," Kurt continued. "We can all share a bottle of Frontier and toast to you. It could be your way of thanking us for helping with your test."

"I didn't pass."

"Yes, but we did help you," he added. "Made sacrifices." Even though we had maintained a friendship, Kurt never missed an opportunity to remind me of the tension that remained between us. The tension that I had caused by running away. Maybe it hadn't been the test after all. Maybe it was simply the fact that he had gotten too close.

"Even though you didn't pass, you're still The Palate. And a very talented taster." His smile was soft, almost pained.

"If I really go there and pick up this case, will you stop asking me to retake the test? Will you accept the fact that, for now, I'm not going to proceed?"

Jackson looked down at the glass in front of him and shook his head, Bill didn't respond, and Darius just stared at me.

"Yes, we will," declared Kurt.

I looked over at Alexis. "Did she leave a number to call her back?"

"No, she said to just come on by."

"Okay." I glanced at my watch. "I'll pick it up and drop it back off here tonight. Sound good? Is that okay, Bill? Can I leave it with you?"

"Of course." His face was emotionless. "There will always be a place at this table when you're ready to come back."

"Thank you." I opened the door back into the restaurant. An unfinished feeling began to wash over me as I left the glasses of wine on the table, unknown and unidentified.

———

For the first time ever, my stomach turned as I drove into the Napa boundary. I put all the windows down and breathed in the scent of the vineyards. The calm sensation returned. I was doing the right thing.

I turned into the parking lot of the sheriff's station and took one step at a time, pulling open the door as I took one last breath of the fresh air.

Dean was near the desk when I walked in.

"Hey, you okay? I heard you were upset last night when you left."

"Me?" I replied with my game face on. "No, I was fine. Listen, is there somewhere where we can go and talk?"

"Katie, I'm working. Can we do this later?"

"No, this is about work. About Tessa."

His face changed and he motioned me through the gate. "We'll go to an interrogation room." He glanced back at me. "Not that I'm going to interrogate you."

I faked a smile and followed Dean through the station to the small room, empty except for a table and two chairs. I sat down as he closed the door. He took the chair opposite.

"What's this about, Katie? Do I need to read you your rights?" He smiled but stopped when he noticed the expression on my face. "What's going on?"

"You know that Tessa was arrested in 2004 for breaking and entering, right?"

"Yes, I've seen her file."

"Tessa didn't break into the house. I need you to know that it was me, not her. She took the blame for it."

"Katie, she was tried for that and spent four months in jail. She admitted to that crime. I don't understand why you're telling me this. What does this have to do with right now?"

"Won't the courts be easier on Tessa if they know that she didn't do that first crime?" The words spilled out of my mouth at a rapid rate. "That she wasn't guilty then, so this was her first offense? It's not her second strike and—"

"Katie," Dean cut me off. "This is sweet what you're doing for her, but if she really killed Seb, you need to let her take the fall for it. It's no good trying to cover for her."

"I'm not covering for her. I don't know what happened with Seb, but I know what happened when Tessa and I were teenagers. It was me. It was all me." I closed my eyes and I was back at my house in Los Angeles, my senior year of high school.

I remembered Tessa sitting on the bed across from me in my bedroom, posters lining the walls.

"My mom had this small statue when I was a kid," said Tessa. "When I would sit in her lap, I couldn't stop staring at it on her nightstand. She'd had it ever since I was born, or something like that. It was a child playing the piano and I remember wishing that I had a piano to play." Her voice shifted to a tone above a whisper. "After they both died, most of their stuff was given away. I don't even know what happened to that statue. I think some aunt got it or something and I'm not going to go back to Ohio to find it."

"I'm sorry." I stared at Tessa's somber face. "I wonder if we can find another one here. That way it will be like your mom is still with you."

"I'd love that."

"Describe it again."

"Small, definitely made out of china, and a girl playing a piano." She shrugged. "That's as much as I can remember."

"Wait, I think I've seen something similar to that!"

"No way, where?"

"At the house two doors down. They have a statue of a small child playing a piano. Like a stand up piano, not one of those long ones. And it's all faded and old looking, right?" I outlined the shape and size with my hand.

"Yes, that sounds just like it!"

I paused for a moment. "Do you want it?"

"What do you mean?"

"Come on, let's go get it." I stood up and put my hand on my bedroom door.

"You're kidding."

"No, I'm serious. It's been dusty for years, they don't even look at it. And I know it would mean so much to you."

Tessa hesitated before a smile grew on her face. "Okay."

We left the house and walked along the quiet cul-de-sac, only ducking into the bushes once we reached the two-story house which sat in total darkness.

"Look, we can go in there." I pointed to a window on the side of the house.

"But how?"

I ran to the window and pushed it up three feet. "It's not locked."

"I don't know, Katie, I think this is a bad idea. Let's go back to your room."

"Fine, you stay here, I'll be right back."

"What if there's an alarm? Katie, don't do this. You don't need to do this."

I climbed in through the window. "Nah, it'll be fine. I'll just be a sec." The house was silent as I crept into the living room. Bookshelves lined half of the room, but I knew exactly where I had seen the figurine. I approached the fireplace and found the delicate china statue on the mantel. It was just as I had described to Tessa, a girl playing a small piano.

"Katie, the cops are here," Tessa said as she scrambled through the window and ran into the living room. "We need to go."

"Hold on, I almost have it." I reached for the statue and pulled it off the mantel, safely into my hands. "Look, it's here. Is this it? Is this like the one you had?"

"Yes, but we need to go."

I took a step forward and tripped on the corner of the rug, the statue falling from my hands, hitting the unforgiving wood floor and shattering into what seemed like a million pieces.

A pounding came from the front door. "Police, open up."

I fell to my knees and tried to gather the pieces, a portion of the china piano in my left hand.

"Katie, stop."

The front door swung open as Tessa grabbed me and pulled me toward the window.

Officers stormed the house as Tessa pushed me outside. "Hide," she said in a loud whisper.

I fell to the ground as flashlights landed on Tessa, her hands up in the air. Tessa stood in front of the window, blocking the policeman's view of the outside as I scrambled into the bushes.

"Check the house," he yelled to his partner.

"There's no one here but me," said Tessa. She gave a slight nod to me in the bushes as she was cuffed, and then she was gone. I stayed hidden until the coast was clear and then made it safely back to my house.

I opened my eyes and looked at Dean. "The owners of the house pressed charges against Tessa. They never knew I was inside. Nothing happened to me."

Dean leaned back in his chair. "You're a lot more complicated than you seem."

"You have no idea."

He looked at the table as he spoke. "I'm not sure what the process would be on that. She pled guilty, she served her time. I'm glad you've come clean, but I'm not sure how it can all be reversed. I can look into it, but I don't know how it would affect this case. We still have video footage of Tessa at Garrett."

I nodded. "At least the truth is out now."

"I didn't really figure you as a criminal."

I shrugged. "I haven't done a thing wrong since that night." I looked up at the ceiling. "Okay, except for maybe a few parking tickets and one speeding ticket."

Dean scratched his head. "I'll let you know what we'll do."

"Okay." I hesitated. "But will you tell Tessa?"

"Sure. But don't you want to tell her yourself? I can take you back there right now."

"No. She won't want to see me, but thanks." I stood up and walked toward the door of the station, pausing to let Peters pass by with three people who had clearly hit the tasting rooms a little too hard already. Mondays didn't matter on vacation. He filed them in the entrance area as I headed down the steps. My shoulders were lighter and the pit in my stomach had disappeared.

As I climbed into my Jeep to drive to Frontier, I remembered my promise to Dean, to tell him before I met with anyone involved in the investigation.

I ran back up the steps. The usually calm entrance area of the station was electric with the energy of the three intoxicated occupants. Two of their shirts were soaked with red wine, filling the air with a thick smell of alcohol. Dean kept one guy from throwing a punch while Peters held another guy, and a third officer I hadn't seen before gently held back a lady even though she was the one putting up most of the fight.

"You bastard," she screamed at one of the guys. "This is all your fault."

"I'm gonna kill you," the man yelled back.

The six people in the room, three drunks and three officers, became a swirling merry-go-round. I stood with my back to the door and tried not to get hit. During a pause, I tried to motion to Dean that I needed to tell him something, but the struggle escalated.

One man managed to free his arm and promptly punched Dean in the face. Dean wavered for a second, gaining his wits, and took the guy down to the ground in one swift motion, his face pressed hard against the linoleum tile. The handcuffs came off Dean's belt and were around the guy's wrists within seconds.

The other two calmed down while the man was being cuffed, but once he was restrained they lunged at each other again.

I wasn't in the mood to wait through all of this distraction. I wanted to get the wine and get back to San Francisco. The drunk man, although cuffed, struggled on the floor with Dean's steady grip on his shoulder.

I stepped to the side of the action and walked through the swinging gate. I felt as though I was betraying orders, a civilian walking through the station, but I would only be a second. I reached Dean's desk and grabbed a pen from the cup holder. A blank notepad sat to the right of his computer screen. I wrote a quick note, *Heading to Frontier to pick up some wine from Vanessa. —Katie.* I glanced at my watch and put *1:43 p.m.* on the top of the note.

I returned to the front of the station where all three fighters had successfully been cuffed on the floor, their hands behind their backs. I managed to lock eyes with Dean for a moment and I motioned that I had left him a note on his desk. He nodded and returned his focus to the three people on the floor in front of him.

I exited the station and started the drive toward Frontier.

TWENTY-FOUR

PAIRING SUGGESTION: BAROLO—PIEDMONT, ITALY

An Italian wine with gripping tannins for gripping situations.

❧

I PULLED UP AT the closed gates of Frontier Winery, a small piece of white paper dangling from the call box.

Problems with the intercom, park outside. I'll meet you in the cellar. –L.

I pushed on the right gate, which opened a few inches but no more. I tried again but knew that although it was at least enough for me to squeeze through, it would not fit a case of wine. A warning registered deep in my gut.

I went back to the note and pulled it off the call box. *I'll meet you in the cellar.* I remembered Tessa's comment about Lisa's lack of work, yet she would take all the credit. Obviously Lisa would make me carry the case back to my car outside the gates. Fine. I could do that.

I parked my car at the side and entered the gates, the gravel driveway crunching under my feet. I relished the moment when I reached the grass and my footsteps became silent.

I headed behind the winery, the entire property absent of movement. I pulled open the heavy right door of the cellar and stepped inside. It banged behind me as the cold air and darkness enveloped me.

"Lisa? Are you here?" My voice echoed down the pitch black tunnel. If Lisa had been inside, the lights would have been on. But then again, maybe not.

A chill went up my neck followed by the sinking feeling that I shouldn't be here. I felt my pocket for my cell phone, to use it as a light, but it wasn't there. It was in my car, as always. When would I learn?

I shuddered and rubbed my bare arms, regretting that I had also left my jacket in the car. The dark had been my foe since I was seven when I accidentally locked myself in a closet. Right now, it wasn't the fact that I couldn't see, it was the thought of *what* I couldn't see. The opaque reality in front of me could possess any number of threats, from spiders and rats to an attacker. Normally I would have turned around and left, but after everything that had happened, I now had nothing to lose.

I searched for the light switch to the left of the door, as I had seen Tessa do. My hand touched the stone bricks but no switch.

I stepped farther to the side and tried again, this time my fingers brushing the small protruding light box. I hit the switch and the lights behind the barrels came on one by one. The tunnel seemed darker than when I had been in there with Tessa.

"Lisa?" I took a few steps. My voice echoed down and back with no response. "Lisa?" I glanced behind me, a sliver of light at the crease where the doors met. A phone call to Frontier would be an easy one to make from my Jeep, to ask Vanessa or Lisa about the wine. Or even walking out of the cellar and knocking on the office door would be more productive than waiting in the cellar alone.

"Back here," said a voice from the deep part of the tunnel.

"Lisa? Can you come meet me up here?" My request was met with silence. I reached into my pocket and took out my wine opener, pulling open the small blade on the end and holding it in front of me as I walked.

I continued into the tunnel, taking one step at a time, my footsteps echoing into the depths of the dimly lit cellar, which left a lot to the imagination. I must have missed another light switch somewhere.

I passed by the alcoves and tunnels that read 2012, 2011, 2010. I continued down the main tunnel until I reached the locked gates.

"Lisa?" My voice echoed down the tunnel behind the gates as the sound of footsteps came from behind me.

I turned around as all the lights went out.

Darkness consumed the area and I gripped the gates behind me, trying to keep my bearings as the blackness spun in front of me. My heart rate escalated as my ears strained to pick up any hint of noise in the eerily silent tunnel.

A bottle exploded near my face, shattering the silence as the force of the glass colliding with the stone wall sent thousands of shards ricocheting around me. From the amount of glass and wine that doused me, it must have missed my head by mere inches.

I dropped to my knees, my wine opener falling somewhere in front of me. I left it and scampered to the side, searching for one of the small tunnels as my heartbeat echoed throughout my body. My hand felt the outline of a tunnel and I crawled in, my elbow banging against two wooden crates stacked on top of each other against the wall. I pushed them in front of me, creating a barrier to protect my safe haven.

My breathing was quick and shallow as I waited. A bottle exploded above my head. I shielded my face with my arm as glass and wine rained down on me. An intense buttery smell filled the tunnel.

A bottle struck my left shoulder, forcing a cry of pain to escape from my lips, as the bottle fell to the floor and cracked, the force softened by the blow.

I grabbed my shoulder as another bottle shattered nearby.

I could cry for help, but the stone cellar went deep into the hillside. No one would hear me. My options were to wait and probably die, or get out. I needed to get out.

The cellar door, my exit to freedom, seemed a long way down the black tunnel when an assailant, who clearly knew the tunnel better than I did, was attacking me.

Two more bottles exploded near me, glass shards hitting my legs. Then silence.

I waited but there was nothing. Perhaps they were gathering more bottles, but I didn't want to wait to find out.

I jumped past the crates, my feet slipping on the debris from the attack. I took one leap and then another, everything moving in slow motion as I ran through the dark abyss.

A rush of air flew by my face and exploded against the wall next to me, glass cascading to the floor.

I put my hands in front of my face and turned around to protect myself.

Another bottle shattered next to me, forcing me to run back deeper into the tunnel, slipping as I ran across the broken glass. I slammed into the iron gate that guarded the back bottles, warm liquid running down my face. Blood.

I felt along the bars until I found the lock. I pulled at it and turned left and right, remembering what Tessa had done on Friday night.

It clicked in my hands and I swung open the gate and jumped inside, closing it behind me. I fumbled with the lock, but it fell out of my hands to the floor.

I reached down and felt along the damp floor. I wanted to secure myself in the tunnel, away from my pursuer, but the lock was gone. I tried again but it wasn't there. I darted away from the gate, my hands in front of me for protection.

I reached the back stone wall and followed it to the right, feeling for a door, staircase, or anywhere I could go. The wall was solid. I was stuck. A rabbit in a corner. No way out.

I sank down in the corner and waited. If my assailant arrived, I would jump and attack, aiming as best I could for the eyes or the groin.

My eyes had adjusted to the dark, but they only gave me enough information to play tricks on me. Movement seemed to be everywhere as the blackness swirled around me.

I waited, my knees aching as I crouched. The cellar was silent. My left shoulder throbbed and my arms stung as if plagued by a hundred bees. I felt my forehead, my hand following the warm stickiness until it reached a gash on top of a welt.

The sound of a bottle rolling down the tunnel like a bowling ball in an alley broke the silence. It bumped the wall next to me.

My attacker was inside the gates.

I silently counted to three and jumped up, pawing at the darkness in front of me. My hands grasped at the air, every bit of force I had pushing forward.

I hit nothing.

I jabbed a few more times and stopped, my hands formed in fists near my face. "I'm here and I'm not afraid of you," I yelled, my voice echoing down the tunnel.

It was silent.

I took several deep breaths to calm myself and then stepped forward, one foot at a time, my hands ready to strike. Each step calculated, my eyes rapidly scanned the darkness for movement. I reached the gate.

I pushed on it, the hinge creaking as it opened. I stopped, not even daring to take a breath. There was no sound in response.

I took a few more steps into the main tunnel, feeling along the side until my hand found an intact bottle. I picked it up and held it above my head like a bat, ready to strike if my attacker returned.

I paused after every step, assuming that each side tunnel had someone ready to jump out at me.

When my eyes could make out the faint line of light from the cellar doors in the distance, I started running, my legs pumping with every stride as I got closer.

I burst through the cellar doors into the cool air.

The lack of activity I had experienced at the winery when I first entered the cellar had been replaced with commotion. Dean's sheriff's car was outside the cellar door with the lights flashing red and blue onto the hill. He stood behind his open door with his gun drawn. "Freeze."

I jumped and put my arms up, my right hand still holding the bottle.

"Katie? What are you doing?" said Dean as he lowered his gun. "Are you okay? You're bleeding."

"Someone was trying to kill me," I said in a breathless voice as I lowered my arms. "Did you get my note?"

"Yes, and then I got a call from Vanessa that someone was in her wine cellar."

"Yes," I took a few unsteady steps toward Dean. "Someone was in there and they were throwing bottles at me."

"Stay here." Dean held his gun in front of him and opened the cellar door, disappearing inside.

I leaned against his patrol car, every muscle in my body tingling with adrenaline.

Dean returned with his gun in one hand and his flashlight in the other. "There's no one in there, but that place is a mess. Did you do that?"

"No, I told you. Someone was throwing bottles at me."

"What's that one?" Dean pointed to the bottle in my right hand.

I looked at the bottle. "I picked it up at the end to use as a weapon. In case they attacked me."

"Detective Dean," a female voice called from the side of the winery. "Did you catch who was in my cellar?"

"It's all right, Vanessa, I think we've figured it out."

Vanessa approached wearing a long white robe, her hair pulled back into a flawless French twist. "Katie, what are you doing here? What happened to your head?" Her eyes lowered to my hand. "And why are you holding my wine?"

I handed her the bottle. "You called me. To come pick up the wine."

Vanessa flinched. "What wine? I didn't call you."

"I meant that Lisa called me. She said you wanted to give me a case." I touched my head, the stickiness turning cold.

"Here," Dean handed me a handkerchief.

I held it to my forehead. "Thanks."

Vanessa emitted a cough mixed with a laugh. "Why would I give you a case of wine? I can't give anyone a bottle, let alone a case. The winery has no money. We need everything we can get."

"Katie," said Dean, "Lisa called you, right? Vanessa, can you please have Lisa join us? We'll figure this out right now."

Vanessa shook her head. "But Lisa's not here. She's been in Sonoma for work all day and won't be back until tomorrow." Her stare fixated on me. "Why are you really here?"

"Honest, I was going to meet Lisa. She called me."

"You talked to her?"

"No. She left a message at Trentino…" My voice trailed off.

Dean motioned to me. "Come on, let's get you back to your car. Where are you parked?"

"Outside the gate."

"How did you get in the gates? And why would you park down there?" asked Vanessa. "If you were really coming to pick up wine, you would have pulled onto the property. Sounds like you didn't want anyone knowing you were here." Her voice was cold.

"But the gate. It's broken. There was a note that said to park outside."

"Oh, please. The gate's not broken," Vanessa scoffed.

I shifted my focus to Dean, but he shook his head. "Gate wasn't broken when I pulled in, it opened fine."

"Listen. There was a note. I'll show you."

The three of us walked down the driveway and out to the street where my car was parked.

"It's right here on the front passenger seat." The driver's window was pushed all the way down, something I didn't remember doing. I opened the door and looked at the front seat. It was empty.

"What happened to your car?" asked Dean.

"Wait, it should be here. It has to be here."

"Katie, what happened to your car? Why is it all damaged on this side?" Dean repeated.

"I got in an accident two days ago." I leaned down to the floor of the car and looked under the front seat. The note wasn't there either.

"Did you report it?"

"No." I glanced back up at Dean. "The note was here. It was right here. Someone's taken it."

Dean's flashlight flooded the car.

"What the …?" I exhaled as the beam revealed multiple bottles of Frontier Winery wine.

"What are you doing with my wine?" said Vanessa, her voice getting louder. "Why is my wine in your car?"

I stared at the bottles, at least fifteen of them, that lay across the back seat of my car. "I don't know. I have no idea why they are there." I looked up at the faces of Dean and Vanessa. "I didn't do this." I pointed to the front window. "Someone knew I was here and did this. Look, my window is all the way down. When I left my car, all the windows were up."

"How could you?" cried Vanessa. "How could you? I trusted you, Katie. But you're just like the rest. Trying to steal what little I have left."

"No. No, I didn't."

"You're a thief and a liar. Is this your role in Tessa's little wine-moving game? Stealing wine from me and selling it to other markets? No wonder you're friends. You both deserve each other." She turned to Dean. "I want to press charges."

Dean hesitated for a moment before he spoke in a soft tone. "Katie, I hate to do this, but I'm going to have to take you in."

"Dean, I didn't do anything."

"I'm sorry, Katie. Please turn around."

The cold metal rings sent a chill through me as the handcuffs clicked around my wrists.

"You have the right to remain silent. Anything you say can and will be used against you in a court of law."

We walked back up the driveway, Dean holding my arm, Vanessa only a few steps behind.

"Why is everyone trying to take advantage of me?" Vanessa cried. "How can people be so cruel?"

I cringed.

We reached Dean's squad car and he helped me into the back, his hand gently covering my head as I ducked under the doorframe. The slam of the door sent a shock into my ears.

Dean and Vanessa continued a short conversation outside the car, but I couldn't make out any actual words.

Finally Dean sat in the front seat and started the car.

"Dean, I'm so sorry."

"Don't," he replied. "Don't say anything. I have to write down everything you say and I don't want to do that. It's better to remain silent."

He glanced back at me in the rear view mirror during the drive, his eyes full of sadness.

TWENTY-FIVE

PAIRING SUGGESTION: SHIRAZ—BAROSSA VALLEY, AUSTRALIA

A dark purple wine that handles spice well.

THE STATION WAS COLD as I sat on the bench in cuffs. Even Peters didn't meet my eye as he cleaned the cut on my forehead.

"Katie, come on to the back," said Dean as he opened the gate. "I'll process your booking." He kept his hand on my arm as he guided me through the office.

"You have to know that I didn't do anything," I whispered. "I told you I got the call from Lisa and went to meet her there."

Dean pointed to the chair next to his desk. "Have a seat."

I sat down, readjusting the cuffs. "Then in the cellar, someone tried to kill me. Just like the other day."

"Other day?"

"The accident. Someone tried to run me off the road. That's why my car is damaged."

Dean shook his head and leaned over a form. "Full name?"

"Katie Kelehua Stillwell."

He looked up. "Sounds Hawaiian."

"My parents were married there."

He continued to write.

"You don't believe me about the accident, do you?"

"We can talk about that in a minute. First, we need to get through tonight's incident."

"Dean, come on. You know I didn't steal that wine. And where is Lisa? We need to find her." My eyes drifted to a beige folder on his desk titled FRONTIER WINERY.

Dean tapped his forehead with the pen and looked at me. "I told you to tell me when you were going to talk to anyone involved."

"I left you a note."

"Not good enough. You're playing a dangerous game with dangerous people. Yet you ignore the warning signs, not to mention your promise to me, and return to the scene of a crime. Then the bottles of wine in your back seat…"

"Someone set me up. They think I'm getting too close."

Dean let out a deep breath. "Katie, you have to stop."

I studied him, his mouth drawn, his eyes not meeting mine. "There's more, isn't there? What aren't you telling me?"

Dean put down his pen. "You're in trouble, Katie. Apart from the wine bottles in your back seat. I don't know how to tell you this but Peters found fingerprints all over Mark's office that don't match Mark or Vanessa. Once I fingerprint you for booking, they're going to run your fingerprints in the system. Am I correct in guessing that there will be a match?"

I hesitated. "Yes, but that's only from the party when I was trying to find Tessa. I haven't been in there since. Lisa mentioned the lodge and I had a feeling that's where Tessa would be, so I went to the office to find out the address. Which I did. And we found her."

"Why didn't you ask me to find out the address of the lodge that night? Why did you sneak into someone's private office?"

I took a large breath. "I wanted to find Tessa first. I wanted to get the truth."

"I could charge you with interfering with the investigation." Dean picked up his pen and placed it in the corner of his mouth. "I need an honest answer from you. Can you do that for me?"

"Absolutely."

He paused. "Did Tessa kill Mark?"

"No."

"Katie, I don't mean because you know her, I mean because of the facts. You're her alibi." He hesitated. "Why were you in such a rush to get to her at the lodge that night? Was it to prep her with information so that she would look innocent?"

"No." My voice escalated along with my pulse. "I just wanted to talk to her. I don't usually . . . I don't ask for help. I'm used to doing things on my own. It was nothing against you or the Pluegers. I needed to find her on my own."

Dean shook his head. "This doesn't look good for you. At all." He straightened the booking papers. "We also did a run on Tessa's accounts. She has a large amount of money in there, which doesn't match her salary record."

I stared at him, not moving. "You mean she took the money?"

Dean shrugged. "I'm not sure. But it looks that way."

I glanced around the office, but there were no other officers in sight. I looked back at Dean and whispered, "If Tessa took the money and Seb was telling people, that could be motive for her to kill Seb. But I don't think she did."

"I wouldn't worry about Tessa right now. You have enough troubles of your own. Now tell me about this accident."

"I was on I-80 and a black truck pushed me off the road."

"Did you get a plate?"

I shook my head.

Dean sat back. "This happened two days ago?"

"Yes."

"Yet you're only telling me about it now?"

I lowered my eyes and nodded.

Dean sighed. "You're entitled to a phone call. Would you like to make that now?"

I stared at the phone on the desk. A cop's daughter wasn't supposed to get arrested, they were supposed to be a shining example for the rest of the community. At least that's what my dad always told me. "No. I need to clear my head first."

"I think we can allow that. Come on, stand up. I'll take you to your quarters."

"You make it sound so fancy."

"I do my best." Dean led me through the door into the hallway of jail cells. He escorted me into the first cell, removed my cuffs, and closed the sliding door, locking it between us. "I hate seeing you in there."

"I hate being in here. You know that I don't belong in here, right?" I waited for Dean to answer, my breath caught in my throat.

"Vanessa is pressing charges. I don't have a choice." He looked down at the keys in his hand. "I like you, Katie, but you're hard to read, and you seem to turn on the charm only when you want something. And then you keep things from me, like the hit-and-run. I don't get it."

A noise stirred from the next cell, but I ignored it. I stared through the bars into Dean's blue eyes. "Dean, I'm sorry. I'm not good at this stuff, but I like you. I do."

"You're saying that now, but I don't know what to believe. What if you've been using me from the start? What if you and Tessa dreamed up this whole thing? You're her alibi for Mark's murder, but what if you're in this together?" Dean shook his head. "It's a rule of mine to never get involved with someone on a case. It's making me waver in what I believe. But not anymore. I'm taking a step back so I can look at the evidence without influence."

I leaned against the bars, the cold metal pressing into my flushed cheek. "Dean, please. Don't believe what is happening, today with the bottles in my car, with everything. Tessa is innocent and so am I. Someone knows I'm getting close and they don't like it."

Dean stared at me, but remained silent.

"If you want to give up on me and believe Vanessa, that's fine, I can handle that." My voice started to shake and I took a breath. "But don't give up on Tessa. She deserves better. She didn't kill Mark and she didn't kill Seb. So please. Help her."

Dean looked at me and back at the keys. He leaned to the left as if he was about to walk out of the cell area.

"Listen," I said, "find out where Lisa is and ask her again about Seb's alibi that night. I still think he was involved with Mark's murder."

"I've already called her about that," said Dean, finally breaking his silence.

"And?"

"Haven't been able to get in touch with her. I've left messages."

"There's got to be something we're missing."

Dean smiled, but his eyes were full of pain. "I have to go. I'll be back in an hour so you can make your call."

He walked down the hallway and out the door. The cell area was silent and reeked with a combination of cleaning fluid and body odor. I sat down on the mattress and stared at the floor, a hollowness inside me that I hadn't felt since my mom died.

"He likes you," said a female voice from the next cell.

TWENTY-SIX

PAIRING SUGGESTION: PINOT NOIR—SANTA BARBARA, CA

A lighter red as things begin to look up.

✍

I STARED IN THE direction of the voice, the concrete wall that divided the cells obstructing my view of Tessa.

"He did. He doesn't now," I replied.

"Dean told me that you came to the station earlier. To tell the truth about when we were teenagers. And now you're in jail, right where you never wanted to be."

I glanced around my cell—two beds and the open toilet—before answering. "I'd do anything for you. Not because of what you did for me, but because we're friends. In fact, I'm glad I'm in here. Maybe you needed to see how far I'd go for you." My voice lowered. "Maybe I needed to see it, too."

"Really?" Tessa's voice came closer, as if she had moved to the side of her cell nearest me.

"Yes, really. You're my family. I need you in my life. You did something amazing for me when we were teenagers. I'd change places with you in a second."

"I never wanted you to be in jail," said Tessa. "You don't belong in here. I don't regret what I did back then. I didn't want you to be in trouble. You had family. I didn't. No one cared what I did, but your dad was so proud of you. I couldn't take that away from you."

I leaned my head against the bars in an effort to get a glimpse of Tessa, but I recoiled with pain, a whimper coming from my throat.

"What happened?"

I touched the bump on my forehead and the wound that I had just reinjured on the bar. "My head … I have a cut and I forgot about it. It'll be fine."

"You okay?"

"Of course. I mean, I won't win any beauty pageants right this minute, but I'll be fine."

"Katie…" Tessa paused. "Why did you tell Dean the truth? You didn't need to do that."

I stared at the tile floor in the hallway, scuffed from years of dragging feet. "I did."

"Why?"

"It was time to come clean. I needed it to be out there. I didn't want that old case to factor in with this current situation."

"But your dad …"

I waved dismissively at the empty air around me. "It's fine. I'll get it figured out."

"Is that why you're in here? Because of the old case?"

I let a small laugh escape from my lips. "No, I'm in here because of what I did tonight."

"Wait, what exactly did you do?" Tessa lowered her voice. "Did you do something naughty to Dean?"

"Tessa!"

"Just asking," she said with a smile in her voice.

"No, someone set me up at Frontier and framed me for stealing wine. Well, that and they tried to kill me."

"Katie!"

"Listen, it doesn't matter right now. But the sheriff's deputies found a lot of money in your account. They think you took it from the winery."

"Katie, I swear I didn't take it." Tessa stopped. "Wait, was that recent?"

"I don't know, why?"

"When I checked my account yesterday, I had a lot of money in there."

"How much money?"

"Not really sure, I was hung over so I didn't really think about it, but a lot more than there should have been. I have direct deposit so money goes in there every two weeks. I figured it was that time." Tessa paused. "But to be honest, it was a lot more than my usual paycheck. I figured I'd finally hit a lucky break. About time."

"Who could have put it in there, Tee?"

"You got me."

I leaned against the bars again, this time more carefully. I could see Tessa's red fingernails resting on her own cell bars. "Someone who had access to your private information, social security, that stuff. Who would have had that?"

"Who knows? I don't give that out."

"Tessa, think. Someone got it from somewhere."

"I don't know, Katie. No one's been to my apartment. I haven't lost my wallet. In fact, I usually keep it very close, right with the twins," she replied followed by the distinct noise of patting her chest.

"Tessa, you never change."

"Why change something so good? I'm like a wine, I get better with time."

"Yes, Tessa. You are like a wine. Sometimes sweet, sometimes bitter."

"Shut it." Tessa laughed.

"Okay, so we don't know who would have been able to get into your accounts." I paused, focusing on the concrete blocks that separated us. "Except with your direct deposit. Who handles the paychecks for Frontier?"

"Lisa. That's part of her job."

"She does all the winery paperwork?"

"Sure, she takes care of that."

"And you said that Lisa and Seb were dating?"

"They were." Tessa coughed. "For a little while, at least. Although I don't know if you could call it dating. It was more sleeping together."

I stared at a crack in one of the blocks, the jagged line nearly separating it in two. "Do you know if Seb was in debt?"

"Katie," Tessa sighed, "how would I know? That's not exactly a hot topic of discussion in the break room."

"What if he was stealing money and when you got blamed for Mark's murder, he tried to blame you for the money as well?"

"You think so? That's kind of a stretch."

"Tessa, you said yourself that he was a jerk."

"I didn't think so until yesterday. I tell you, Katie, the whole weekend is starting to blur together and not because of alcohol."

"Okay. We're going to use some advice from my dad and treat the money and the murders as unrelated crimes. I think Mark's murder and you being under suspicion for it gave Seb the perfect opportunity to blame you for the missing money."

"You sound like your dad."

I nodded. "Yeah, I guess I do." I sat down on the floor closest to Tessa's cell, ignoring whatever filth or grime I might possibly be sitting in. "Tee, is there anything else you need to tell me? You've told me about the affair, but is there anything else? I just want to make sure."

"No way, I'm being honest. One hundred percent honest."

"Okay, good. Now that we've got that out of the way, let's figure out who could have killed Seb. Did anyone have any animosity toward him? Or was upset at him?"

"No. Not that I can think of."

"I think if we can figure out who killed him, that will lead us to who killed Mark."

"You still think the murders are related?"

I nodded as my eyes traced the tile floor. "Yes, I do. We need to figure out who is trying to frame you. Actually, frame both of us. So we need to think." I looked at my watch. "And we have all night."

"This reminds me of…" Tessa trailed off. "Never mind."

"I was thinking," I started, "that this reminded me of when we were thirteen and stayed up all night talking about boys and eating Sour Patch Kids. I miss those times."

"I do, too." Tessa's hand pushed through the bars in the hallway, her hand waving up and down as she spoke. "We need to do that again. Even if we're both working a lot, we need to make time. I'm glad you're back, Katie."

"I never really left, Tee. You can tell me to leave all you want, but we're family and that means we stick together."

"I like that. But hey, how are we going to solve this from jail? We both know there's no one to bail me out…" Her voice fell away.

I glanced down at the hallway, absent of movement. I knew what I needed to do. "I'll make the call. He'll be disappointed, but he'll bail me out."

"Are you really going to call your dad for bail? He'll be pissed! His daughter in jail? What about your image?"

"Maybe it's time to lose the perfect image. We both know it wasn't true anyway. And besides, bad girls have more fun."

"Yeah, we do."

I took a deep breath and stretched my neck on both sides. "Okay. I'll tell Dean I'm ready to make my call."

When Dean returned, he opened my cell door. "Rules say I need to cuff you to take you to the phone, but I'm going to play the trust card and know that you won't run. Right?"

"Only the guilty run." I exited the cell, the scent of Dean's after-shave floating in the air.

"Pay phone is there. You have five minutes. Do you know who you're going to call?"

"Yep." I picked up the phone and dialed zero to call collect. I had never called to ask for this type of help before, but sometimes you can't figure out the story alone. Sometimes you need help.

———

The sound of metal sliding on the tile floor stirred me awake. A thick haze occupied my mind, as if I had gone straight to bed after too many bottles of wine. Or worse, a bottle of cheap tequila.

"What time is it?" I sat up and rubbed my eyes, the haze remaining as I glanced around the cell.

"Seven," said Dean. "Breakfast time." He pushed a tray under the bars. "Did you sleep okay?"

I looked down at the rough cotton pillow, its shape still intact from when I first arrived. "Perfect. Like a five-star hotel." I reached for the tray and put it down on my lap as I sat on the mattress. "What is this?"

"Eggs and toast," replied Dean as he walked to the next cell, the sound of metal again on the tile floor.

I pushed the meal around with my fork. The eggs didn't move while the toast melted into itself. "Seriously?"

"It's like rubber," yelled Tessa from the next cell.

"Exactly." I put the tray on the floor. "Tee, are you going to eat this stuff?"

"Nope," said Tessa. "I'm going to fit back into that little black dress from high school."

Dean returned to the cell door. "I don't mean to interrupt your breakfast, but your visitor is here."

"Where is she?" said the familiar voice from down the hall.

I raced to the bars. "You came."

Bill's cheerful face appeared at the cell door. "Of course! My favorite wine taster needs to be bailed out of jail, where else would I be?"

"Thanks, Bill. I really appreciate it."

"I would have come last night, but you said to wait till this morning."

I motioned to the next cell. "I wanted to stay with Tessa."

"You hungry?"

I glanced back at the uneaten eggs and toast on the tray. "Starved."

"Jenny's making breakfast back at the house. I gave her a quick summary of everything you said on the phone. She's ready to give any legal advice you may need."

Dean unlocked the door and I wrapped my arms around Bill. "Thanks so much. And I promise I'll pay you back."

"You don't need to pay me back, just don't skip bail," he laughed. "I want to get my money back, and I need you for work this week."

"I promise I won't get into any more trouble." I stepped in front of Tessa's cell. "I'll be back. Remember what we talked about."

Tessa's hazel eyes met mine and she gave me a thumbs-up. "Thanks, friend."

I gave her a thumbs-up back. "You'll be out soon and we'll go grab a burger."

"Oh my God, that sounds so good! That's so mean, though! I'm hungry now."

"Sorry." I paused. "I'll see you soon."

"Don't be a slowpoke," Tessa muttered as she sat back on the mattress.

Dean motioned for us to walk up the hall and we entered the front office.

Deputy Peters held up a large manila envelope. "We're able to return your phone, which was in the car." He emptied the envelope, my cell phone sliding onto the counter. "I'm sorry, but your car is still impounded as evidence."

"Awesome. Can you repair the dents and paint it for me?" My comment was met by silence. "Sorry. Bill, can you drive me…"

"Of course. Whatever you need."

Dean stepped forward. "Be safe out there."

"I will." I touched his arm but avoided eye contact.

I knew all too well that once a wine is spoiled, nothing can make it better.

TWENTY-SEVEN

PAIRING SUGGESTION: MALBEC—MENDOZA, ARGENTINA

A velvety wine with high alcohol and bold fruit flavors.

❧

BILL PARKED IN THE driveway of his white two-story house located in the Sea Cliff area of San Francisco. Several homes in the area had picturesque views of the Golden Gate Bridge and the bay and it appeared that Bill's would be no different.

The front door opened and a tall woman with perfect posture stepped onto the porch, her flaxen hair pulled into a ponytail.

"That's Jenny," Bill said as he got out of the car. "I don't think you two have met before."

"No, I don't think so." I exited the car and smoothed out my sweater as she approached. I extended my hand to Jenny. "It's so nice to meet you."

Jenny firmly shook my hand, the morning sun glinting off her black-rimmed eyeglasses. "I'm sorry for what you've been through the last few days, but we're going to get it sorted out. I'm sure Bill's told you that even though I deal in family law, I'm certain I can help."

"Yes, thank you." I glanced at Bill. "Both of you. I really appreciate it."

"Here, come in."

I stepped inside the house, a smell of lavender and freshly baked bread in the air.

"Are you hungry?" Jenny motioned toward a doorway into the kitchen. "I'm almost done making eggs and waffles."

"Sounds amazing."

"Would you like to shower first?"

I glanced in the hallway mirror, my face spotted with remnants of blood from the cut on my head and my hair sticky from the wine. "Yes, that would be great."

"There's a bathroom in here." Jenny pointed to a bedroom off the hall. "I'll be right back with a set of clothes you can borrow."

"Thank you so much, I don't know what to say."

"You don't have to say anything," said Bill as he chuckled. "Just be quick so we can all eat. I mean, come on, it's waffles."

I closed the door to the bathroom and took off my coat, small pieces of glass falling onto the floor. My hair shed more glass as I showered but by the time I was done, I felt like myself again.

I wrapped myself in a white towel and opened the bathroom door. As promised, Jenny had laid clothes on the bed, a pair of white pants and a black top. I dressed and tied back my wet hair before opening the door.

Jenny flipped an egg over in a pan as Bill stood across from her in the kitchen. She looked up and smiled at me. "Feel better?"

"Much. I don't think there are even words."

"Bill will show you to the dining room," said Jenny. "I'll be out with the food in a minute."

"This way." Bill led me through the kitchen to the dining room, the dark wood highlighted by the sun that streamed through the window. The top of the famous red bridge peaked through the fog in the distance.

I sat down at the table as Jenny entered the room and placed a plate of eggs and waffles in front of me.

"I don't think I've ever been more hungry than I am right now."

"When you're finished, I'll have you go over every detail from this weekend." Jenny sat down, a yellow legal notepad and pen in her hand.

I nodded as I covered my waffle in syrup. I cut a piece and placed it in my mouth, the warm syrup flowing over my tongue. I closed my eyes. Breakfast had never tasted so good.

After eating a second waffle and two helpings of eggs, I spilled every single detail of the last four days. Bill listened intently as Jenny filled page after page of the notepad with black ink.

"And then I called you this morning." I took a drink of orange juice.

"You poor thing," said Jenny as she flipped through the eight pages filled with her notes, her eyes skimming the words. "That's quite a weekend."

"Seriously."

Jenny read a few lines on the second page. "Don't be concerned, I think everything will work out fine."

"For me or for Tessa?"

Jenny gave me a warm smile. "For both."

"She's very good at her job," said Bill. "She's modest about her success, but she's won many high-profile cases." Bill's voice dropped to a whisper. "Don't let the sweetness fool you, she's a tiger in the courtroom."

I nodded and leaned back in the chair as my eyes skimmed the room. A large grandfather clock stood next to a wooden cabinet with polished wineglasses hanging from the top section.

I pointed to the glasses and smiled. "It's not even ten thirty. I guess it's too early to drink."

Bill laughed. "Are you kidding? After what you've been through? It's not only allowed, it's encouraged. Let me get a bottle from the wine fridge." He disappeared through a side door.

"You're his favorite taster in the group," remarked Jenny. "He's always impressed with your calls."

"Thanks. But not good enough to pass the Certified Exam."

Jenny waved it off. "I didn't pass the bar the first time. Big deal."

"So what happens next?"

Jenny held the notepad in her hand. "We need to narrow down the suspects. Your talk with Tessa last night was interesting. I think we're almost there." She stared out the window. "I agree that the two cases are separate."

"The two murders?"

"No, the murders and the finances. It appears to me that Seb took advantage of the situation and used it as an opportunity to blame Tessa."

"But why was he killed?"

"A few reasons. One"—Jenny counted on her fingers—"so he wouldn't be able to tell the truth, that he had laid the blame on Tessa. Two, to put Tessa back under suspicion. You said she had been cleared in Mark's murder that morning?"

"Yes."

"This was a way to implicate her again." Jenny adjusted her glasses and made another note.

"Why did someone want so badly to take her down? She didn't do anything to deserve that."

"You can't take this personally, Katie. She was their opportunity." Jenny flipped to the front page again.

Bill returned with a bottle in a brown paper bag.

"Seriously?" I leaned back in my chair. "I can't just drink?"

He winked. "If I'm going to pour you a glass, I might as well make it interesting. Besides, this will prove you can taste under extreme moments of stress."

I forced a smile. "Great. Thanks."

Bill poured white wine into the glass in front of me.

"You know," I remarked, "I've always thought certain white wines would go well with waffles."

"I couldn't agree more," said Bill as he sat down across the table from me and picked up his phone, swiping to the timer. "Clock starts whenever you're ready. And no *if*s, right? Be certain with your calls."

"Believe me, no *if*s. Things are different now." I reached for the glass and swirled it, the golden liquid climbing the sides in an effort to reach freedom, but never quite reaching the top. "This is a white wine with medium viscosity and a golden straw color." I put the glass to my nose and sniffed. "Lemon." But I stopped after the first word and held the glass in front of me, my eyes fixated on the wine.

"Stumped already?"

I looked at Bill, my eyes growing wider as the pieces came together in my mind. "No. I think I've figured out who the real murderer is and who tried to kill me last night in the wine cellar."

"How can we help?" said Bill.

"Can I borrow your car?"

TWENTY-EIGHT

PAIRING SUGGESTION: BORDEAUX—BORDEAUX, FRANCE

A red wine constructed from a blend of five grapes:
Cabernet Sauvignon, Merlot, Cabernet Franc, Petit Verdot, and Malbec.

I WENT OVER THE last-minute advice from Jenny as I drove along I-80. I had one chance to get this right and I didn't want to mess it up. When I made the transition onto Highway 29, I dialed Dean's number. His phone rang three times and went to voicemail.

"Dean, it's Katie. I know who killed Mark and I know how to prove it. The answer is in the wine cellar. I'm heading to Frontier right now. I know you don't believe me, but please meet me there. It will all make sense, I promise."

I ended the call and dialed Vanessa's number. It rang, was answered, and went dead. I tried again. This time the call went straight through to voicemail.

"Vanessa, it's Katie. I know you don't want to talk to me, but I know who killed Mark. I'm on my way to Frontier. Meet me in the cellar so I can show you. I know you don't trust me, but you can. I'm here to help."

I put down the phone and gripped the wheel, my fingers turning white. I would be at Frontier Winery in about fifteen minutes. Everything was in place, I just needed it to work. If it didn't, I could lose more than just my job.

A tractor blocked the road as I approached the winery and cars came from the other direction, making it impossible to pass. I sat back and waited as it crawled up the street.

When the tractor finally passed the driveway of Frontier, I was able to make the turn, stopping in front of the gates and pressing the call button. It rang once, twice, three times, and then went silent. I pressed it again, but the sequence repeated.

The gates were locked and I looked around, glancing at the stone wall that lined the property in both directions. I calculated the height of the wall and the height of Bill's car. It could work. I moved the car alongside the wall, two of the four wheels on the small strip of grass that separated the property from the road.

I stepped up on the tire and onto the roof of the Lexus for two steps before jumping for the top of the wall. My forearms and elbows barely reached the top, my legs dangling below.

I hoisted my right leg up on the wall and pulled myself up, the round stones digging into my knees. I cringed at the damage I was doing to Jenny's white pants, especially after she had been so helpful. I would buy her a new pair. And a bottle of wine.

I stared at the drop into the vineyards below me, the ground seeming much farther away than the side I had just climbed.

Not a problem. Knees bent then stick the landing. I jumped off the wall, my feet striking hard into the ground as my knees absorbed the force of the fall. I nearly fell forward, but managed to stay standing. I was about to put my arms in the air like a gymnast, but thought better of it and started running up the gravel driveway.

The sprawling oak trees cast misshapen shadows on the dirt and everything seemed drearier than before. I stopped when I reached the winery. No one was in sight, even on a Tuesday, when workers should have been milling about. Instead the entire property was vacant, an eerie emptiness surrounding it.

Vanessa must have heard my phone message, or at least the call from the front gate, but she was nowhere to be seen. I gave up waiting and ran to the wine cellar.

I pulled one door open, the cool air smacking me in the face as I stepped inside.

The door slammed behind me, making me jump. The lights were on in the cellar, but there was no one there, at least not that I could see. "Vanessa? Are you here?"

I made my way deep into the tunnel until my feet crunched on broken glass, signaling that I had reached my destination.

I crouched down, positioning myself so I wouldn't block the overhead light illuminating the broken bottles that had been thrown at me yesterday. Using my pointer finger and thumb, I carefully pulled up a label, large pieces of sharp glass attached to it. I held it up to the light, studying the paper square still damp with wine. Bingo. I had my answer.

The sound of a gentle click came from the tunnel to my left. Judging by the proximity of the sound, it was only about three feet away. It might not have been recognized by anyone else, but I knew the noise well. I had heard it multiple times throughout my life and could remember each instance.

When I was five, visiting my dad at the station. When I was seven and tin cans were lined up on the brick wall in the back garden. When I was twelve and my dad decided I should learn how to protect myself.

One doesn't forget the gentle yet haunting sound of a gun being cocked.

TWENTY-NINE

PAIRING SUGGESTION: PETITE SIRAH—NAPA VALLEY, CA

A dark red wine ideal for intense situations.

❧

"I KNOW YOU'RE THERE. And I'm not going to make any sudden moves, but I am going to turn to face you. We need to talk. I'm only here to talk. About Jeff." I slowly turned my head to see the barrel of a gun.

"Sorry to disappoint you, Katie," said Jeff with a drastic difference in his voice from our previous conversations. "Life isn't always what it seems."

I kept a stern, unwavering appearance, my game face on. "I knew you would come," I replied as I stared directly at Jeff, ignoring the ominous black circle that invaded my line of sight. "It's nice to see you again."

Jeff raised his eyebrows as he lowered the gun slightly, before repositioning its aim at me. "I don't know what you're talking about. I'm simply protecting the winery from a thief. You stole before, you'll steal again."

I let a small laugh escape from my lips. "That's funny. You can be set up for stealing just like you can be set up for murder. Isn't that what you did to Tessa?"

"I don't know what you're talking about." The gun barrel shifted.

"Sure you do, Jeff. And you had the perfect alibi. Me. I was with you when Mark was killed. Or at least that's what everyone thinks. But I still knew it was you. How about that?"

"Liar. You couldn't have known it was me."

"Jeff, you don't trust me? That's a shame." I locked eyes with him, looking past the barrel of the gun, which seemed to inch closer and closer. It was the first time I had a gun pointed at me and although I didn't like it, a wave of calm swept over me. I was composed and my senses were acute. It surprised me, but I would have to analyze that later. For now, I needed get a hold of the situation. "I liked you. I liked talking about grapes and wine with you. In fact, so much so that I ignored all of the blatant clues." I glanced at the cellar door, hoping Dean would burst through any second. The tunnel was silent.

"There weren't any clues." Jeff's green eyes looked black in the dim light of the cellar.

"Sure there were, Jeff. In fact, Lisa gave me a great one right at the beginning. Be wary of grapes that shouldn't be growing together. There were a lot of ways I could have taken that." I placed my hand on a bottle next to me.

Jeff pointed the gun at a nearby bottle and fired.

I threw my hands over my face to protect myself as the glass exploded and fell to the ground around me, the gunshot ringing in my ears.

"Keep your hands up," said Jeff in a terse and stressed voice.

I lifted my hands. "I'm surprised you destroyed a bottle without checking what type of wine it was."

A guttural sound came from deep in Jeff's throat.

"But," I continued, "as I was saying, Lisa gave that great clue. It could have meant Tessa and Mark, or Garrett and Vanessa. But what I think it meant was you and Seb. Seb didn't work directly for you, but he would listen anytime you said anything. Always looking over his shoulder, waiting for you. What did you have on him? What made him so loyal to a vineyard manager when he was an assistant winemaker?" The gun inched closer.

"Come on, Jeff, you have me here. You could at least talk to me. You know, like old times. Let's pretend we're sharing that '69 Chateau Margaux and talking about wine." I smiled. "So what made him so loyal?"

"Respect," said Jeff. "You could learn some of it, like not breaking into wine cellars."

"That's cute. Cute that you still believe I think you're innocent." I pointed to a nearby crate. "Mind if I sit? I've had quite the twenty-four hours. I was in jail, you know."

Jeff didn't reply, but I lowered myself onto the crate. "What did you have on Seb that he became your little errand boy? Did you do him a favor once? Save his life? Did he owe you a great deal?" I tilted my head. "Or was it more of a blackmail situation?"

Jeff didn't move.

I smoothed out my pant leg, large marks from the walls on both of my knees. "Pretty quiet now, huh? Maybe we should talk about grapes instead? I'm going to take a stab in the dark here and say it came down to money. You caught Seb stealing money from somewhere, maybe here, maybe not, and you've been blackmailing him."

"Stupid kid," growled Jeff. "He should have known better than to steal from where he worked. But catching him doesn't mean I did anything wrong."

"No, it doesn't, but it sure made Seb eager to pin the whole thing on Tessa." I pointed to the gun. "Since I might only have a few minutes to live, can you fill me in a bit more about Seb? Tessa has money in her account that she didn't put there. And Seb already came to me at the restaurant and accused Tessa of stealing. It was a little too perfect."

Jeff narrowed his eyes. "As I said, a dumb kid. Got himself into debt and tried to use the winery to get him out of it. That's why he started dating Lisa. She had access to all the account info. He started submitting invoices as a fictitious business that provided wine barrels, or so he said. He would have gotten away with it, too, if he hadn't submitted an invoice for a new trellis wire. Lisa came to me asking if it arrived and I figured out what he was doing. I covered for him, and he's been my little errand boy ever since."

"Was," I corrected him. "So then you helped him pin it on Tessa?"

"Nope. He did that himself."

I leaned forward. "You really had nothing to do with that?"

"Nothing," he replied softly, back to the Jeff I'd met at the Frontier party just a few days earlier. But the facade quickly vanished and he steadied the gun again. "I bet he figured Tessa was going down for the murder, so why not the rest of it. He was opportunistic like that," Jeff added.

"Okay," I continued in an effort to delay the inevitable gunshot, "then mysteriously Seb ends up dead. Almost as if to keep him quiet. Was he going to confess to the accounts? Was he going to reveal Mark's murderer? What was the reason to kill him?"

"I didn't kill him," grunted Jeff.

"Oh that's right." I waved my hand. "I can believe everything you say. And, if I may ask, where is Lisa?"

"She's a little busy." Jeff sat down on a crate across from me, keeping the gun pointed at me from his knee. "You still have nothing on me."

"True, but let me share my theory. I think this isn't the first time we've been in this wine cellar together. I think you were here last night, throwing the bottles." I leaned back against the solid stone wall. "They were all white wine. I could smell the buttered popcorn. Red wine doesn't have that smell and in fact, I didn't smell any red wine last night." I pointed to the shattered glass at our feet. "Frontier doesn't produce white wine, but Garrett Winery does. May I?"

Jeff scowled as I reached down and picked up the same shard of glass I had held before, the label still attached.

"Buttered popcorn is a big indicator in California Chardonnay. The same kind they make next door." I pointed to the colors of the Garrett Winery label.

Jeff's eyes shifted to the label and then back at me.

I motioned to the racks of wine around us. "The white wine is placed in random order around here with no large groupings together. Which means the person in the cellar last night knew how the cellar was organized and cared about the wine made here at Frontier. Certainly there were red wine bottles that would have been closer to throw instead of the multiple bottles of white, but the assailant didn't want to waste the red wine. The Frontier wine." I leaned forward. "And you don't like to waste Frontier wine. Not even a single drop."

Jeff twisted his mouth and then smiled. "You must be a fool," he said. "You think you're in charge here? Who's holding the gun? News flash, it's not you."

"Such a strong man." I shook my head. "And we almost had something. But I don't think you're as innocent as you say. That text was sent to Tessa after Mark was already dead. And that would take out your alibi, which is me." I shrugged. "Tessa got the text at the party and disappeared. Immediately after, you stood by me and didn't leave my side until the body was discovered."

I took a breath and continued, as if I was explaining the wine list at dinner. "Since the text had the code, which Tessa and Mark had only set up two days earlier, it had to be someone who had overheard them plan it. Someone who had easy access to the winery where they made the plan. Perhaps someone who had been delivering grapes? So tell me, Jeff, why did you kill your boss?"

He stayed motionless.

"Oh please, Jeff, I'm about to die. You're going to kill me. I get it. You can at least tell me why you killed Mark."

Jeff leaned back against the wall, the hand with the gun resting on his thigh, the barrel still pointed at me. "Mark found out I bought Pinot grapes from McPherson Winery up the road. He didn't like that. Said it messed up his estate labeling. I told him it didn't matter. That no one would know and it made the wine better. Richer. Full-bodied." He shook his head. "But he got all up on my case about it. Said it wasn't right to go behind his back and misguide people who buy his wine. People who only want wine from grapes grown right here on the property."

Jeff wiped his forehead with his free hand and laughed. "There I am, getting a speech from a man who says you shouldn't go behind people's backs, and there he is, cheating on Vanessa. Prancing around with girls like Tessa. He was ruining his marriage, and all I was trying to do was to improve his wine, yet I'm the bad guy." Jeff looked at me as if I would agree with him.

Even though agreeing with him could possibly lighten the situation, I wouldn't give him that satisfaction. I kept my game face on. "There's got to be more."

He breathed out and nodded. "I caught him putting a move on Lisa at the party. I don't know if it was the first time or not, but they were in the winery together. After Lisa left, I called Mark out on it. Told him he had no right to treat Vanessa like that." The gun moved in Jeff's hand as he talked and I felt myself twinge with the worry that it could go off.

"He fired me. Right then. After everything I had done for him and his winery, and he was firing me." Jeff's voice grew sharper. "I got upset. I pushed him."

"So you killed him because he was firing you?" I muttered to myself as much to Jeff.

"No, it was an accident."

I scoffed. "I doubt a jury will believe that."

"I only wanted to push him, but he fell and hit his head against the fermentation tank. Pretty bad, too. He wasn't going to make it, I could tell. But I needed to buy time, so I put him in the tank and found you at the party."

I studied Jeff as the events of that evening went through my mind. "And Tessa's wine opener?"

"It was on the grass. Since I was the one to pull him out of the tank, it was easy to stick it in his back."

"So you killed Mark by accident." I debated using air quotes, but I refrained. "Yet now you're going to kill me." I put my hands on my knees. "Wait, why did you kill Seb? What was that about?"

"What if I didn't kill Sebastian?"

"Right. Like I'm going to believe that." I sat up as a sudden realization dawned on me. "But, Jeff, since you don't like to waste a single drop of Frontier wine, why would you ruin a whole batch of wine with Mark's body?"

A wicked grin formed on Jeff's face. "I gave him a good old taste of those McPherson grapes."

A noise came from the main tunnel and a wave of relief fell over me. I turned to the darkness, waiting to see Dean's face. Instead, a different face appeared. One filled with hatred and spite.

But it shouldn't have been a surprise. Because that's the thing to remember with blind tasting. You can't ignore the clear indicators.

THIRTY

PAIRING SUGGESTION: SAUTERNES—SAUTERNES, FRANCE

*Made from grapes that struggle with a fungus called Noble Rot,
eventually producing a sweet and sugary wine.*

❧

VANESSA'S COLD EYES CAME into view, a soured smell of jasmine filling the area. "You jump to conclusions, Katie. That's your problem," she said as she crossed her arms and took a place next to Jeff. "I'm glad I don't have to play the grieving widow anymore. That was taxing."

"You? You're involved in this?" I looked from Vanessa to Jeff, who still held the gun and seemed unfazed by Vanessa's presence.

"Yes, my little friend who is so eager to help yet so unaware." Vanessa rubbed her hand across Jeff's back. "Now that Mark is dead, I'm the sole owner of this winery. Poor Mark couldn't divorce me; he would have taken the winery with him. It'd been in his family for generations, so the courts would have never sided with me. What can I say, I've never been a fan of lawyers." She brushed her hand against Jeff's cheek. "But I found someone who loves my wine as much as me. We're going to create beautiful wine together."

My mouth dropped and my hands opened in front of me. "I can't believe I missed it. Be wary of grapes that shouldn't be growing together. She didn't mean Jeff and Seb, she meant you and Jeff. You're having an affair."

"Wow, you really are slow, aren't you? To think poor Jeff had to pretend he liked you. Sickeningly sweet." Vanessa shook her hair back. "I should have driven you off the road when I had the chance. There were just too many witnesses on the highway. But there's not now. Jeff, get rid of her."

"Wait," I started, "what about Lisa? She called me yesterday. She knows the truth."

Vanessa threw her head back and laughed. "You really think that was Lisa? You are a fool."

"Did you kill her, too?" I asked. "String her up in a vineyard like Seb? Waiting for her body to be found?"

"There you go again, Katie, jumping to conclusions. What makes you think that Lisa's in a vineyard? That would be so tacky to commit the same crime twice. Do you think I'm that unoriginal?" Vanessa's mouth drew into a thin-lipped smile.

I was tempted to answer, but decided to leave it alone. "So where is she? I'm going to assume she's no longer alive."

"Of course. Because you couldn't stop killing, Katie." Vanessa's eyes were cold and glaring, a far cry from the downtrodden lady I had met for coffee. Whatever goodness I had seen in her that day was long gone, the theatrical side no longer an option.

"Yesterday, a lone truck ran into a ditch off a road in Sonoma. No one's discovered it yet, but when they do, they'll find poor Lisa's body in the driver's seat, her last effort scrawled across the seat. 'It was Katie.'"

"You really think you can blame all of this on me?"

Vanessa laughed. "Of course. I always get what I want."

"But why kill Seb? Why him?"

"Because he was too good. His conscience got to him. He wanted to come clean about everything." Vanessa put her hand back on Jeff's shoulder. "As I said, I always get what I want and right now, I want all this mess to go away. You're the vehicle to make it all disappear." She turned to Jeff and whispered in his ear, "I'm bored, finish it. I need to call the authorities." Vanessa took a step forward and looked at me. "In fact, I'll call Detective Dean. I think you know him? I need to tell him there was an intruder in my cellar again and my trusty vineyard manager came to my rescue, taking down the culprit as she attacked a poor, defenseless widow." Vanessa turned down the tunnel.

"Wait, I'm not the only one who knows. There are others."

"No one is going to believe Tessa, sweetie," said Vanessa. "She's as guilty as you are." She disappeared into the darkness.

Jeff raised the gun. "I'm sorry," he whispered. "I really did like you." His eyes narrowed. "But this is business."

"Jeff, please. Don't."

But it was too late. The noise of a firing gun filled the air. This time, the sound was deafening.

As the noise ricocheted through the cellar, bouncing off the tunnel walls, I hit the floor and shielded my face, broken glass cutting into my legs.

Everything inside told me to get up and run, but as much as I wanted to listen to my gut, my experience at the Academy had proven it would be pointless. No matter how fast I ran, no matter how quickly I jumped to my feet and sprinted down the tunnel, I couldn't outrun a gun. My hands flew over the back of my head as I waited for more bullets to come.

Faint footsteps followed by yelling in the distance, or perhaps it was closer, I couldn't tell. My muted hearing gave little clues as to what was happening around me.

"Freeze!" said a booming voice. I lifted my head enough to see a pair of shoes disturbing the broken glass near me.

"Don't move," said the voice. I looked up to see Dean standing next to me, his gun pointed at Jeff.

"Put your hands up," he barked.

"You must be joking," said Jeff as he pointed his gun at Dean.

I slid back, the glass under my knees scraping against the floor as I moved.

The two men stood about four feet apart, both of their guns aimed at each other, neither one of them moving.

"You okay, Katie?" asked Dean as he kept his eyes on Jeff.

I checked my face and body for any signs of an entrance wound from the bullet. My face was intact and the only pain I felt came from where the glass had cut me. "I think so."

"Get to a safe place."

I scrambled to my feet and stepped back in the tunnel, out of the line of fire.

"Put the gun down, Jeff." Dean's powerful voice came through louder this time as the muffled sensation in my ears dissipated.

"I'm in control here," said Jeff. "You put your gun down."

"Don't make things worse for yourself. You can come out of this okay, you know."

A movement down the tunnel distracted my attention. I turned to see Vanessa creeping away from the commotion into the other end of the tunnel. "She's getting away,"

"We'll get her later," said Dean.

Vanessa disappeared in the shadows toward the gated area of the cellar where it stopped at a dead end. I focused on the darkness, waiting for her to reappear.

"Jeff, I'm giving you one last chance. Put the gun down. I'll say you surrendered easily. You can be the good guy in this. Listen, you're in trouble here. I can help. Let me help make this an easy transition for you. Things can only get worse if you don't."

Jeff hesitated before placing his handgun on the floor in front of him.

"Good." Dean stepped forward and kicked the gun farther into the tunnel, the sound of metal echoing against the stone. "Put your hands up and keep them up as you lie down."

Jeff got to his knees then onto his stomach, his hands over his head.

Dean took his handcuffs and pulled Jeff's right hand behind him, then his left. I kept an eye on the darkness to my right, but there was no sign of Vanessa.

"You sure you're okay?" Dean looked up at me once the handcuffs were secured.

"Yeah." I pointed to the tunnel. "But Vanessa, she's involved in this too. She went that way."

"I'll take care of it. Get Jeff's gun and watch him." Dean took off down the tunnel.

I picked up the gun, the base still warm from Jeff's hands. I pointed it at Jeff, who lay motionless on the floor, his head up, facing me. "Don't move."

Jeff laughed. "Sure."

"I'm serious. I'm not afraid to use this."

"You're not going to fire that," Jeff said in a voice strained by the stone floor underneath him.

"Maybe you don't know me as well as you think, Jeff." I steadied my aim. "My dad's a cop. I've been shooting guns since I was twelve. I'm a sure shot."

"Right." Jeff got to his knees. "I'll buy that. Didn't Tessa tell me you flunked out of the Academy? Couldn't even hit the target?"

"Stop it. Get back down. I will shoot."

"No, you won't." Jeff stood up. "You're weak, just like your friend." He lunged toward me.

I pulled the trigger and fired.

THIRTY-ONE

Ideal for wrapping up a long meal.

☙

JEFF STUMBLED BACK, HIS whole body contracting in pain. "You shot me. I can't believe you shot me."

"Oh please." I shrugged. "I grazed your shoulder. You're fine."

Dean ran up the tunnel. "You okay? What happened?"

"He came after me, so I gave him a warning shot."

"You shot him?"

"Yes." I continued to point the gun at Jeff. "Only his shoulder. If I'd wanted to kill him, I would have. But I didn't."

Dean grabbed Jeff and held him by the cuffs, glancing at his shoulder. "Looks like a shallow wound. You'll be fine."

"She shot me," Jeff repeated. "She really shot me."

"What about Vanessa?" I motioned to the dark tunnel. "Did you find her?"

"She wasn't there. The whole place is empty."

"But that can't be. There's no exit that side. I've been down there."

"No, she's gone. There's no one there, I looked."

I stepped to the side and stared down the dark tunnel. "What if she's hiding?"

"No, there has to be an exit, because she wasn't there. If she's escaped, Peters is outside watching the property. If she's still in here, I'll make sure someone stays by the door in case she comes out later. Either way, we'll get her." He pushed Jeff forward. "Come on, let's go."

The three of us walked down the tunnel to the cellar exit. I held the door open as we reached the crisp afternoon air.

Three squad cars with flashing lights were parked outside. Another deputy stepped forward and took Jeff from Dean, guiding him toward one of the cars.

"Anyone else in there?" said a deputy I hadn't met before.

"No, but take a look just in case," replied Dean as the deputy entered the wine cellar.

I put the gun flat on my palm and held it toward Dean. "Here, you might want to take this. I don't want anyone to think I'm a threat."

Dean picked up the gun from my hand and gave it to another deputy. "You sure you're okay?"

I looked down. Small dots of blood were sprinkled around the ripped knees of my borrowed pants. "A few cuts on my legs. Nothing that won't heal in a few days." I touched my right ear. "Well, except for my hearing." I snapped my fingers next to it. "I think it might take a while for that ringing to stop."

"I'm really glad you're okay. That could have been bad."

I took a deep breath. "I know. And when that first bullet was fired, I thought I was a goner. I don't know how he missed me."

"The first bullet?"

"The one right before you arrived. Jeff shot at me."

Dean shook his head. "I fired as I approached you both. That bullet was from me."

I paused, my heart rate increasing. "That's what saved me. He was about to shoot me. You saved my life."

Dean swayed awkwardly as if he wasn't sure how to act. He tapped his badge. "Doing my job."

I reached out to hug him but lowered my arms back to my sides. "Thanks for being there. I'm glad you got my message."

"Yes, I did," Dean replied. "I'm not happy about you coming here, especially right back to the place where you were just arrested. The last time you were here, you were attacked."

"I know. I know."

"But"—Dean paused—"I'm glad at least you let me know. We headed straight out here. I figured something bad was going to happen. I was right."

"I'm sorry, but I needed to get it solved today. I was worried he might try to run. I guess both of them." I glanced up at the stone winery and then to the vineyard on the hill. "This is such a beautiful place. So sad that it had to be the scene of so much tragedy."

"By the way," said Dean, "all of the money in Tessa's account was transferred the night of the murder."

"By Seb, I guess."

"But you knew Jeff did it? How?"

I nodded. "I figured out he was involved because of the wine in the cellar and the little details that didn't quite add up." I paused. "But I didn't see the Vanessa thing coming. That surprised me and I don't like being surprised." I shook my head. "I was convinced that Jeff was playing Vanessa. That he was roping in this poor defenseless woman. I was wrong. I should have seen it."

"Don't beat yourself up about it. People are hard to read. You're not so easy yourself."

I held out my arms, holding my wrists together. "I guess you have to take me back to jail now. I'm sure I've violated some code or rule, especially with being out on bail."

"I don't know, I think we can figure it out." Dean smiled. "For both you and Tessa."

Deputy Peters ran up to us, sweat pouring down his face. "I can't find Vanessa. I've been all over the hills and she's nowhere."

"That's okay, I'll put out an alert. We'll get her soon enough."

"Okay," said Peters as he wiped the sweat from his forehead. "Want me to drive the suspect back to the station?"

Dean looked at Jeff in the back seat. "Nah, I've got it." Dean opened the front passenger door of the patrol car and locked eyes with me. "Want to ride in front?" He winked.

"Yes. I'd love to." I slid into the front seat and closed the door. I turned around to Jeff, who sulked in the back as Dean came around to the driver's side. "Aw, cheer up, Jeff. I can still help with the harvest next week."

THIRTY-TWO

PAIRING SUGGESTION: OLOROSO SHERRY—JEREZ, SPAIN

To end on a sweet note.

❧

THE NEXT MORNING, I walked into my blind tasting group, all four participants greeting me with smiles.

"Look who's out of jail," said Darius. "I heard you had quite the weekend."

"That would be an understatement." I put my bag down at my seat. Five glasses of wine sat in front of each person, each glass containing a different wine. The fifth glass at each seat was empty, waiting for me to pour my bottle.

"I thought you weren't coming back," said Jackson. He shook his head. "You're too good of a taster to give up after only one try."

"Let's just say I'm not quite giving up."

"Did everything work out with Frontier?" asked Kurt. "Bill told us about it. I'm sorry you were in jail."

I nodded as I took out my wine, its identity hidden with a paper bag until the group used the blind tasting method to deduce what it could be. "It did, thanks to Bill and his wife."

"I don't know what you're talking about," said Bill as he winked at me. "You solved that on your own."

"You're free then, right? Not out on bail?" said Jackson.

I poured my wine into the empty glasses on the table. "All charges were dropped against both me and Tessa. Jeff's in jail, waiting for his court date, and I just heard from Dean that they picked up Vanessa. She'd cut and dyed her hair and was on her way to Seattle, but they got her." I filled the last glass and put the bottle on the floor. "So everything is back to normal now. I used to think normal was boring. Now I'm glad for it."

"What about Frontier? What's going to happen there?" asked Kurt.

"Alan, the winemaker, is taking over the operations and he hired a great assistant. Tessa." I sat down as the silence that always kicked off a wine-tasting session fell across the room. Everyone seemed to stare at the five glasses in front of each of them, waiting to see who would go first. Going first was difficult, especially as one hadn't had any wine yet to cleanse the palate, their taste buds still affected by the morning's toothpaste or a flavorful and greasy breakfast.

"Okay," said Kurt, breaking the silence. "Who wants to go?" He leaned back against the wall of the private dining room and clicked his pen.

"I'll go." I reached for the first glass of red wine. "Who brought this?"

"It's mine," remarked Jackson.

"Jackson brings the tough ones," whispered Darius. "I'll switch with you if you want, and I'll go first."

I returned my attention to the glass of wine in my hand and swirled it. "No, it's okay. I'll go. Jackson, you ready?"

"Yep." Jackson picked up his pen and placed it on the paper grid in front of him, ready to write down everything I said about the wine so the group could break down my deduction.

"Great. Let's start."

"Ready?" Bill clicked the stopwatch. "Go."

I swirled the wine, little droplets running down the inside of the glass after each swirl. "This is a red wine, it is a clear wine, with medium viscosity, and a ruby core with a purple to violet rim. There are no flaws on this wine."

I held the glass to my nose and took a deep breath. "On the nose, black cherry, black raspberry, blackberry, black plum, chocolate cake frosting, turned earth, baking spices."

I took a long sip and swished the wine around my mouth. The flavors danced on my tongue, sending a combination of fruits to my brain. My mind raced to identify the different elements before I paused for a moment and focused on the deductive method. Is there cherry? Yes. Is there cranberry? No.

I picked up the paper cup in front of me and spit the wine into it, licking my lips before I spoke. "On the palate, confirm the black cherry, blackberry, black raspberry, chocolate cake frosting, turned earth, baking spices. Acid medium plus, body medium plus, alcohol medium plus, tannins medium plus, complexity medium plus. Initial conclusion, this is a new world wine, one to three years."

I stared at the glass in my hand, a small amount of ruby colored wine still swirling at the bottom. "Possible varietals—a Malbec from Argentina, a Shiraz from Australia, a Cabernet from California."

My mind raced from Shiraz to Malbec. It could easily be a Shiraz with the color and the descriptors, but it could also be a Malbec. I needed to trust my instinct. But what was my instinct telling me? Think. What was different? There was cake frosting. Definitely cake frosting. I made my decision.

"Final conclusion, this is a 2014 Argentine Malbec from Mendoza, quality level good." I looked up at Bill, who stopped the watch.

"Three minutes, twenty seven seconds. Nicely done. Jackson, how did she do on the grid?"

Jackson looked down at the paper in front of him. "Good job on the grid, you hit all the areas, just don't forget to confirm on the palate what you said on the nose. You didn't confirm the plum. Other than that, nicely done." He looked at the other members of the group around the table. "Anyone want to argue?"

Kurt shook his head. "Katie, I think you're right. I also got plum, chocolate, and cherry as well as a tar quality. 2014 Malbec is a good call."

Darius nodded. "Agreed."

"Well done," said Bill. "Don't forget to take a deep breath and go slower. Your time is great, so you can slow it down in the future. Then you won't miss anything." Bill motioned to Jackson. "Jackson, the reveal."

Jackson held up the paper-covered bottle and removed the bag. In his hand was a 2014 Argentine Malbec. He beamed at me. "You're an excellent taster."

Heat rushed to my cheeks. "Thanks." I took another deep inhale of the glass, the scent of Malbec clear now that my deductions were confirmed.

"You're still The Palate," quipped Bill as he picked up the second glass of wine. "So, the next Certified Exam." He paused. "Have you registered?"

I looked at the glass in my hand and swirled it, the remaining Malbec climbing the sides. "Not yet," I said as a smile spread across my face. "But I'm going to."

THE END

© Matthew Semerau

ABOUT THE AUTHOR

Nadine Nettmann, a Certified Sommelier through the Court of Master Sommeliers, is always on the lookout for great wines and the stories behind them. She has visited wine regions around the world, from Chile to South Africa to every region in France, but chose Napa as the setting for *Decanting a Murder*, her debut novel. Nadine is a member of Mystery Writers of America, Sisters in Crime, and International Thriller Writers. She lives in California with her husband.